Echoes Down a Dark Well

Ric Wasley

Echoes Down a Dark Well

Copyright © 2015 by Ric Wasley

Printed in United States of America

Printed by

Tell-Tale Publishing Group, LLC
5174 Peri Street
Swartz Creek, MI 48473
www.tell-talepublishing.com

Nightshade Imprint

NIGHTSHADE

Dedication

I would like to thank my publisher, Elizabeth, and my editor, Laurie, for their help and advice and as always my wife and dedicated 'First Draft' reader, Barbara.

Chapter 1

I awoke at the same moment a screaming, wild-eyed Saxon split my head with an axe.

As a knight of William the Duke of Normandy, I'd had nothing but contempt for the Saxon King Harold's dull-witted blond *huscarles* who made up his royal bodyguard. I had been trained as a warrior since birth, unlike the bulk of the army standing next to their king atop a low rise who were mostly *ceorls*—farmers and peasants. True they were sworn to come to his aid whenever he levied the *fyrd* for his army, but most of them were more familiar with a plow than a sword. Whereas I had killed my first man at fifteen, and was awarded a war horse and a knight's status before I turned eighteen.

Perhaps that made me overconfident.

But for the first half of the battle outside Hastings, I had seen nothing that induced me to be cautious. We charged them twice, and each time I'd ridden down scores of farmers armed with whatever bits and pieces of weaponry they could glean. My massive destrier cut through Harold's first line like a predator through a flock of sheep and left them screaming on the blood-trampled grass.

It wasn't until the third charge that the unthinkable happened. I was unhorsed.

I will admit it now, I was cocky and careless and never thought that the mounted knight's greatest nightmare could befall me. But it did.

One minute I was leaning from my saddle, swinging my long-sword and cleaving their helmets. And the next a skinny Saxon stripling with nothing but a rusty old spear had slipped under my horse and thrust the tip into her belly.

The horse screamed and wrenched violently. I landed flat on my back on the ground, just managing to get to my knees in time to slash the hand of the boy carrying the spear, taking it off at the wrist. But before I could regain my feet, one of Harold's personal house troop rushed at me. He swung his deadly four foot, two-handed ax.

I tried to deflect the blow, but the massive ax sheared through my blade. And the last thing I remember was the sound of my own skull splitting . . .

. . . So much for that life.

I sat up in bed and rubbed my eyes, droplets of cold sweat dampening my fingertips.

I got up and walked over to the window. The streetlight was still making that sputtering sound that reminded me of bugs frying in the bug zapper my dad had hung over the back porch the summer I turned thirteen.

The summer the dreams started.

Back then they had scared the hell out of me—they still did sometimes, but by now at least I was used to them. You'd be scared too if you had them every night of your life. Every damn night.

I went into the bathroom, filled the sink and pushed my face into the cold water. It felt good—washing away the night sweat. But it couldn't wash away the dreams. Nothing could do that. Hell, I'd been trying to do that for thirty years, and nothing even made a dent. Not drugs or booze or women or music or—blood. And I liked all of those—though not necessarily in that order.

I sat down on the bed, propped up a pillow against the wall and reached for a cigarette. My hand hesitated a moment. I was vaguely considering getting into one of my quitting phases, maybe the tenth or twentieth—hell who was keeping count, not me. I put the pack down on the nightstand, then said, "Screw it," out loud to the empty room. If I checked out of this incarnation early, no one was gonna shed a tear, least of all me.

I lit the cancer stick and leaned back against the wall. Maybe it was time to help things along. I glanced over at the silver automatic on the nightstand next to the ciggys. It was a Desert Eagle Mark XIX .50-caliber Action Express with the upgraded finger groove grip—the biggest freakin' practical automatic pistol in the world. And right now it was loaded up with seven big fat .50-cal AE rounds. If I stuck that great big barrel in my mouth and pulled the trigger, whoever found me wouldn't even know it was me. I'd have no head.

I chuckled and ran my fingertips down the silver steel barrel, "Hey, Babe..." That was what I was calling my constant companion this time around. Not that unusual, a thousand years ago I talked to my swords, too. "Whadda' ya say, Babe? Wanna give me a good night kiss?"

The gun didn't answer—they never do—but it didn't stop me from asking. And the night they answered back then I probably really would eat the barrel. But not tonight. Tonight the big nasty hand cannon was just a cold, inanimate piece of steel waiting for its master to get out of bed and put it to work doing the job that we'd been paid to do—very well paid.

I sighed and crushed out the cigarette on the nightstand. No ashtrays 'cause the roach motel I'd been staying in for the past two weeks didn't allow smoking. I glanced around the grimy room made seedier still by my dozens of cigarette butts burned into various pieces of cheap furniture. Hell, what did I care? When I left this time, I wouldn't be coming back.

I got up, pulled on my jeans and grabbed a black tee-shirt from the half dozen in my nylon gym bag. I slipped my feet into a pair of black Reeboks, shoved one arm into my black leather jacket and with my other hand grabbed the gym bag. I was all packed and ready to go to work.

A half hour later I was sitting in a rented Buick—grey, non-descript. The look I always strived for. It was cold—probably down in the twenties—but I resisted starting the engine and turning on the heater. Noise, exhaust vapor and those tiny red dashboard lights you could never get rid of without rewiring the whole panel—they'd give you away. Besides, I was used to cold. Sitting in a thirty-degree automobile? Hell that was nothing compared to sailing across the frigid North Sea with Günter 'Skull-Splitter' to plunder another rich monastery and send the mewling monks on a one-way journey to see their "nailed" god, which was the Vikings' derisive term for Christ. One thing I learned as a Viking—keep your mouth closed and keep rowing.

I risked a brief check of my watch and pushed the button that lit up the face. Three thirty-seven AM. He'd be coming home soon from whatever club he'd been snorting coke and lapping up the 'Dom' in. Maybe he'd have a woman with him—maybe not. It didn't really matter, though I always tried my damndest not to kill a woman. Unless she was the target. But most of the time they were just poor dumb sluts, or rock star wannabes, or high-class hookers or, occasionally, just some bad-luck kid in the wrong place at the wrong time with most definitely the wrong guy. The one who I was being paid to kill.

I had my code, too. I always sort of had it in the back of my mind, but when I saw that movie *The Professional* with Natalie Portman and that French actor—I can never remember his name—I liked his line and adopted it as my own. It kinda' gives me a kick when I say it to my employers, "No women—no kids."

I wasn't that way in the early days. Hell, when you rode with Attila or Genghis Kahn, you pretty much just killed everything that moved. But now . . . Well, at least I'm trying. Though it's pretty friggin' obvious that it hasn't been good enough, I keep coming back. But trust me, I'm doing my best. And yeah I know the punch line—"Compared to what?"

OK, it's not much but it's something. "No women—no kids."

Besides, every time I have a woman in my sights the thought always runs through my mind, *What if it's her?*

It's made me hesitate and has almost gotten me killed a few times. No, make that *has* gotten me killed a few times. For instance, that Hungarian Countess bitch in the Fifteenth Century . . . Elizabeth something? Elizabeth Bathery, that was it. The whack job who thought she was a vampire and was quite literally bleeding the countryside dry with her obsession for bathing in the blood of young peasant girls. I was a mercenary then, a landless knight with a sword for hire, and a frantic farmer gave me everything he had to find out what had become of his daughter after she went to serve the countess.

I found out all right. She and a dozen or so local girls had been hung up like hogs and bled dry to fill the countess' bathtub, and while I was deciding if the farmer would be satisfied with the head of the woman who'd murdered his daughter, that bitch countess had her maid sneak up behind me and stick a dagger between my ribs. A split second after that first stroke, I had my sword out and was about to plunge it between a pair of very attractive breasts before she could take a second swipe at me, but I hesitated. I thought I saw something in her eyes. And while I was realizing that the only thing I saw there was someone who was crazier than a rabid bat, the bitch pushed the dagger through my doublet and straight into my heart.

So much for compassion, huh?

But still . . . I just can't afford to take that chance. Any one of them could be *the girl*.

Down through the centuries she's been tall, short, petite, heavy, every nationality, every ethnic group and every age—from a child to an old lady. In 1909 she was even a precocious four-year-old who sat on my bony old knee as I rocked out my last heartbeats at the Old Soldiers Home for Confederate War Veterans in Mobile, Alabama. And I remember what she said as I closed my eyes on that incarnation. She whispered, "Don't worry, Lucas (my name in that lifetime). We'll be together soon."

That's what I'm waiting for.

I checked my watch again. Any minute now. I stared at the Upper East Side brownstone where Anthony "Little T" Valboni, Jr. would be arriving shortly in a Beemer iseries that he always liked to drive his latest squeeze home in to impress her. However, from two weeks of surveillance I also knew that he was followed two or three hundred feet back by a black Mercedes that rode heavy 'cause it had been retro-fitted with bulletproof glass and the latest hi-tech armor. Little T was a showoff and a loud mouth, but he wasn't stupid.

On the other hand he hadn't come up the hard way and wasn't half as tough as his old man, "Tony Bags," nicknamed for his penchant for cutting up his rivals and dropping off parts of them in trash bags all over New York City. In fact, if my contract had called for Tony Bags, I'd be charging more—a lot more. Fortunately for me and the rest of the Five

Boroughs, Anthony Senior was doing five to twenty Upstate, leaving his obnoxious kid next in line for everything–including me.

The guy who was paying me to make Little T go away had gone to great pains to make sure I didn't know who he was. He always worked through one of his *amigos* from the old neighborhood back in Columbia. But he could have saved himself the trouble. I knew who he was. I knew all about him because I never work for someone I don't know. Before I take the job I make sure I find out as much about my employer as I will about whoever it is they want me to eliminate. It tells me what level of low-life I'm working for, and makes the job that much easier if it happens some day that their name comes up on my list. I just don't tell them that. Maybe that's why they always look so surprised to see me. They usually blurt out something like, "Hey wait a minute—aren't you the guy I paid to take out . . . ?" And I answer, "Yup. And now someone is paying me to take out you."

They usually die with an expression of incredulous bewilderment at the unfairness of it all. But it's rarely unfair. Most of them are simply getting what is long overdue. And what with my all-too-intimate association with Karma, I have to admit I've rather come to enjoy helping give the wheel a little push in the right direction. I think they see that in my eyes, and that's what scares the hell out them in those last moments.

As I watched the empty street, another pair of eyes drifted through my mind. The only eyes that scared the hell out of *me*. I don't see them very often, which is one of the few things I have to be thankful for. But when I do, I always wake up with my heart threatening to burst from my ribcage. And there's a good reason for that because, over the years, there's only one time I can count on that face in the fog appearing—the moment of my death. I've often wondered if he was coming to help me on to the next incarnation or merely to gloat?

Sometimes his expression is anger, sometimes pity, but most of the time it's disappointment. Kind of like, "So you blew it again?"

His face is always staring back at me from the smoke or mist or fog or rain. I keep trying to get a good look at it—see who it is haunting me, but the image wavers and dissolves, and I can never quite make out the features. Except for the eyes. Those bore right through me. They're pale, but glow with a terrible intensity—angry and accusing. They make me want to apologize. But for what? I keep wondering, *Is this someone I killed? A former client pissed at finding himself next on my hit parade?* Somehow I don't think so. His eyes contain too much depth of soul for that.

Yet in some ways, although the image continues to haunt me, those eyes are not the ones that affect me the most. It's the girl's.

When I have the really bad dreams—the ones that I'm almost ashamed to admit leave me waking up with big fat tears streaming down my face, it's always the girl's eyes that do it. In the worst, and what may be the dream where it all started, she's always clothed in a shapeless brown sack of a dress and I see her, thin hands outstretched in supplication — pleading. I can't make out what she's saying, but I see it in her eyes. Those great big luminous eyes. Pleading, imploring me from a thin pale face. She's asking me for something, but at the same time offering me something too — salvation.

But I never get it, that much I know.

Because I think I killed her.

Chapter 2

Auschwitz-Birkenau Concentration Camp—November, 1944

Boris, the pot-bellied red-faced *Unterscharführer* from the Ukraine was in a fine mood despite the steady pelting of precipitation that couldn't seem to decide if it wanted to be snow, rain, sleet or a combination of all three. But the grinning *SS* guard didn't seem to mind. He stood watching the pathetic trembling and doomed human cattle blink up in confusion and terror at the glaring white spotlights piercing the murky night and the snarling dogs that strained at their leashes. Most of the guards were cold and cranky and wanted nothing more than to get back to their warm barracks, *weisewurst* and schnapps. But not Boris. He always met each incoming train of prisoners with a big beaming smile.

Those prisoners who were lucky—or unlucky, depending on your point of view—to survive the initial "selection" process quickly came to know the smiling guard by the nickname the prisoners had given him the day after he arrived with a new detachment of non-homeland auxiliaries to Himmler's prized *SS-Totenkopfverbände*. Those were the Death Head units responsible for administering the death camps. Most of the so-called Auxiliary units were staffed by anti-communists or other dissidents who'd had problems in Stalin's USSR or merely thought that serving the *SS* was preferable to becoming cannon fodder for Uncle Joe's Red Army. But Boris was different—he loved it.

That's why the prisoners referred to Boris as, *Das Tier*—The Beast. It was a nickname he was proud of and strove each day to live up to—like now. He stood grinning ear to ear, slapping a long black club—perpetually crusted with dried blood—against the top of his gleaming black boots. No matter what the weather or how muddy the marshalling yard,

Boris's boots were always polished to a mirror-like shine. He kept a half a dozen former shoemakers busy making sure that his boots were always perfect. And they did—all of them. Because those who didn't were summarily beaten to death in front of the others. Boris was quite the motivator, indeed.

I smacked my hands against my black leather trench coat and stamped my jackbooted feet against the frozen ground. It was bloody fucking cold, and I too wanted to be back in my room gratefully using a bottle of schnapps to anesthetize the last dismal scraps of my conscience. The dreams had been growing steadily worse.

They always started on the night of my thirteenth birthday. And they always scared the hell out of me, bursting into my mind with a thousand confused images of different times and different palaces but always dripping red with violence and death. Soon enough, I learned to sort out the jumble and realize that they were memories of past lives. My lives. And so it was this time too. But this time it seemed their legacy of war and conquest would serve me well because by the time I began my teenage years, a grand new spirit had swept my fatherland. Adolph Hitler had just become Chancellor. I had been part of the New Germany's young people's organizations and so, along with the rest of my schoolmates, joined the Hitler Youth. I loved the sports and military training and because I was the only thirteen-year-old who had spent a hundred lifetimes with a weapon in his hands, I was soon promoted to squad leader. And by the time I was ready for my secondary schooling my parents were delighted when I was accepted into the Adolph Hitler School.

I was likewise delighted in the action, military tactics and acceptable place to channel my increasing aggression and desire for combat. But most of all it was the uniform.

I had worn many uniforms of many armies. From Roman to Huns and Goths, Frankish armor and the Great Kahn's leather and plate, the helmet of a Viking, the bluecoat and braid of Napoleon's army, the flak-jacket of a grunt in 'Nam and the homespun butternut of a Confederate soldier. But I have to say that none of them had the style and sheer ability to strike terror as the black and silver uniform and peaked Death's Head cap of an *SS* officer. When I was fifteen the girl I used to walk home from the movies on Saturday, Gretchen Muller, told me that when she finally "gave herself" to a man to have a child for the Fuehrer, he would have to be wearing the dashing uniform of an *SS* officer. I applied for the Adolph Hitler School the next day.

And the first time I called on Gretchen in my new uniform with silver lieutenants' pips on my collar tabs she was true to her word. That was the high point of enjoyment my uniform brought me. It brought terror and hatred to many who saw it afterwards but never again love.

Now I didn't even want to look at my reflection in the mirror each morning when I went out for roll call and inspection. I only glanced in the mirror to make sure my cap was straight and I hadn't forgotten to shave after a long night with the bottle. But I didn't want to see my eyes staring back at me. I was afraid of the vision. Those eyes had seen too much.

And they were about to again. The newly arrived sad collection of Jews, Gypsies, Slavs and other assorted political prisoners were being herded down the *Himmilstrasse,* the ironic name bestowed on the street that lead to the gas chambers—the "Street to Heaven."

Boris, his gleeful smile beaming, yelled at the prisoners to form lines so the *SS* doctors could inspect them. Doctors—a detestable collection of washed-out or bottom-oftheir-class medical students and butcher's boys I wouldn't have let treat a rabid dog. But here they had the power of life and death over the trembling, frightened people waiting unknowingly for a quick death or a lingering one. The ersatz doctors stood self-importantly in front of the throng, giving each a few seconds' glance to decide who would live and who would die—at least for now.

I could hear them barking out, *"Rechts ! Links!"* sending the poor bastards to the right to be worked to death or to the left to be gassed immediately.

Every so often, Boris would help some sick or elderly person along with a friendly kick—always delivered with that big, beaming shit-eating grin. After smacking a mother hunched over trying to protect her two small children, he happened to glance up and notice me watching him. The grin dropped for a moment and he snarled at the woman with the children to hurry into line. He then straightened his tunic and made a stab at what he may have thought was the serious professional expression of a dedicated servant of the Reich. He waited a few moments before glancing back to see if I was still watching him. I was.

I didn't like *Unterscharführer* Boris Ulnakov, and he knew it. I had dressed him down in front of the entire troop, and in return he whispered little tidbits into the Commandant's ear at every opportunity about my being too soft on the prisoners. The Commandant didn't care for me either, and I returned the feeling.

But Boris had to be careful. He was a lowly *Untersharfuehrer,* and I was a *Sturmbannführer.* An officer of the Waffen *SS* and highly decorated war hero wounded at Stalingrad and again in "heroic" rearguard action against the Red Hoards who where even now kicking our asses across the Baltic states and chewing up the miles towards the Fatherland itself. So Boris was being careful not to give me any excuse to smash his grinning face in. I, on the other hand, was becoming increasingly careless with everything that had to do with the posting to which the Reich had invalided me in order to give my wounds a chance to heal so I could return to combat to collect more for the glory of the Fatherland. It was a posting that had landed me among the perverts and sadists who made up the crews that manned the *abattoirs*—the ones the little worm Goebbels, in charge of our propaganda machine, called "re-education" camps. Yeah, we "re-educated" them all right—right out of existence.

The wind blew a gust of ice pellets against my face, and I pulled the collar of my leather trench coat up against it and shifted away from the stinging blast. That's when I saw her.

She was small and thin and frightened. She looked to be about thirteen or fourteen, but I recognized her eyes instantly. The same luminous eyes, dark and liquid, with a depth of understanding unlike anything I'd seen throughout all the long ages. I know that she is born each time with full knowledge of who she is and who I am, but that doesn't mean she can instantly recognize me from afar. It also doesn't mean she doesn't get scared or hungry or feel pain, and now she was experiencing all three. So when I saw her huddled in her thin coat and shivering with the January cold that scoured the Polish countryside, I knew I had spotted her before she recognized me—and there was a large part of me that wanted to keep it that way. But despite what I knew she would probably feel for what I represented to her in her current life, I knew I had to help her.

The penalty for aiding a Jew was death for the average citizen of the Reich, and even for an *SS* Officer the consequences could be severe, but I didn't care. Truth be told,

I was pretty damned sick of the Third Reich and everything in it—including me.

I took a dozen striding steps to the guard pushing the *links* line towards the complex where they would be stripped and gassed. He stiffened to attention as I approached and I barked, "That girl in line—bring her to me." He hesitated. "Now, you *schiese!*"

He jumped and screamed at one of the Capo's—the Jewish guards we used to do the herding of the prisoners to their final destination—and the guard grasped the girl and pulled her out of line. The SS guard grabbed her elbow and pushed her towards me so that she fell sprawling at my feet. I struck him backhanded with my gloved fist. He opened his bleeding mouth to protest, but the look on my face stopped him cold. He swallowed the blood in his mouth and then turned back to abusing the prisoners. It didn't matter—I couldn't save them all, but if I could save her . . . I bent down and gently helped her to her feet. It felt strange—I hadn't touched anybody gently in a very long time. "I'm sorry," was all I was able to say. I also hadn't said those words in an even longer time. She looked at my face and ran a tiny finger down my jaw and over the shrapnel scar from a Russian grenade. Then she studied my eyes for several moments and broke into a shy, sweet smile.

"It's you. You've come for me, haven't you? Out of all of these suffering millions, somehow you found me. And somehow I always knew you would. You are a good man." She touched my chest with her fingertips. "Despite the uniform you wear and the things you feel you must do—you are good, Luc . . . " She stopped as if catching herself before she could finish the sentence.

I frowned. "What were you saying?"

She bowed her head. "Nothing."

I put my fingers underneath her chin. "You were about to say a name. Was it my name? Was it a name you knew me by before—in another life?" I paused, feeling lightheaded and strange. Was she remembering me from the first life—did she know what I had done—how it all began and, maybe, how to end it?

She shook her head. "I—I don't remember."

"That's a lie!" I shouted and raised my hand. She didn't flinch but looked at me with a gaze so sad that I felt more ashamed than I have at any time before or since.

I lowered my fist and said hoarsely, "And so you see what I am. What I have become—a monster."

She took my hand in her soft tiny one and kissed it. "No— you are not. And by saying that, you prove the evil you serve has not succeeded in crushing the goodness I know you have."

I closed my eyes and felt my cheeks burning despite the cold. Cold . . . The poor child was freezing. Without thinking I opened my coat and drew her into the leather folds next to me. She huddled gratefully against my body, and I felt a peace so profound I almost smiled. Then I remembered where I was.

Glancing around I looked to see if anyone was watching. Sure enough, The Beast had his mouth open, his beady little eyes taking in every gesture. I glared at him and dropped my hand to the butt of my Luger pistol. He quickly looked away, pretending to count prisoners, but I knew he had seen everything. Shit! I had to get her away from there before he had a chance to tell anyone what he'd just seen.

I stiffened and whipped my coat away from her. "You—Jew! You will come with me. You have information, and I am going to get it if I have to beat it out of you!"

She caught on instantly and meekly bowed her head as I grabbed her arm and propelled her toward the officer's compound. The other guards grinned, assuming I was going to beat her or rape her or both. But I knew our little ruse had not fooled Boris, and I was going to have to move quickly in order to save her.

Once in my quarters I stripped off my still-warm coat and bundled it around her, then poured two schnapps and held one out to her. "I know you're a little young for this . . . I'm sorry, I don't know your name."

"Sara—my name is Sara."

"Well, I don't know if they let you drink at home Sara, but this will help to drive the chill out of your bones."

Despite all that she had been through, she still managed to smile mischievously up at me and say, "Oh I have drunk the Passover wine for years. And on occasion even shared a schnapps with Poppa." The smile faded. "Poppa is dead. They killed him when he tried to stop some Arrow Cross men from beating my sister."

"I'm sorry," I said, but she seemed not to hear me.

"In the end, they beat Poppa to death and my sister, too. Then I was deported along with most of the other families on our block in Budapest to a series of detention centers and finally to Krakow where we were loaded on cattle cars and sent here."

She said it all very matter-of-factly, as if this was just the way of the world and one more bit of suffering to be endured. And she was stoically far better than I could have been in her place. But then again she'd had many lifetimes to practice enduring—and forgiving.

I put my arms around her and held her. At first she was stiff with remembering past sorrows, but after a few minutes she sighed and relaxed against me. Snuggling deeper into my arms, she said, "We've been like this before haven't we? It's always so nice but always too short."

Memories flashed through my brain, almost overwhelming me. Good memories, sweet memories of the times we had been together as man and wife, and other times we had been fleeting star-crossed lovers. Each one was like a shinning jewel, but in this incarnation I had suppressed them, buried them under a pile hate and death and self-loathing. Now they were back, and my heart ached so much I thought it would shatter into a thousand pieces and spill out at her feet.

She tilted up her head to kiss me. I drew back. "Sara—no, it's not right—I'm a twenty-five year old man, and you're still a child."

She looked at me from under long lashes. "I'll have you know, good sir, that I am not a child, I'll be fourteen in two months."

I put my head in my hands. "The Fates are really doing it to me this time. I find in this hellhole the only woman I've ever loved, and she is a thirteen-year-old-girl."

"Almost fourteen," she said with a smile.

I sighed. "Very well. I'll smuggle you out of here and take you back to Dusseldorf. I know of a very nice girl's school there. That is, if it's still standing. You can spend the next four years there—I'll visit every weekend, and then when you turn eighteen we can be married. What do you think of that?" The words were pouring out of me like I was a lovestruck schoolboy.

She smiled again and took my hand. "I think that sounds wonderful," she answered, but there was a strange sadness behind the smile.

No matter—I was still a German officer, and if there's one thing we were obsessed with, it was planning.

"All right then, to business." I went to the desk, got out paper and pen and began making a list of what we would need for the journey, listing the checkpoints to avoid and the ones where I knew my rank would carry us through.

"There are warehouses filled with coats and clothing from former prisoners. I'll have one of the Capo's hunt you up a warm coat and . . ."

I saw the sorrow in her eyes and stopped myself then shook my head and whispered, "Sorry. I've served so long with monsters that it's hard to think like a human being."

She walked over and kissed me. "It's all right. You'll see, one day everything will be all right."

I touched my lips where she had kissed me. "Thank you." Then I straightened up—all business again. "Very well, I've still got my field jacket from Russia, and you can wrap up in my greatcoat. Now, as to supplies . . ."

There was a knock at the door. *Damn!* I threw the pen down, strode over and yanked the door open. It was one of the Commandant's guards.

"*Herr Sturmbannführer*, SS Commandant Kremer requires you immediately."

Shit! Had that son-of-a-bitch Boris already ratted me out? I looked around and realized the guard was staring at Sara. I stepped in front of him, barking, "This is a very important prisoner. She has knowledge of an escape attempt. I want you to post a guard at this door and let no one in until I return— understood?"

His boot heels crashed together. *"Ja sächlich!"* Another thing we Germans knew was how to obey.

I closed the door on him and took Sara in my arms. "Don't worry, I won't be long. Kremer hates my guts, but he fears my rank and hero's record. On the way back, I'll requisition a *kübelwagen*, and we can leave tonight."

She nodded, then just before I opened the door, hugged me fiercely and whispered, "I love you."

I nodded and stepped out into the night. I wish I had told her that I loved her, too.

"**Ah** *Herr Sturmbannführer* Baumann, so kind of you to accept my invitation—please sit." The Commandant smiled sarcastically and gestured to a low chair opposite his long oak desk. The bastard had kept me waiting for over an hour, so I was in no mood to play his little game of cat and mouse. I stood.

He frowned for a moment then turned his gaze down to the desktop and shuffled through a sheaf of stacked papers. Finally locating the one he was looking for, he pulled it delicately from the pile by his fingertips as though it was somehow contaminated.

"It seems you have been quite busy, *Sturmbannführer* Baumann."

I remained silent.

He picked up the paper—a transfer request form—then cleared his throat and began to read aloud. "Therefore due to the gross mismanagement and un-soldierly like conduct of the entire staff of Auschwitz-Birkenau, I strongly request an immediate transfer back to frontline duties."

The Commandant let the piece of paper drop from his fingers. It fluttered to the corner of the desk. "I do not appreciate slurs on my management of this facility, *Herr Sturmbannführer*."

I shrugged. "And I don't appreciate serving with a bunch of perverts and sadists." He gritted his teeth and smashed his fist down on the desk. It would have been far more effective if he hadn't gasped with pain and tried to surreptitiously rub his sore hand a moment later. I said nothing but knew he could see the contempt in my face.

"So the 'hero' of the brave *Waffen SS* doesn't care for the crass company of the

Totenkopfverbände, eh?"

I didn't speak.

"Well, hear me, *Herr Sturmbannführer* Baumann, this request puts my entire operation in a bad light, and I will not stand for *Reichsfuhrer-SS* Himmler being burdened by defeatist and negative reports during this trying time."

I shrugged again. "Then sign the transfer."

He came around the desk, sat on the edge and leaned forward. I had to stifle an impulse to unsheathe my *SS* Honor Dagger and shove it into his balls.

"Let me make myself quite clear Herr 'hero of the Reich' *Sturmbannführer* Baumann.

You will withdraw this request for transfer and refrain from sending further requests, or . . ."

"Or what?" I snorted derisively. "You'll send me to the Russian Front?"

His pinched, weasel face narrowed with spite. "No, *Herr Sturmbannführer*, I shall have you arrested for consorting with a Jewess!"

I tensed and glared at him.

"Oh yes, I know all about the little girl you pulled from the selection line. But according to the sacred word of our *Fuhrer*, Adolph Hitler, "No *SS* man shall be allowed to have relations or consort with a Jew under any circumstance." He paused for dramatic effect. "Under pain of death."

No choice now but to bluff it out.

"I don't know from what sewer you dredge your information, Kremer, but I'm afraid someone has made you the victim of a jest in questionable taste. The 'Jewess' to whom you refer is nothing more than a very valuable potential informant in an escape attempt—that had it succeeded I might add, would not have reflected well on you or this camp." I glanced over at him—he wasn't buying it. But on the other hand, what could he really prove? Nothing. I wasn't worried.

I should have been.

"Ah, so." He straightened and moved toward the door. "Perhaps then we should both talk to your informative Jewess." Before I could say anything he threw open the door and yelled, "Bauer!"

The same guard who'd come to my quarters stuck his head in and clicked his heels to attention. "*Zu Befehl, Mien Commandant!*"

"Go to the *Sturmbannführer's* quarters and fetch his little Jewess."

The guard hesitated. "But Herr Commandant—you already sent for her." My stomach turned over.

But Kremer seemed remarkably unfazed. "Really—then where is she?"

The guard shifted uncomfortably from one foot to another, stammering, "But is she not here, Herr Commandant? The *Unterscharführer* who came for her told me you had ordered her delivered to your office."

I took two steps and grabbed the lapels of Kremer's coat. "*Unterscharführer?* What *Unterscharführer*?" But I already knew and started running for my quarters, my blood colder than the bitter wind that froze the brief spark of hope I'd felt. I barely heard him when he called after me, "*Unterscharführer* Boris Ulnakov."

I did little more that glance into my empty room. I knew she wouldn't be there, and the knot in my gut told me where she would be. But I was wrong. When I burst into the *Unteroffizier's* barracks Boris was waiting for me. No doubt he felt secure surrounded by fellow sadists and back room bully-boys. He didn't even try to deny it.

"Where is she?"

"You mean your little Jew whore?" His tunic was unbuttoned, and his belly protruded from between his suspenders. He'd obviously been drinking, as a half dozen empty bottles of schnapps and lager littered the table. They all were drunk enough not to be intimidated by my officer's pips. He belched and winked at his compatriots. "You were very selfish *Herr*

Baumann to keep that tasty little piece all to yourself. After all, don't we men of the *SS* share everything through our sacred bonds of blood?"

I took a step toward him, and he backed up. "The only blood I'm going to share with you, you fat piece of *schiess*, will be when I paint yours all over these barracks walls." I grabbed his undershirt and pulled his face close to mine. "What have you done with her?"

"You'd best get your hands off me, *Herr Sturmbannführer*. I was merely following the orders of *Herr Commandant* Kremer."

Kremer! That bastard—he'd set me up.

"Where is she?" I tried to keep my voice from shaking and my hands from ripping him apart before he told me, but even then I think I already knew.

He flashed me his famous malicious grin. "Why, we sent her on her way, *Herr Sturmbannführer*. And of course before we wished *Gott* speed on her journey, we thought it only fair that she 'entertain' us in return."

My hands grew numb, my breath came in short sharp gasps.

"And being all brothers of the *SS*, we naturally took turns with her." A few of the others guffawed and nudged one another. "But I was surprised to see that you had not trained the little Jew slut how to be a good whore. Why, *Herr Sturmbannführer*, you surprised me. You had not even had her. She was a virgin."

"But not for long!" shouted one of the men from the back of the room.

"*Ja, Ja*, Claus, true enough." Boris laughed. "She bled the first few times but not after the third or fourth time." He looked puzzled for a moment. "But she never cried. In fact, she never made a sound." He shook his head. "Strange creatures those Jews, don't you think *Herr Sturmbannführer*?"

I smashed my fist into the side of his head and he went down. "What did you do with her? Where is she?"

He glared up at me from the floor, malice gleaming from his tiny black eyes. He spat out blood and sneered, "Why just as I told you, *Herr Sturmbannführer*, we sent her on her way. She is on the *himmelstrasse*. On the road to meet her God." He pulled a heavy gold pocket watch, spoils from some prisoner, from his pocket. "Yes, and just about now they should be dropping the Zyklon B into the air vents."

As I raced from the barracks he called after me, "Maybe if you hurry, you can collect her body for your use before they remove her hair and gold fillings."

As I ran across the frozen parade ground I prayed for the first time in several lifetimes. *If you're really up there you better damn well save her!*

It wasn't much of a prayer, was it? And it got just about the results I'd come to expect from my prayers.

I tore down the cement steps to the false shower changing room and past a dozen startled Capo's sifting through the clothes that would never be returned to their owners, skidding to a stop at the thick iron door at the other end of the room.

"Get that door open!" I shouted at the stunned guard.

"But *Herr Sturmbannführer*, we must allow the gas time to vent—if you open that door now, we would all be killed."

I slammed my hand against the wall. "I don't care! I don't care if every miserable fuck in this camp dies. I'm going to save her!" I pulled my pistol, jammed it under his chin. "And if you don't open that fucking door right now, I'm going to start with you."

"Please sir—there is no one left alive in there. Listen."

"I don't hear anything," I snarled and pushed him aside, beginning to turn the heavy wheel that sealed the door.

He put his hand on my arm. "That's because they're dead. All of them."

He was right. It was silent as a tomb—her tomb.

I think I went a little insane then. I hit him in the face with the barrel of my pistol and screamed at the rest of them, "You bring her out, do you understand me? You bring her body out of that charnel house. You handle her gently. She is not to be touched except reverently. I will be back for her. And if I find she has been defiled in any way, I will kill each and every one of you." I was panting, sweat dripping from my face. "Do you understand me?" I screamed.

They all nodded—guards and Capos. They were terrified, and with good reason.

I walked back across the parade ground in a red haze as images flashed through my brain. Her sweet smile and gentle touch. Then rough hands grabbing at her, tearing at her clothes, raping her, brutalizing her, laughing at her pain. But she didn't cry. The swine Boris was puzzled because she didn't cry. My only love—she didn't cry.

But I did.

For the first time in almost two hundred years I felt an uncontrollable flood of cold liquid freezing on my face. Sara, sweet gentle forgiving Sara. She always forgave. But I didn't.

I kicked in the barracks door. Some were surprised to see me, but Boris was not. He was seated in straight-backed chair while one of the men held a cold compress to his face. "Don't bother with that," I said to the man and motioned him away.

Boris stood up, grinning his malevolent grin. "I knew you'd be back, *Herr Sturmbannführer*, so I've already informed the Commandant. He should be here any minute to arrest you."

Now it was my turn to smile. "Then I'll have to work fast, won't I, Boris?"

He paled, and for the first time fear showed on his florid features. He glanced around quickly to make sure of his backup, but in that second I moved and as his head turned back toward me, I smashed my elbow into the same place I'd hit him before and kneed him in the groin. He went down with a high-pitched squeal, and I dropped on top of him, my knees pinning his shoulders to the floor.

"So she didn't scream, Boris? Let's see if you can be as brave, you pig." I pulled my black-handled *SS* Dagger with my right hand and gripped his hair with my left. "And you like to smile so much Boris, why don't I make sure you'll always have that big, shit-eating grin on your face?" I slashed down with my dagger. Once. Twice. And he screamed. Very, very loudly.

One of the other *Unteroffizier's* started toward me, but I pulled my Luger and shot him in the stomach. Screaming, too, he went down.

"All of you," I snarled, "to the back of the room. The first man who moves gets the same." They moved back against the wall, and I went back to my work. I took Boris' eyes next. One at a time. As I popped them out with the tip of my blade, I whispered in his ear, "My Sara had beautiful eyes. Now she is dead and you have none."

And then he was past listening, so I took his ears. By that time his screams had become so high-pitched they were becoming inaudible. I had nothing left to say, and he had no ears left to hear it. So I cut his throat.

I got up dripping with blood, still clutching the bloody dagger, and started toward the men huddled at the back of the room. One held up his hands in a supplicating gesture, "Please, *Herr Sturmbannführer*, it wasn't our idea. We never meant to hurt the girl, we just . . ."

He got shot between the eyes. The others put their hands up as if they could stop the hail of bullets I was about to unleash. But they were wrong about the manner of their deaths. I had other plans.

I walked over to the glowing red hot stove in the center of the room, opened the firebox door and kicked it over. Cherry-red coals tumbled over the floor, immediately beginning to smoke and then burst into flames.

Two of the men tried to rush me. I shot them both and they fell into the fire. The remaining four called out to me for mercy. Mercy—mercy for the sadists. When I didn't answer, one ran to the single window and smashed his hand through the glass. The sudden draft of fresh air drew the flames, and he went up like a torch. A screaming, crying torch.

As fire enveloped the room, I called to the three men choking in the back, "Give my regards to *Reichsführer* Himmler when he joins you in Hell." Then I walked out of the burning barracks to pay my respects to Commandant Josef Kremer.

By this time sirens were going off all over the camp, guards were running everywhere, and from the north tower I heard the chatter of an MG 42 Machine gun. They thought it was the prisoners trying to escape. No, I was the only one who was going to escape.

I was almost to my quarters when I saw Kremer running toward me with a squad of black-helmeted guards. I slipped the Luger out of my holster and inserted a fresh clip.

When he was twenty feet away, he slowed. "Baumann, you're under arrest for high treason against the Reich."

He motioned to the first two guards, and they started toward me. I shot them both in the chest. Then I had to duck and roll as a fusillade of nine millimeter *Schmeisser* MP Forty-three machine pistol bullets tore up the frozen ground, following me as I dove into my room and kicked the door shut. More bullets smashed through it, reducing it to little more than a web of splinters held together by two cracked crosspieces. I tipped the cot up and crouched behind it as the next two guards came crashing through the broken door. I shot them both, but not before they stitched three bullets across my right leg and side. Warm blood soaked my uniform, but I didn't care. I checked my clip. Only two bullets left. That was all right, too. They were enough.

I heard Kremer's voice call out, "Come out Baumann, you've nowhere to run. Come out now, and I'll give you a quick death."

Liar.

I didn't answer. In a widening pool of my own blood, I lay next to the bunk as if dead. I heard his boots on the steps, and then through my eyelashes saw him nudge one of the bodies aside. He walked toward me but paused a few feet away. *Herr* Kremer was cautious. The report of his pistol was deafening in the room, and I felt the slug bury itself in my chest, but I never flinched—I needed a clear shot. Just one clear shot.

Satisfied I was dead, he came closer and nudged me with the toe of his boot. That was all I needed. I grabbed both his feet and pulled. He went down hard on his ass. Raising my Luger, I smiled at him.

"This is for Sara." I shot him in the face at point-blank range.

His blood and brains spattered over me, blinding me for an instant, but I struggled to my knees and wiped a bloody hand across my face. I heard the sound of voices and jackboots. The enemy was approaching my door.

This time I said it. "I love you, Sara."

I put the still-warm barrel of my Luger into my mouth and pulled the trigger.

Chapter 3

1238 - The court of Baldwin II, Emperor of Constantinople

The Ambassador of Louis IX of France paced the small antechamber just outside Emperor Baldwin II's Privy Council Chamber. He'd been waiting for hours and could not understand the delay. The 'gift' from the Emperor to his master the King had been agreed to before he'd left France three months before. So what was the difficulty? All he had been told to do was to journey to the fabled city of Constantinople, express his Majesty's undying friendship and gratitude and then bring the gift back safely to his king. What could be simpler?

Instead, he had been cooling his heels for the past three days, waiting for an audience that had not yet happened. He would have preferred going back to his ship, sailing out through the Bosporus and returning to France, but he could not. Not without the gift.

His pious Royal Majesty was very anxious to receive the gift, so here the ambassador stayed, waiting and pacing. And he would continue to do so until the Emperor finally deigned to receive him.

Suddenly the door to the antechamber opened, and a liveried servant spoke longed-for words—"The Emperor will see you now."

An hour later, the ambassador emerged carrying a beautiful gleaming chest studded with diamonds and rubies and chased with solid gold filigree. But he was still puzzled, for as the Emperor had handed him the golden chest, he'd lifted the lid and placed a plain wooden box inside the larger, glittering one, admonishing the ambassador to guard the contents of the chest with his life. And, if need be, part with the golden one if he could but save the wooden one inside.

"That," the Emperor had said, "is the true treasure."

The slam of a car door woke me.

Damn it! I must have dozed off. A dangerous and often fatal mistake in my business. For a moment I wasn't sure what I'd been dreaming about, then it all came rushing back to me at once, and I gave a strangled groan. The camp, the ovens—*her*. Shit—that was one of the worst ones ever. The one that, almost seventy years later, I was still trying to drive from my memory. Maybe that was why who or what had cursed me always made sure that it came in so clear—my own personal nightmare in wide screen plasma, vivid HD.

I touched my face—wet. Perfect. The tough-guy mercenary assassin had been crying. Hell, stuff like that might get me drummed out of the assassin's and killer's guild. Right.

I desperately wanted a smoke but couldn't even risk the glow of the car lighter. Maybe some Meth would perk me up. No. I needed to stay calm and focused. I wiped my eyes, still envisioning her sweet, trusting gaze. Gritting my teeth against the pain of that memory, I gripped the steering wheel so tightly that I heard the vinyl crack.

Fortunately, I was saved by the sound of another car door slamming. Crap. I had literally been sleeping on the job. The second car of Little T's entourage had just pulled up in front of the brownstone. That meant Little T was already inside. I checked the magazine of the Desert Eagle then screwed a silencer into the big barrel.

Time to go to work.

I waited until the three mega-steroid using, iron-pumping, leg breakers finished scanning he streets for people like me then slid out of the Buick's passenger-side door.

The Brownstone's front door closed behind them, but I knew Little T had entered via an elevator that ran from the garage underneath the brownstone to his bedroom on the third floor. That was where he played.

I'd done my homework, I always did—that was I why I was still alive in a business whose practitioners had notoriously short life spans.

Little T would have a girl with him—he always brought one home. Like I said, usually she was a hooker or a girl who fooled herself into thinking she wasn't a hooker. Even though she went home with creeps like Little T because he had a nice car and plenty of money he didn't mind spending on pretty girls stupid or greedy enough to accompany him home where he liked to play. The problem was, these girls found out too late that Little T liked to play rough. He was one of those twisted fucks who gets off on making girls moan— but not in a good way. That's why he usually stuck to hookers. They were used to it and wouldn't go to the cops. And they already had a pretty low opinion of men and were accustomed to 'rolling with the punches' as it were.

I didn't know if he'd have a pro or an amateur with him tonight—I kinda' hoped it would be a pro. They knew how to make themselves scarce when things got nasty, and it was liable to. I always tried to do things as quietly as possible, but sometimes my target didn't cooperate, and I had a feeling Little T wasn't the strong, silent type.

I'd studied his three goombas and knew their specialties and MOs. All three were there tonight. Sometimes they brought their own entertainment home to while away the small hours of the evening while their boss was otherwise occupied. Regrettably, this was not one of those times. So my choices were to take them all out or avoid them. I don't kill needlessly, so I chose to avoid.

They would probably be playing pool on the second floor or watching the big screen on the first. That meant I'd have to go straight to the third floor, and I had already planned out how. I opened the trunk from which I'd removed the bulb— just as I always did with all of the door lights whenever I used a car. I took out a coil of thin but very strong and lightweight nylon rope and then a small but powerful crossbow pistol. I walked down a block before I turned the corner and approached the building from the back. There was a brick wall which I scaled and on the other side a small patio with a chef-sized gas grill. Above that was a small wrought-iron balcony and a pair of French doors that led to the third floor bedroom. Where I was going.

A large oak tree grew about twenty feet from the back of the brownstone, and someone in charge of security had had the foresight to remove all the lower branches making it impossible to climb. Or so they thought.

I uncoiled the rope and clipped one end to a steel crossbow bolt. Then I picked a spot about three-quarters of the way up the tree and shot. The specially sharpened bolt buried itself halfway into the tree trunk. I gave the rope a couple of tugs, braced my sneakers against the trunk and began to climb. When I was opposite the balcony I swung over and landed lightly on the railing then looped the rope once around it and got out my lock picks. A few seconds later the lock clicked open, and I cracked the door and listened. I always listen before I enter a room.

Grunting was accompanied by a low, throaty feminine voice that sounded like asideline coach urging a player toward the finish line. There was a particularly loud grunt, and

I assumed that Little T was done. I heard the murmur of voices being raised and then the sound of a slap and a pair of feet hitting the bedroom floor in the next room. I opened the French door another inch and saw a slim, naked blonde storm out. She crossed the sitting room facing me and went into the bathroom, slamming the door behind her.

A male voice called from the bedroom, "Get back here, bitch. I'm not done with you." When there was no response he called louder, "Did you hear me, you fucking whore? I paid you two grand, and your ass is mine for the night. The whole night!"

The bathroom door opened, the girl stuck her head out, extended her middle finger and yelled back, "Fuck you, Tony!" and slammed the door again.

I heard the bed creak, and a moment later Anthony Valboni, Jr. aka Little T came out of the bedroom pulling up his red silk boxers. He crossed to the bathroom, put his shoulder against the door and pushed. On the third try the lock gave way and the door burst open with a splintering crash. A few moments later a knock sounded on the bedroom door and a voice called from the hallway, "Hey T, is everything okay?"

"Mind you own damn business and go back to jerking off, Paulie!"

"Jeeze, pardon me the fuck for caring." I heard the voice mutter from the hallway then footsteps descending the stairs. A few seconds later, Little T emerged from the bathroom dragging the blonde by her long hair.

He pulled her into the bedroom, and I heard a half dozen more slaps followed by a sobbing, "Okay, okay! Christ, whatever you want."

I heard Tony, Jr. tell her what he wanted and then the sound of her body hitting the wall when she obviously didn't comply fast enough.

The last ten minutes had been an assortment of screaming, hitting and door shattering. The boys had been told to M.Y.O.B. and they were. It was perfect. Time to go to work.

Easing the French doors open, I slipped silently into the sitting room. Hearing the sound of contented grunting, I guessed that the blonde had gotten down to business. Across the room I peeked into the bedroom. She was down on her knees giving Little T his money's worth. I hated to interrupt the tender scene, but my time was money, too, and I had my own job to perform. At least Little T would die happy. I stepped into the room.

"Who the fuck are you?" Anthony Valboni, Jr. said by way of greeting. "You got two fuckin' seconds to get the fuck outta here before I blow your nuts off!"

"Sorry, Mr. Valboni." I like to keep a professional demeanor when I work. "I'm afraid you're in no position to blow anyone's nuts off but your own." I looked down at the girl. "Sorry Miss. I hate to interrupt a professional when she's working."

"Fuck you." She got up wiping her mouth, went over to a chair next to the door and flopped down, throwing one leg over the arm. I turned back to Little T.

"I think you'll find this easier if you turn around. It will be quick, clean and relatively painless, though I can't entirely guarantee the latter."

That was actually just a little bit of final comfort that I threw in for free. Truth is, I remember all of my deaths, and almost none of them had been painless. Then again, most of them were violent.

He didn't move, just stood there searching for something to say to buy him a little time and, of course, he asked the question they all do.

"Who's paying you? Is it that fuck Mendoza? Whatever it is I'll double it—no, triple it."

They always say that, too.

"I'm sorry Mr. Valboni, but I value my reputation and professional integrity. A contract is a contract. After all, we all have our standards to maintain. Now you may turn around or not, as you prefer, but I'm going to count to three, and when I'm finished I'm going to pull the trigger."

I braced the big Desert Eagle in a shooter's position. As you might imagine, a .50- caliber anything packs one hell of a recoil. I began to count. "One..." I took a deep breath because I'd learned from experience that most targets when told they will be shot on three will bolt or try to attack on the count of two. So that's when I always pulled the trigger. One last surprise.

But I never got to *two*, because as the word formed on my lips and my fingertightened on the trigger something smashed against the back of my head and I went down.

People always assume that tough guys never get concussions when brained with a heavy object. That's not true. Depending on how heavy the object is, a guy can wind up in the hospital, or in a coma or dead. I should know, since I've been hit on the head by a ten-pound Norman mace.

But this time it was a table lamp and fortunately one coated with thick brown hand-tooled leather, so I was probably only out for a couple of minutes. Long enough. I woke up just as Little T's three goons came bursting into the room. The biggest and fattest one hauled me to my feet and braced me up against the wall. I turned my head and stared at the girl. She shrugged and gave me the finger. I sighed. Even though I'd always been fond of whores, I should have remembered, you can never trust 'em.

Little T pointed my gun at me, saying over his shoulder, "Me and Vinnie will take care of this guy. Go check the place and make sure he doesn't have anyone else with him."

They nodded and clomped down the stairs. "Frisk 'im, Vinnie, and then stand back. I always wanted to try out one of these big canons."

Vinnie grunted at me, "Put yer friggin' hands behind yer neck." I complied.

He patted my arms, pulled the cuff of my jacket back, saw my black diver's watch and continued to slip his hands over my arms, chest, back and so on until he was satisfied I was clean. He turned me so my back was against the wall to make a real good target, then turned to Little T, who was drawing a bead on me with my Desert Eagle.

"I'm gonna kneecap you with this before I kill you, you bastard. Turn 'im back around, Vinnie."

He thumbed back the hammer and took aim at my left knee. That's when I slipped the five-inch, black OTF jungle combat knife from the underside of my black watch band, pressed the thumb release and let the dagger blade that I'd modified with a heavy-duty industrial grade spring shoot forward and burry itself in Vinnie's carotid artery. As he died, I grabbed him and pushed him in front of me. He went stumbling into Little T just as T pulled the trigger. The .50-cal slug caught Vinnie in the chest and spun his two hundred and fifty pounds around like he was a marionette. Blood exploded in a shower, splattering Little T, blinding him. I sidestepped the falling body and twisted the gun out of his hand.

"This concludes our business, Mr. Valboni." I squeezed the trigger.

I sensed movement behind me and whirled around. The blonde was pulling on her dress and stuffing the bills from Little T's wallet into her purse. She looked up at me. "What? A girl's gotta eat, too, ya' know."

Shaking my head, I walked out of the bedroom. Time to go. Someone would be up soon to investigate those shots. I pulled open the French doors and felt a hand on my arm. "Please let go, Miss. I have a feeling you're going to continue to need that hand in your line of work."

"Christ, Mister, give a girl a break will you? Those guys are gonna be up here in two minutes, and when they find him dead, they're gonna beat the shit outta' me on general principles."

"You've got to be kidding. Why in the hell should I help you after you sucker-punched me with a lamp?"

"Look, I didn't know you, and I thought it would get me in solid with Tony." I stared at her. "Hey, I know he was creep and a nasty shit, but he paid well."

When I didn't answer she opened her mouth to speak, but I said it for her. "And a girl's got to eat."

"Well, she does." She pouted.

I tipped up her chin and stared into her eyes. Yeah, I know. Pretty damn unlikely, but I can't afford to miss anyone. *The Girl* could be anyone. Anyone.

But not this girl. When I looked into her eyes all I saw was greed, deceit and a little fear.

"Hey, Little T, Vinnie. Everything all right up there?"

When there was no answer, I heard heavy footsteps start up the stairs. The blonde looked at me. "Please?"

I grabbed her by the elbow and hustled her onto the balcony, then wrapped the nylon rope around my right arm and my left around her. Two figures appeared at the open doorway. I kicked off the balcony railing, swung down to the grass below and with one motion boosted the blond over the wall and myself after her. Three minutes later we were in the grey Buick heading uptown, and I had apparently found myself a new roommate.

Chapter 4

"So are you gonna screw me, or what?"

She had told me her name was Clarisse. Clarisse Fontaine.

I glanced up from the TV. She had come out of the bathroom with one towel wrapped around her hair and another around her slim body. Now she moved in front of the TV, so I was forced to consider something I hadn't been quite ready to consider.

On the surface it seemed to be an easy choice. To get laid or not get laid—not much of a question. I liked girls and I liked sex, so what was the problem?

Well, for one, she presented me with a connection to the life of another human being that I really didn't want right then. A few hours ago, I'd scattered Little T, Anthony Valboni, Junior's brains all over the bedroom of his expensive brownstone, and by now the word had surely reached Anthony Senior in his upstate cell. He'd certainly put out a contract on a guy described by Tony Junior's ex-bodyguards as around six feet, medium build, grey eyes and mean looking.

That was why I didn't want any entanglements. I needed all of my concentration to be focused on running, and I hadn't run anywhere near far enough or fast enough yet.

My guess was that Big Tony would assume I'd be running to the gentle climes of the sunny South, or the wide open expanses that ran out three thousand miles towards the setting sun west of New York City. So I headed northeast to New England.

We arrived in Boston just as the sun was coming up, and I checked into a small Back Bay hotel that had been converted from a stately granite-front home I'd first stayed in on a brief visit to the city in 1888. I'd used it from time to time since then but never so many times in one life that I'd be recognized or remembered. And the sleepy night clerk who was just getting ready to go off duty barely nodded to me when I paid for two nights in advance with cash. I would be leaving before dawn the next morning, but I wouldn't be checking out. It would take Tony's men at least that long to have the slightest idea which way we went. And in the unlikely event they were able to trace us to Boston, we'd be long gone before they even discovered the hotel.

I say "we" because after reluctantly bringing the blonde with me, I now couldn't simply dump her in Boston and go on my merry way. One thing whores do better than screwing you—in more ways than one—is talking. To anyone who will pay them. And just because I'd saved her from getting her pretty little ass kicked, I had no illusions that she wouldn't rat me out the first time money crossed her perfumed palm.

So I had to keep her with me at least until I got to the tiny cabin in northern New Hampshire. From there, I planned to sneak over the Canadian border and on to Montreal where I had a place to hole up in the Old Quarter. I hadn't planned what to do with the blonde after we got to the cabin, but my plans did not include taking her to Montreal.

Presently she stood in front of me making me an offer I didn't want to deal with but wasn't inclined to refuse.

She unwrapped the towel from around her head and shook out her long hair, then pulled on the towel suspended from her breasts and let it fall to the floor. I noticed she was a natural blonde. She put one hand on her hip and arched her eyebrows.

"Well, like what you see?" I nodded. "Want some?"

I looked her up and down. Seeing her fresh out of the shower with no makeup, I upped my original estimate of her age from late twenties by at least a decade. She had a few lines around the mouth and eyes. Her body, on the other hand, was almost flawless—breasts, butt and skin taut, firm and smooth—well almost. There was a long, thin red scar running from her left breast to her navel, and as she saw me staring at that she lifted her right arm and showed me a half dozen red, puckered round scars about a quarter-inch in diameter on the underside.

"Not bullet holes," I said. "Too small."

She shook her head. "Cigarette burns." Her hard eyes were flat and cold. "The first and last guy I was in love with wanted me to make him a little extra cash. When I told him I was nobody's whore, he showed me why I was."

"What about the one on your stomach?"

"That was from the night I tried to leave him."

"What finally happened? You're not still with him?"

"No. The big cosmic irony is that I finally did what he wanted me to and found a client who was tougher than he was—much tougher." She walked over to the nightstand and lit one of my cigarettes. Took a long drag. "I watched him die and went into business for myself."

"And how's business?" I asked only a little sarcastically.

She answered the same way, by turning and looking mockingly back at me over her shoulder. "What do you think?"

"I think I'd like to take you up on that offer." I patted the bed beside me . . .

. . . She may have been a pro and sarcastic and cynical, but she made love like something different. More like a real woman than a lot of women I've known who were supposedly "good girls" and who were supposed to be doing it for love, not money. Maybe I was just flattering myself, but I could have sworn that at one point she actually gave a tiny sob. And yeah it could have been nothing more than a hooker's trick to get repeat business, but for some reason I didn't think so.

Now before anyone starts thinking that it's the typical story about the hard-on-the-outside hooker with the heart of gold, I should mention that when I awoke two hours later, I found her fully clothed, standing at the dresser going through my wallet and stuffing the cash into her purse. I waited until she was through and had her hand on the doorknob before I flicked out the blade of my OTF knife and sent it thumping into the doorjamb six inches from her head.

"Try that again, and the next one goes straight into your cute little ass."

She had guts, I'll give her that. She shrugged, threw the wad of bills carelessly onto the dresser and walked back to the bed. "Tell you what, I'll give you another for free."

"Really? I wasn't aware that the first one was anything but."

She shook her head. "Nope, that was payment for taking me with you."

"Okay, then what's this one for?"

She shrugged out of her dress and straddled me. "This one's for not killing me."

Clarisse then proceeded to nearly kill me, though in a most pleasant way. Later she slept. A cold sea breeze was blowing in the half-open window. I closed my eyes and began to dream.

November 27, 1812—The Berezina River—Russia—with the Partouneaux Division of the Grande Armée of Napoleon Bonaparte

I was freezing to death.

Those of us from Marshall Victor's Corps who were still in reasonable fighting condition clutched our muskets and waited for the attack. The Russian forces under Tchichakoff had taken command of the heights on the opposite bank of the river, and the continual barrage of shells from Wittgenstein's artillery closing in behind us meant the entire Grand Army was trapped between the partially frozen river and the rapidly advancing Russian forces from the east. We had been "chosen" for the great honor of rear guard for the fleeing remnants of the half-a-million men that had so confidently entered Russia only six months before. Now there were fewer than half that, and our division was about to add its name to the rolls of the illustrious war dead.

A shell exploded overhead, raining down chunks of red-hot iron that sizzled as they struck the snow. One landed inches from my arm, and I actually held my freezing fingers over the steaming hole it left. I think if the fragment hadn't buried itself so deeply, I would have picked the damned thing up and put it in my pocket. I was that cold.

It seemed to me I'd been cold forever, though it had only been six weeks or so since the Russian winter surprised us with the sudden onset of frigid temperatures and ever-increasing snowfall. Marching into Russia behind our ever-victorious general, we'd had such high spirits. We were the favored soldiers of a bright new empire currently in the process of making all Europe, nay the entire world, France. At least that was what Napoleon told us. And that was what the officer had said to me and my dozen young friends—sons of farmers, cobblers and bakers—when he stood in front of our village tavern on that bright spring morning five years earlier. Oh, how the drums had rolled and the fifes had played as they unfurled the tri-color of the Republic. The gold braid shown on their new uniforms, and the silver medals and brass buttons gleamed in the sunlight.

That morning we all enlisted.

Now the sun was gone—shrouded behind clouds of swirling snow and dirty black smoke.

I heard the sounds of screaming behind us and turned to see the pontoon bridge our engineers had cobbled together for our evacuation break apart in the middle, spilling men and horses into the freezing, ice-choked river. Horrified, I watched as men cried out and horses tried to scramble onto chunks of ice, only to slip back into the black water.

"Shit," Francois muttered beside me through chattering teeth. "Now we'll never get across."

"Pah," the big, color-sergeant from Caen spat. "Marshall Victor never had any intention of letting us cross. Didn't you hear him? We of the Partouneaux Division are to be sacrificed for the greater glory of the Empire. More likely for the personal glory of the Emperor himself."

"Hush yourself, Jean. That kind of talk is treason!"

"You are a child, Francois. There will be no time to stand me up before a firing squad because by tonight we will all be dead."

I put both ice-cold hands under my arms in a vain attempt to glean a little warmth. It merely served to make my body colder. "I only wish I could harness all that hot air both of you are spouting to warm my damn hands."

Jean laughed and poked me. "Don't fret, Christophe. You'll be plenty warm soon enough when we all meet in hell." He moved off toward where a company was trying halfheartedly to raise a barricade from shattered artillery carriages.

"A bundle of cheer that one, eh?" Francois said gloomily.

I never got a chance to answer for at that moment several volleys of musketry cracked out, and we saw Big Jean frantically waving us forward.

"They are attacking our left flank. Come on the run!"

We rushed forward to the makeshift redoubt. I had just dropped behind it and fired my musket into the swirling smoke when there was a blinding flash followed by a deafening roar. The world exploded in my face.

I awoke to the shock of icy water stabbing through my uniform like a thousand tiny knives.

"Come on Christophe, you must help me. Kick! Kick your feet!"

I gazed around groggily. We were in the middle of the river, clinging to a splintered pontoon. Francois must have dragged me there and pushed us out into the current. Now he wanted me to kick my feet to help propel us to the far shore. A request that was both sensible and reasonable. The problem was I couldn't feel my feet. They were like chunks of inanimate lead. I tried to move them. Nothing.

The current kept sweeping us farther and farther away from our straggling army across the river. François kicked franticly, but we were making no progress.

"Please Christophe, you must kick or we will die."

I muttered a desperate prayer and began to force the two pieces of lead attached to my legs to move. And somehow through the snow and smoke and cannon fire we made it across the Berezina River and managed to crawl onto one of the few remaining retreating wagons.

Not without cost, however. Francois caught pneumonia, which plagues him to this day, and I lost all the toes on my right foot and three on my left, as well as two fingers on my right hand, all from frostbite. But we had survived the retreat from Moscow.

I sat up in bed with a gasp. Slowing my breathing, I took a deep breath of the cool damp air and looked at Clarisse sleeping next to me, hair spread out on the pillow like a dark-golden fan. She almost looked innocent.

Sighing, I laid my head back down. Clarisse yawned and nuzzled my shoulder sleepily. I didn't think I'd be able to sleep any more but within minutes I did. This time, although the dreaming continued, the path my life took was different.

Near Reims, France — September 1844 — Abbey St. Germaine

When we finally returned to our village outside Reims, I could no longer work the fields of my father's farm, so I became a priest.

Surprised you, didn't I?

During my long convalescence from the effects of fever, starvation, frostbite and amputation, I'd had a lot of time to think. I decided soldiering and lifetime after lifetime of violence didn't seem to be getting me anywhere. Plus there was that prayer in the middle of the icy river. Had God really heard me? Was He ready to forgive me for whatever it was I'd done? It was certainly worth a shot to find out. The last dozen centuries hadn't seemed to have gotten me anywhere.

So after several years at the monastery I became Farther Christophe. I was a familiar sight hobbling around the village on my twin briarwood canes. On more than one occasion I was told I was a comfort and example for those afflicted by doubt or disease.

"If Father Christophe can keep a cheerful countenance with his war wounds and constant pain," people would say, "surely I should not complain about my bunion."

And I was glad my suffering brought strength of spirit to others. I was becoming quite the Christian paragon of virtue, wasn't I?

Then God decided to really test me. He sent me Sister Madeleine.

It was on the first day of May, 1844 that I saw her. Finally at peace with myself, I was just about to celebrate my fiftieth birthday with more joy than I could remember ever feeling down through the long centuries of death and slaughter. Nothing could ever force my crippled feet from the paths of righteousness again. Or so I thought.

On that soft spring morning I'd taken the oxcart to the monastery to bring back some chickens and flour for the next day's feast. I was to preside over a hearty meal for the poor and homeless of our community.

When I reached the monastery complex, one of the brothers helped me down from the cart. "*Bonjour* Father Christophe. Before I forget, the Abbot would like to see you."

I smiled and shrugged. "Then there is no time like the present. If you will be so kind as to load my cart, Brother, I will proceed to his office straight away."

When I got there the Abbot rose, beaming. "Ah, Father Christophe. Your ears must be burning, my son, for I have just been extolling your virtues to your new assistant."

"Assistant? Forgive me, my dear Abbot, but I do not recall requesting an assistant."

"Perhaps not, but the Bishop and I discussed it at length, and we both agreed. As you are now getting on in years, and what with your war wounds and all, you should have an assistant who is light of foot. To help you in your many duties, especially those of the parish school for girls. And it just so happens one of our diocese's most generous benefactors has a daughter who after many years of teaching at the girls' seminary in Reims has requested a parish with a quieter environment."

"But Reverend Abbot, I do not need an assistant. I assure you, I am quite able to . . ." He held up his hand. "Please Father Christophe, it has been decided. Come."

He turned toward the single chair in the room, directing my attention to the nun I now noticed for the first time. Eyes downcast, she rose from the chair. She was tall—as tall as I was—and had a plain but well-worn rosary in her hands. She didn't speak or look at me. "Father Christophe, this is your new assistant, Sister Madeleine."

She finally looked up and raised her large brown eyes to mine.

It was *Her*.

We passed the entire ride back in silence. I had a thousand questions on the tip of my tongue but could ask none of them. Several times I opened my mouth to speak, but each time I peeked over at her silhouette, her face obscured by the enveloping cowl of her elaborate habit, my mouth became dry. I told myself I'd just imagined what I thought I saw lurking behind that brief glimpse of brown eyes.

In fact, by the time we reached the village I had almost convinced myself and had regained much of my composure. That is until I went to help her down, and she thanked me with a modest nod and a brief flash of depthless eyes.

All that night I prayed on my knees for the strength to keep my priestly vows, but by morning I knew if I looked into those eyes once more I would cease to be a priest and most likely drag her down into sin with me. So as the sun came up over the chapel spire, I did something I'd never done before. I ran.

But I didn't run very far. Only to Reims, where I stayed for a month and served at Mass with my old friend Francois who had followed my example into the priesthood. And in the end it was Francois who persuaded me to return to my parish and my duties. I didn't tell him who Sister Madeleine really was and our history together down through the ages. All I told him was that she and I had loved long ago, before I became a priest, and that I feared if I saw her again, my vow of celibacy would evaporate like mist in the morning sun.

"Perhaps," he told me with a smile. "But as I recall the act from years ago, doesn't it require the participation of two people?"

"You mean to remind me that she may be more devoted in her vows than is my poor weak flesh?" I answered wryly.

"Come," he said, taking me by the arm, "I have half a bottle of very nice Bordeaux left. Let's you and I finish it and give thanks to the Lord that we are not in Russia."

We did, and I left Reims the next morning with a feeling that, for the first time since the long nightmare of my eternal consciousness began, I was finally going to get the opportunity to prove myself to whatever power seemed to ceaselessly test my ability to rise above my base nature. I would go to Sister Madeleine and confess that I knew who she was. I would tell her I was prepared to treat her like a true sister and fellow servant of God. We would become partners in his service. Platonic soul mates, friends instead of lovers. Over the years to come she would gradually reveal to me that which I had always been too impatient to wait for—the answer to the riddle of my existence. And now for the first time I had the strength of will and steadfastness of purpose to pray and atone for my many sins and finally make peace with God. I would attain true repentance and true forgiveness, and this time when I died I would ascend to Heaven. There would be no more weary cycle of rebirth and struggle and failure. I would at last be free. At peace.

I may have actually been humming as I rode into the village, but near the church, the weeping women with black shawls over their heads stopped me cold. They swarmed me when I climbed down from the cart.

"Pray for us, Father, my baby is dead!"

"My husband is dead . . . My brother . . . My father, my best friend . . . "

"What has happened?" I asked, stunned.

"Cholera," was the answer.

It had started two weeks before, and now half the village was down with it. There had been over one hundred deaths so far and more every day. The church and the schools had been turned into makeshift hospitals, but so many of the priests and monks who had come to nurse them were sick or dying that many lay untended in the hallways and on the steps, gasping out their last breaths. Many of the dead had not even been buried because the survivors were afraid to touch them.

"Is there no one left to tend them?" I asked as I walked past the stricken wretches lying on the chapel steps.

"Only Sister Madeleine," answered one old woman who followed me in. "She has been a saint since the illness started. She works tirelessly. Cooking, cleaning, serving and praying with the dying both day and night."

I bowed my head, overcome by guilt. I should have been here working alongside her instead of running away like a cowardly schoolboy. Well all that would cease now. I was back, and God had surely sent me here today to prove myself. I would work at her side. Together we would save each body and soul that we could, and our friendship and bond would grow stronger over the years. Pure and true love.

"Where is Sister Madeleine? Please take me to her. She has need of me, and I am now here to help."

The woman buried her face in her handkerchief and wept. "Oh yes, Father. You are so right. And somehow the good Sister knew you would come. She told me so at dawn today. She said she could not go until you returned."

"Go?" I said, fear chilling my missing finger and toes. "Go where?"

"To Heaven!" she wailed. "She said she could not die until you returned to give her the Last Rites and to pray with her."

"Take me to her," I cried, clutching the woman with my good hand. We threaded our way through the bodies to a corner where sunlight cast by the stained-glass window bathed in red, green and golden light the form of a tall, thin nun.

I knelt beside her and took her hand. She smiled up at me. A beautiful, radiant smile.

"I knew you would come, Father Christophe." She touched my face. "You have never let me down."

I felt hot tears welling behind my eyelids. "Once. I think I must have let you down terribly, once."

She smiled again and touched the wetness on my cheek with her fingertip. "Yes, Christophe. Once."

"And so you cannot go, Madeleine. You must stay with me, help me. Pray with me. And I will serve God and you. I will be your servant, your loving brother—anything you want—only please, please dear Madeleine, do not go and leave me all alone here in darkness."

The light was fading from her eyes like a candle burning down to the last few guttering flames, but the sweet smile was still on her lips. "No Christophe, I will never leave you. And remember that it is you who have the power to banish the darkness forever."

"How, my beloved Madeleine?" My tears dripped onto her pale hand as I kissed it. "Only you can tell me how." But she couldn't.

"I love you," she whispered, and the candle went out.

I opened my eyes and looked at the late afternoon sun shining in the hotel room window. The bed beside me was empty, and I heard the shower running. I got up, went over to the dresser and checked my wallet—all there—then sat at the window to watch the setting sun. It was almost time to go. I poured a shot of Grey Goose vodka into the cheap hotel tumbler and slugged it back. As I continued to stare out the window, my mind filled with that last image of Sister Madeleine and the weeping priest holding her hand and praying for her not to die.

So much for prayer.

Chapter 5

We left Boston at the tail end of the rush hour just after dusk. It wasn't that I liked traffic, but the more cars on the road the less likely anyone looking for us would be able to pick us out from the angry honking throng of motorists fleeing the city for the suburbs and a dinner of Hamburger Helper and mindless TV.

I maneuvered onto Storrow Drive and inched onto Route 93 North. It was bumper-to-bumper all the way to the New Hampshire border. I kept checking for a tail, but all I saw in the rearview mirror were fellow motorists cutting one another off and giving each other the finger.

The traffic thinned out once we passed Merrimack, and by the time we'd put Concord behind us we had most of the road to ourselves. I glanced over at Clarisse. She was curled up in her seat, head on her shoulder, asleep. I didn't know how soundly she was sleeping, but I needed to find out what was going on in the big, bad, nasty world in which I operated, so I decided to risk a call.

Reaching into the back seat, I fished out one of a dozen disposable phones from my gym bag. I always carried a supply of them because real cell phones which real people buy because they want to reach out and touch someone and be touched back—those could be traced. And I never made a call from any phone that could be traced, not even a pay phone. So I bought these things by the dozen. Use 'em and lose 'em, that was my motto for just about everything.

I dialed one of very few numbers I had memorized. As I had no friends or family, there were few numbers to recall

On the third ring, a voice answered. "Is that you?" When I answered, "Yup," he knew who it was.

"Man, you sure as hell stirred up a shit storm," he said by way of greeting. "Tell me about it."

"When Tony Bags heard you capped his kid, he went nuts. Threw a chair into the recroom TV and put out a contract on your ass."

"How much?"

"Quarter Mill. Cash."

"You got any plans to get rich?"

He laughed. I trusted him. As much as I trusted anyone, which was as much as I had to. His name was Charlie Walker, and in Iraq—and later in our merry little band of mercenaries—his nickname was Chuckles because he always smiled when he killed. But I'd saved his life outside Bagdad, so I trusted him at my back.

"I don't know where you are and don't want to know until you need me," he stated.

"But I'm gonna assume you have some place to drop out of sight for a while?"

"Yup. I'll check in with you in a few days. Keep your eyes open in the meantime." I reached for the *End* button but heard him say, "Hang on. I got a message from a friend of friend that someone wants to know if you're available for a gig in a week or so."

"I might be. Who is it?"

"Don't know, but I'll find out. Call me back tomorrow."

"Copy that, and tell him I want his real name. No hiding behind aliases and front men, or it's no deal. I don't work for anyone I can't check out. And make sure he knows—no women, no kids."

I really didn't have to tell Chuckles that—he knew the way I worked—but it never hurt to put in a reminder. He hung up, and I powered the cell phone off, hit the *Down* button on the window and tossed the phone out onto the middle of the highway. In the rearview mirror I saw it hit the blacktop and split open before a big semi traveling about a hundred yards behind me ran over it, scattering it into a million tiny bits of plastic that swirled into the empty bottles and fast-food wrappers along the side of the road.

Clarisse woke when I turned off the blacktop onto the dirt road that led to cabin, and she woke up cranky.

"Where the fuck are we?"

"And good morning to you, too."

"It isn't morning," she grumped. "It's the middle of the fucking night."

"You know, I thought *I* was a negative, nasty shit. But you make me look like a little ray of sunshine."

She shrugged and folded her arms, slumping further down in the seat. "What the hell do you expect, dragging me outta a warm hotel bed in the middle of the goddamn night to go to East Butt-Fuck Nowhere."

"Hmmm . . . Don't hold back now, Clarisse. Please feel free to share your true feelings."

"Well, I'm just saying, is all. I mean, I left New York for this?" She pointed to the darkened windshield just as the car dipped into a large pothole and bottomed out on the shocks, then snorted as if vindicated. "See what I mean?"

Just then we crested a rise and there on the other side, nestled between two enormous pines, was the cabin.

I got out of the car, walked up to the thick pine door and unlocked a heavy padlock. There was no electricity because I didn't want any utility bills that could be traced, but there was a kerosene lantern, and I lit it.

Footsteps sounded behind me.

"Christ, what a dump! Like I said, I left New York for this?"

Now I was getting annoyed. "First of all, I don't recall inviting you. And second, you had such a great career there blowing guys for quarters?"

She grabbed my arm. "Hey! I got two grand a night, sometimes more."

I took her hand off my arm. "And from such a refined and high-class clientele." She stormed over to the other side of the room and flopped down on a faded old couch. "Oh, go fuck yourself."

"I guess I'll have to 'cause I don't have two grand just now." That was lie. I had over a million in cash and gold resting in a fireproof safe on the other side of the stone fireplace. But that's definitely not something you tell a girl with a penchant for rifling through your wallet for twenties.

"I'm hungry." She pouted.

"Then I suggest you open a can of whatever is in that cupboard and start cooking."

She looked at me as though I had just asked her to sprout wings and fly. "You've got to be kidding."

"Oh, and don't forget, it's a wood stove, so you've got to get a fire going first."

"You *are* kidding. Right?"

I sighed, walked over to the stove and got a flame going in the firebox. I found a can of Chef Boyardee Ravioli and tossed it and an old hand can opener to her. "You do know how to open a can, don't you?"

"Yeah, yeah," she muttered grabbing the ravioli and crunching down on its lid with the opener.

"Ah, you might want to stand at the counter while you do that," I said as she turned the opener and in the next moment spilled down the front of her dress. "Shit!"

"I warned you."

"Goddamn it!" She stormed to the counter and slammed down the can. "Here, you do it!" On her way to the single bedroom, she stopped. "Damn, I don't have anything to change into."

I unzipped my gym bag and tossed her a plastic bag containing a sweater and jeans. "While you were in the shower back at the hotel, I visited the shop next door. I had to guess at the size."

She emerged five minutes later.

"Looks like I guessed right." Actually, I'd guessed small and tight, but neither of us was complaining. She looked almost pleased.

"Okay, where's the bathroom?"

I nodded toward the back door.

She opened it. "What . . . ? I—There's nothing here but woods and some little shack. I don't see any bathroom."

I walked up behind her and said, "You'll need this," as I put a flashlight into her hand. "Aw, shit!"

"Yup. Out there will be the place for it."

We didn't have sex that night. She was still fuming about the accommodations, and I still thought it best to maintain the illusion that I didn't have two thousand dollars. Besides, in the morning I was going to leave her. I'd blindfold her, drive her out to the main road, head down the blacktop a mile or two and then give her the keys, the car and some money for gas, and it would be "*au revoir*, Clarisse." Then I'd cut back through the woods, pick up a couple hundred thou from the safe, wait for dark and slip over the border into Canada by an old hunting trail I knew. It was a nice, clean and well-thought out plan.

I should have however remembered what Robert Burns wrote to me when he sent me his new poem back in 1786— "The best laid schemes of Mice and Men oft go awry."

Just before we were ready to leave, I called Chuckles.

He answered on the first ring. "Shit man," he snapped, clearly agitated. "You know you really should give me the number of one of those cells."

"Why?"

"Oh, like in case someone is on their way to kill you, and I've been waiting all morning to warn you. But I couldn't 'cause there was no way to get hold of you, and now they should be there any minute."

"How? How did they manage to tail me? You know how careful I am."

I stared out the door at Clarisse, leaning against the car smoking a cigarette. But she hadn't been out of my sight for a minute. Except . . . when I ducked around the corner to buy her those clothes. She could have called Tony Bags then. The little bitch.

Well, I was gonna take care of that problem right now.

I got out the Desert Eagle then thought better of it. No sense in splattering her all over the place in big messy bits. It would take too long to bury her in that condition. Instead, I attached a silencer to the Sig-Saur nine millimeter. As I went outside, she flicked away her cigarette and started to open the car door.

I stamped out the butt. "Smokey the Bear doesn't like forest fires, and I don't like little girls with big mouths. Start walking, Clarisse."

She opened her mouth to give me a smartass comeback, but when she saw the Sig in my hand her face paled. "What's going on? What the hell did I do? You're not gonna . . . ?"

"I said start walking. I can shoot you here if I have to and drag you body." She began to stumble toward the woods. When we got about a hundred yards from the cabin I told her to stop and turn around.

She was crying. "What did I do?"

"I saved your ass, and you sold me out to Tony Bags. His crew is on their way here now. But they won't find me and they won't find you, Clarisse. There will be no big payday."

"No . . . No! I didn't! I never would. You did save me, and you may think I'm just a fucking whore who can't be trusted, but it's not like that." She was really crying now. "I just never had anyone I could trust, except my sister. Shit, Cody, you treated me nice. You never hit me once. You—you even bought me these clothes." She ran her hand over the sweater. "No one ever bought me clothes unless it was something to wear while I fucked 'em."

She dropped to her knees sobbing and held her hands out in front of her. "Please, Cody. You gotta' believe me. I'd never rat you out. I, I think maybe I'm kinda' falling for you."

"Nice try, Clarisse. Is that one for free, or do you charge for that, too?"

She slumped back on her knees. "Okay, Cody. Then there's nothing else I can say." She looked up at me with her tearstained eyes. "I guess I'd rather be killed by you then beaten to death by some twisted John." She closed her eyes a moment and whispered something, almost as if in prayer, then opened them, looked straight at me and said, "Go ahead. I'm ready."

I thumbed back the hammer and started to squeeze the trigger. My finger froze. There was something in the way she said it, in the way she looked. She had pleaded but then seemed to accept death. I felt sweat break out on my forehead and under my arms. I didn't know why, but I couldn't do it. Sure she was a whore, a thief and a liar. But for some reason I believed her. She hadn't ratted me out.

But if she didn't, who did? No one knew the location of this cabin. No one. So how the hell could they find . . . Location! Damn. Location!

I left her there on her knees and went tearing back to the cabin. I flipped up the hood of the car and scanned the engine compartment. Nothing. Then I got down and crawled under the chasse, running my hand over the frame. And there it was, under the rear bumper. Its tiny red LED winked mockingly at me. A homing bug. Christ, just like some dumb-ass spy movie. Those two guys from Little T's crew must have spotted the car across the street when he told them to check and see if I was alone. And when they saw a car that would make a good surveillance vehicle, they must have planted the bug, just in case. And in this instance it had paid off. I started to remove it, then stopped. I'd better try to at least get it away from the cabin.

I ran into the cabin, pulled open the hidden safe and stuffed bundles of cash and a roll of gold half-ounce Eagles into my bag. Then I ran out to the car. Clarisse was standing there. "You're not gonna kill me?"

"No time. Got places to go, things to do. Have a nice life." I started the engine and put the car in reverse, but before I could move she opened the passenger door and got in. "I don't recall inviting you."

"You didn't. Too busy, remember?"

I sped down the dirt road and glanced at her. She was smiling a quirky little half smile, and for some reason I found myself oddly pleased.

When we got to the main road I floored it and ten miles later pulled into a little gasand-grocery parking lot. I got under the car and popped the bug off then scanned the rest of the lot. Spotting a car that looked enough like the Buick to maybe get them to follow it, I slapped the bug on it then took off back the way we'd come.

Two miles past the dirt road to the cabin, I pulled off onto an old, overgrown farm road. I stopped about ten feet up and pulled brush behind us, then drove until the road crossed over a small gully. I ran the car down into the gully then covered it with brush. With any luck they wouldn't discover the road. Or if they did, they might not find the car and so would have no idea if or where we got out.

The gym bag slung over my shoulder, I climbed back up to road where Clarisse was waiting. Then I crossed the road and into the woods on the other side. She followed.

All afternoon we made our way north, and about three o'clock I found a hollow with a little stream where we could wait until it got dark enough to cross. I got out two cans of the ravioli and opened them with my OTF knife.

"Here, have something to eat, and we'll grab a few hours of sleep while we wait for the sun to go down."

She looked at me with curiosity. "What made you change your mind?"

"About killing you?"

She nodded.

I shrugged. "I don't know. I guess I figured out it wasn't you."

"Uh, uh. You decided not to before that. Why?"

That was a good question, and one that I really didn't have a good answer to. "I'm not sure. Something in the way you looked at me. That look, it reminded me of someone."

"Who? An old girlfriend? A wife? Someone you killed?"

"Yes. No. Maybe. I'm really not interested in discussing it. Just forget about it and get some sleep."

I rested my hand on the butt of the Sig and leaned back against a big pine tree. I could feel the cushion of pine needles beneath me, and their clean, astringent smell filled my nostrils. I closed my eyes.

Chapter 6

The Cumberland Gap—Indian Territory, East Tennessee—1782

I heard the soft sound of dry pine needles crunching underneath my moccasins and smelled the sharp scent of the low-hanging pine boughs. I moved the largest carefully and quietly, making sure I didn't snap any of the thin, brittle branches radiating from the trunk.

The last ten yards I covered at a crouch and slowly worked my way between two low bushes until I had a mostly unobstructed view of the clearing. There were four white men and at least a dozen Indians—looked like Cherokee. Or could have been one of those bands of Chickamauga Cherokee that had followed the war chief Dragging Canoe during the Second Cherokee War back in '76. Though the peace treaties of 1777 had supposedly ended hostilities, it was the opinion of many men along the frontier, as well as mine, that bands of those Chickamauga Cherokees were being egged on by British and Spanish agents to raid outposts and lone farms. They also had few qualms about ambushing and dismembering small groups of travelers. I'd learned that on a steep mountain trail a fortnight before when I'd nearly lost my life.

Again.

They had attacked as we were struggling to maneuver an oxcart down a trail that was in truth little more than a deer path. While our men were hauling on ropes and blocks to slow the cart's descent, at least two score had attacked from the dark bowels of the forest.

Our muskets were in the cart or slung across our backs, and the Cherokees were well armed with British-made Brown Bess muskets. Before we could even return fire, half our party was dead. As it turned out they were the lucky ones. Outside of the half-dozen children they took to raise as their own and a few of the younger women they took to be slaves and second wives, those remaining were bound and tortured for the next two days. I know, because I watched it all from under a pile of bodies where they had thrown me thinking I was dead, too. I almost was. I'd taken a ball through the shoulder. The wound had bled profusely, covering me with blood, which was probably what saved me in the end.

Whether or not I'd survive was a near thing for a while. When they'd finally slaked their lust for inflicting pain, they tomahawked most of the screaming victims. But a few they left tied where they were to die by inches.

When they were gone, I crawled out from under the bodies and over to where the poor wretches writhed in agony. I felt queasy when I got a close-up look at their condition. Scalped, flayed, missing fingers, toes, noses, eyes . .

. Those who could still speak begged me as a Christian mercy to kill them.

I did.

Since I didn't have a musket and wouldn't have risked a shot if I had, I used a long skinning knife. Their end was as quick and clean as I could manage. One blessed me as I cut his throat.

I buried them and marked their grave with a crude cross. It was the best I could do. Then I heated the knife and dug the ball out of my shoulder.

When I came to, I bound the wound and passed out again. For three days I burned with fever that I quenched by crawling to a nearby stream and rolling myself in the water. Eventually the fever broke. I found some hard biscuit the Indians had overlooked and gradually got my strength back.

On the tenth day after the attack, a pair of Indians happened upon the camp. While they were sifting through the broken and burned remains for useful loot, I crept out of my hiding place, snatched one of their muskets, shot one through the chest and stove in the other's head with the musket's brass buttplate. I put together a good traveling kit from what they had and left them as they lay, figuring any other Cherokee who stumbled upon them would assume they'd fallen in the raid.

For the next week I pushed west navigating by my compass and the crude and mostly inaccurate map of my Continental Service Land Grant.

Though two months shy of my twenty-fifth birthday, I was a veteran of almost eight years of war. I had served with

Knox all the way from Fort Ticonderoga to Dorchester Heights outside Boston. I froze with Washington during that terrible winter at Valley Forge and had been with our victorious troops when we forced the surrender of Cornwallis at Yorktown.

Since the new Congress had been unable to pay us except in the almost worthless Continental Dollars no merchant in his right mind would take, they'd bribed us to stay and fight by promising us land in the Ohio and Tennessee valleys that they weren't quite sure they owned. I was one of the first ones to take mine and muster out shortly after Yorktown. Damn good thing I did. The poor souls who stuck around until the formal peace was declared were told that the Congress they'd fought eight years to protect had just sold their land to speculators to pay for the bloody war debt!

Governments—never trust 'em.

But come hell or high water, Continental Congress and all pettifogging government lackeys everywhere, I was going to get my land. I had fought for it and bled for it, and the only way they could stop me was to kill me. And God knows they were trying. Now as I crouched in the bushes watching the group of whites and Indians around the campfire, I began to realize that my fight might have just begun.

. . . They were speaking in low, terse tones as if discussing something no one could agree about. I strained my ears to listen.

"I say, Chief," came the clipped accent of a British officer. "What you ask is clearly impossible. Even as we speak, my superiors are drafting a treaty with the bloody Americans to turn your lands over to them."

There was an angry murmur from the Indians around the fire as one translated in angry, guttural tones what the Brit had said. Several put their hands on their knives and tomahawks, but the Englishman held up his hand.

"However, the Colonials are very weak now. Bled dry from fighting a long war they couldn't afford." He stood up and motioned another white man to come into the firelight. Two others carrying a large wooden crate followed. They opened the crate, displaying dozens of brand new English Tower and Brown Bess muskets.

I thought so. Ever since I'd crossed the mountains I'd been hearing rumors of British agents stirring up and arming the Cherokee. At first I wondered why, since they had obviously now lost their Colonies, but one of the men in our former party reminded me that they still had Canada and still held onto the goal of dominating the North American Continent.

I had backed away from the fire, travelling all night to put as much distance as possible between me and that raiding party. But I also vowed on the bloody corpses of the men, women and children I'd left North Carolina with that I was going to warn every settler I could.

Two days later I got the chance.

It couldn't rightly have been called a village—there were just three farms that shared a small green valley—but I stopped at each one and told them what I'd seen and heard. The last farm was owned by a plump Dutch farmer from Pennsylvania who commented "*Ja, Ja*" to everything I said but seemed not to take it very seriously. He had a pretty teenage daughter who winked at me and begged her papa to invite me to dinner, which he did, but I had at least six more hours of daylight and wanted to push on.

Just before I left, his wife came out onto the porch and gave me a slice of ham on a warm loaf of bread.

"You're sure you won't stay for dinner?" she asked me in a low, pleasant voice. She was wearing a calico dress and a wide bonnet, and under its brim her smile shone sincere and welcoming.

"No ma'am, but thank you kindly. Please, for your sake and your daughter's, try to persuade your husband to take you on up to Jonesboro or at least band together with the other families in this valley until this raiding party has passed."

"I'll try," she said quietly. "But Hans can be very stubborn sometimes."

Well it wasn't up to me to make them listen and act. All I could do was warn them. I'd done that. So, I waved to the woman on the front porch, followed the early afternoon sun westward. And hoped I'd been wrong about the danger.

But I wasn't

Just before dusk, as the long rays of the sun were casting shadows on the eastern slopes of the hill I was traversing, I came to the top and looked back toward the valley. Just below the horizon, I could see the smoke from their chimney fires. I thought of a hot dinner in a warm house and wished I'd stayed. About to turn back, I noticed the smoke spreading out over the valley was too thick to be from kitchen fires. I stared a few more moments. It was from a cabin. More than one was burning.

This time I ran toward the trail leading back down the mountain.

It was the very raiding party I'd warned them of, of course. Once I'd descended, I paused to take in the situation. The two farms at the far end of the valley were already in flames, and I could see half a dozen Indians tossing lighted brands into the Dutchman's barn. Soon it began to smolder, and moments later orange tongues of flame were licking up the sides.

But they hadn't been able to fire the house. Yet.

The Dutchman and probably his wife kept up a steady stream of musket fire, so it looked like they must have had several guns loaded. Even as I watched, the house fell silent. They were obviously reloading their weapons, and that was all the raiders needed. Two strapping Cherokee braves approached from either side. As the barrel of a musket poked from the window, one of the braves leaped forward, grabbed it and with one short, savage jab, pushed it back into the owner's face. I heard a scream from the cabin followed by a woman's wail. The pair of Cherokee put their shoulders to the door, and I knew it would only be moments until they broke it down and slaughtered any inside who were still alive.

I was outnumbered at least twenty to one, but I had one ace up my sleeve that I was pretty sure none of the war party had run up against. Something I'd taken off a dead grenadier outside Yorktown.

A small ledge overlooked the edge of the woods where the main part of the band was rampaging. I ran for the vantage point, knelt down and pulled from my pack a round iron ball about the size of my fist and packed with gunpowder. I lit the fuse with a spark from my pistol's flint, and as I watched it sizzle I wished the Grenadier had lived long enough to tell me how long I was supposed to hold the damn thing before I tossed it. But I couldn't ponder that at length because the fuse was burning down alarmingly fast. I waited one more second and tossed it into the middle of the raiders readying to rush the cabin. It exploded before it hit the ground, and I was more than a bit alarmed to see that if I'd held it one more second I would have been little more than a small, greasy spot on the landscape.

But the affect was wonderfully devastating. Those of the raiders who weren't killed outright by the concussion of the blast and deadly shards of iron shrapnel were skewered by splinters of the pine and oak ripped from the surrounding trees.

One of the English agents mistakenly screamed, "Cannon!" and when the smoke cleared, those Indians that were still standing howled and high-tailed it back into the woods. The Brit yelled at them to re-form, but that crew was having none of it and kept right on going. He pulled his pistol and started towards the house, apparently prepared to finish the job himself. But he was too intent on that and never heard me come up behind him and slit his throat. I scooped up his pistol and ran toward the house.

By this time the two braves on the cabin porch had recovered their wits and were both raising muskets at me. I paused, raised my own gun to my shoulder, and dropped the one on the left. But the one on the right had me in his sights, and I knew I couldn't reach him with a pistol shot. I had no cover and no shot. I was dead.

But just as the Indian cocked the hammer, the front door flew open and a mighty blast from something that sounded like a shotgun struck him. His arms flew up as he pitched forward off the porch. The Dutchman's wife stepped out holding an old fowling piece, stood there a moment, then slumped against the battered door.

I caught her just before she fell and helped her into the house. There I saw the pretty teenage girl draped in a bloody blanket, lying on a settee. I put my head down on her chest and listened for a heartbeat. There was none.

The girl's mother bowed her head. "They shot her as she churned butter on the porch." Then she turned and knelt beside her husband. I knelt alongside her. I didn't have to check his heartbeat. One look at the side of his head where the butt of a musket had stove it in told the story.

"Oh Hans," she whispered. "Why oh why could you not have listened to someone else's advice just this one time?"

She folded her hands in prayer, and I waited until she was done before helping her up. "I'm sorry for your loss, ma'am." I didn't know what else to say.

She nodded and finally looked up at me. Her hair was a reddish auburn with streaks of grey and hung in tangles of disarray around her shoulders. Her heart-shaped face was sprinkled with freckles. Age lines bracketed her mouth and cheeks, yet her skin still shone with health. She looked to be somewhere in her forties, but life on the frontier often made it hard to tell. All and all, though, she was still a damned handsome woman. I decided to help her bury her husband and daughter and then accompany her to the nearest settlement and resume my travels.

She finally glanced up, directly into my eyes. The first time I'd met her, the deep brim of her bonnet had shaded her face. Then in the stress of events I hadn't really looked, not at her eyes. Deep, round and hazel with tiny flecks of green, they stared back right into my soul.

She was The Girl.

As it turned out I never did get my land. Fool that I was, I had put my faith in the word of officials and a piece of paper. Like I said, never trust a government.

But for the time being the journey to my grant was temporarily on hold. After years of searching and staring into the eyes of every female I met, I'd finally found her again. And for the moment that was all that mattered. The fact she was twenty years my senior bothered me not at all. She had fire, intelligence and grace. We'd known one another in so many guises that we hardly even noticed what visage we saw. What glowed behind the eyes was most important. Still, she was a damn handsome woman, and as we had so many times before we began to fall in love.

Yes, we had loved before, but never for long. In each incarnation it seemed the search lasted too long and the time together was all too fleeting. I should have remembered.

That first night together we spent on the porch wrapped in a quilt watching the stars spin through the night sky. Just as we had together so many times over the long centuries. As they faded out one by one and the black velvet of the night sky lightened to pearl grey, she took my hand and spoke.

"And so, my love, once again the good Lord has closed one door but opened another."

The events of the day had caught up with me and, as delighted as I was to be once more in her company, I had begun to doze. I said somewhat groggily, "What do you mean?"

"I mean that, although God has seen fit to call my husband and daughter to Him, He has sent you back to me."

I stood, stretched and yawned. "I don't think your deity had anything to do with it. What saved both of us was a well-placed toss of a pound of black powder and steel taken off a dead Grenadier."

She jumped up and took both my hands in hers. "You mustn't say that . . . " She laughed. "I'm sorry, what is your name this time?"

"Josh—Joshua Campbell. And yours, Ma'am?"

"Abigail. Abby Van Duinen, although Hans was actually my second husband. Samuel, my first, was taken by the flux, along with our dear baby, Susanna." Her eyes grew sad. "And now I've lost another daughter and husband."

I gave her a wry smile. "If I were a betting man, I might say that the odds of reaching as ripe an old age as your husband do not seem good. But then I never was one who cared much about long odds."

She tried to smile but her lower lip quivered, and I felt like an insensitive bastard.

Again.

"I'm sorry, Abigail. I was trying to make you laugh. That was a stupid thing to say." She dabbed her eyes with a handkerchief as I took her free hand. "But I guess you're used to that quality in me by now."

She rested her head against my chest. "Yes, and I forgave you long ago."

I took her by the shoulders and stared at her. "What do you remember of that . . . of that first time we met? Did you have to forgive me then? What did I do?"

She put a finger to my lips. "Hush, Joshua. We'll have many days and nights to speak of such things. For now, we must see my husband and daughter receive a proper Christian burial."

I nodded. "Of course. You prepare them. I'll find a peaceful spot and see if I can carve a suitable marker."

And so we buried them. She read a Biblical passage because, despite my brief occasions as a man of God, I've always felt a bit uncomfortable with that book. Perhaps I feel that too many of those, "Thou shalt not's" were aimed at me.

I knocked down the burnt parts of the barn and rebuilt it and began to settle into married life. No we didn't actually get married because there was no one around to marry us. The nearest settlement with a resident preacher was Jonesboro, and that was farther away than we wanted to travel with raiding parties still likely active in the area.

So we lived as husband and wife, friend and lover, man and woman, and the seasons changed. The days grew short. Fall became Winter, and through the long, dark nights seated close to one another before the fire, we filled in the missing gaps of our lives and all of those lonely years when we had not found one another.

It was mostly I who had the gaps. For although she was born each time with full knowledge of who she was, mine didn't occur until the onset of puberty. This meant that if I died before then, I'd never know who I'd been. And throughout most of human history the majority of children died before their thirteenth birthday. So when that happened there was no way of finding out who I'd been, when I'd been born, or where I'd lived. Hell, for all I knew I could have been born a dozen times and died in infancy. All I knew was that there were gaps between many of my lives, and although she didn't know either to which parents or in what town or city or country I might have been born and died before the age of thirteen, she could and did relate to me her own existence during the years since we'd last been together.

I think we grew closer that winter than we'd ever been and, oddly enough, I forgot all about my eternal quest and question. Or maybe I just didn't want anything else to intrude upon our happiness. Besides, I reasoned there would be years ahead for those answers.

Fool.

When spring finally came, a peddler passed through the valley and brought news, or I should say lack of it. Apparently our rout of the raiders had induced them to disband. At least that was the local opinion, for no word had been heard of them anywhere throughout the surrounding countryside.

And so I decided to renew my journey to my land. Oh, this would not be to settle. There would be a return to the farm, the valley and the woman with whom I planned to spend my life. I suppose it was wanting to find completion of a task long delayed or perhaps simple curiosity that drove me to leave.

Well, remember what curiosity got the cat.

On the day I set out she hugged me fiercely and whispered, "Come back to me. Promise that you will always come back to me."

I laughed with the confidence and faith in my own young life and said, "Don't take on so—I'll only be gone a fortnight."

The worst kind of fool is one who never learns from his mistakes.

What with so-called roads that were little more than forest trails and rivers and swamps where there weren't supposed to be any, it took almost a fortnight just to find the claim. Though I'd only covered a few dozen miles as the crow flies, much of the time was taken up stopping for compass readings then trying to align them with the few landmarks sometimes positioned correctly on the map, but more often not. As I said, the maps were crude and mostly inaccurate. So I should have been better prepared for the nasty surprise when I finally did find it. Plunked right next to the only potable fresh water stream on the acreage was a squat, ugly log trading post.

I checked my compass and the map coordinates again, and as near as I could see there could be no question of a misaligned boundary. Whoever had built the trading post had put it right smack dab in the middle of property that was supposed to mine.

Filled with righteous rage and clutching my ridiculous piece of paper issued by an equally ridiculous Continental Congress, I stormed inside and demanded to see the owner.

He was an oily sort of gent in a fashionable but soiled suit, and when he smiled it was a big toothy grin with equally stained teeth.

"Can I help you, Son?"

"Yeah, you can start by telling me what the hell you and this place are doing on my land!"

"Your land? I think you must be mistaken."

"No mistake, Mister. Look here. I've got a government land grant from Congress." I slammed my deed down on the rough plank bar and glowered in righteous indignation. "Go ahead, read that."

He did and gazed up at me with amusement. "Very impressive, Son. Almost as impressive as this."

He pulled a piece of paper from his jacket pocket and unfolded it before me. It was also a land grant. And it was also signed by Congress. The only differences were that it postdated mine by six months, and it assigned not only my land but the surrounding 10,000 acres to the Grenville Land Development Company. He held out his hand.

"I'm Ambrose Grenville. Pleased to meet you."

I pushed his hand away. "My claim still pre-dates yours, so I've still got the stronger title."

He pointed to a paragraph about halfway down the page on his document. "Be it known to all men that this deed and Grant supersedes all previous claims and titles made against this parcel described herein."

Those government bastards had sold me out.

I stared down at his claim and my now-worthless piece of paper. Oh, certainly I could trek back over the mountains and appeal the backstabbing I'd received to the same people who had held the dagger. But I knew that despite whatever pious noises they might make or smarmy excuses, it would change nothing. Better to take my lumps the way I always had and go back to the valley and Abby and forget all about it. But it galled me all the same.

Maybe that's why I did what I did next.

Grenville filled a small tumbler with whisky from a stone jug on the bar and pushed it toward me. "On the house."

I downed it in one swallow and studied the keg sitting next to the jug. "This is mighty good whiskey. You must have one hell of a lot of stills to fill up a keg of that size."

He laughed. "That stuff never went into the jug you just sampled. The raw corn squeezings in the big keg are for the Cherokees and them renegades what raid with 'em."

I glanced at the cases of English Brown Bess Muskets stacked against the wall. "I see.

So you sell 'em rotgut whiskey and British guns. And what do you get in return?"

"Me? Why trade, of course. I told you, Son, that's what I am. I'm a trader."

"Oh yes, I know what you are. But I think you're most likely more of a traitor than a trader."

He pushed his chair back and put his hand in his coat pocket, but I dropped my hand to the butt of my pistol and he stopped, eyed me and slowly withdrew it.

"I think you best have a care as to how you wag that tongue, young man. Especially where you wag it."

I should have known better and shut up then, but just because I'd lived a hundred lives and learned many hard lessons didn't necessarily mean I could profit from them. When it comes right down to it, a twenty-five-year-old hothead is still a twenty-five-year-old hothead, no matter how many times he's lived.

So I stood up and said with all the self-righteous anger of youth, "Maybe the constable up in Jonesboro would be interested in your business practices."

"Really?" The trader raised his eyebrows. "And is that where you're planning on heading next?"

"Maybe."

"Well I'd be careful, Son. The trails north of here are mighty winding and steep, not to mention all the dangerous critters in the forest."

"You mean the kind of *critters* that walk on two legs, drink cheap-jack corn liquor and carry smuggled British guns?"

His eyes narrowed. "A bit of friendly advice, Son. If I were you, I'd be less concerned with poking my nose into other folks' business and more concerned with keeping that widow woman you been holed up with safe and sound."

Without thinking, I whipped out my hunting knife and drove it into the tabletop. "If you even come near her, I'll cut your guts out and wear 'em for garters."

Smiling, he pulled my knife out and gently placed it down on the table, point toward me. "Come near her? I think you've got me wrong. I'm just a merchant and a homebody. Why, I doubt if I've traveled more than a mile or two from this place since we opened."

Moving to the door, he looked outside. "No, all I'm doing is giving you some neighborly advice. One Christian to another, as it were." He pointed. "Them trees are filled with heathen savages bent on murder and plunder. You can never tell where they might show up."

He was pointing south, the way I'd come. I felt a cold knot in pit of my stomach. "You bastard, I swear the law will hear about this."

He smiled again. "And I'll be sure to watch for him when he makes his next circuit through these parts . . . In about six months or so."

He laughed as I turned and started for the path back to the valley, calling after me as I trotted to the edge of the woods, "Take care, Son. You best keep a wary eye to the forest. You never know what critters may be lurking there."

I broke into a run.

I ran, and the miles fell behind me. I was young and strong and motivated by fear— not for myself but for her. I couldn't lose her again. Not this time. Not when we'd finally found one another and were going to build a life together. Yes, she was older, but I was sure we could have children and we could have many happy years.

Fool. The worst kind of fool.

As I ran I looked for any signs of a raiding party but saw none. However, that didn't mean they weren't there. Finally, I settled into an easy trot that I could keep up all day, and as my feet kept a steady measure on the twisting path, I had plenty of time to curse myself. Why couldn't I have kept my mouth shut? I'd practically invited him to kill us . . .

. . . The more I thought about it the more I realized I'd played right into his hands. I'd given him all the excuse he needed to send his English and Indian raiders to massacre us. Then he could buy Abby's homestead for pennies and add it to his wilderness empire. And I'd no doubt he routinely bribed the local officials to look the other way. Hell, he was probably in business with the very sheriff I'd threatened him with! I should have remembered that young hotheads fight wars, but it's old men who profit from them.

I ran on.

If I kept up my pace, I was sure I could be home before any raiding party he sent after me. While the Cherokee would have no trouble matching or exceeding my speed, I very much doubted their English commanders could. But what if they sent half a dozen swift young braves to run me down while the rest of the party caught up? I decided not to stop and sleep for the night. I would push on until dawn, then hole up and sleep for an hour or two and be gone again.

I calculated that if I could keep that up, I could be home by the next night.

And I was right.

But I was also right about them sending a small party of warriors after me because only ten or fifteen minutes after I stumbled across the cabin threshold, sweating and trembling with fatigue, five Cherokee braves came bounding out of the forest thinking to rush the cabin before I could recover. But like I said, I was young and strong, and as soon as I caught my breath I explained to Abby what had happened and what was likely to.

She'd loaded the other muskets and the fowling piece, so I let the raiders get to within twenty paces of the cabin and then shot them, one with my musket, another with her dead husband's. The last two were almost through the door when I let them have it with a double load of buckshot.

Only one had a musket, which I took before pushing the bodies off the front porch. I left them lying in the yard where they could be seen in the moonlight as a warning to the rest of the party. Not that I really expected it would stop them. But it might caution them to wait 'til morning to attack.

No such luck.

For the next two hours we held one another and tried to cram everything we wanted to say into such a short time. I think we both knew what was coming, and I couldn't lie to her.

Along about midnight they arrived. They were that anxious.

They made two charges that night, but I'd learned to be a marksman during eight years of war. With Abby reloading, they couldn't get close enough to fire the cabin. By the time dawn broke, the clearing was littered with at least a dozen bodies, but they showed no sign of giving up. Someone was paying them well.

I was dozing by the window when Abby came to me with a horrible discovery. "Joshua, we have no more buckshot or musket balls."

I rubbed my eyes, got up and reached into my pouch. Six rounds. "Isn't there any bar lead?"

She shook her head. "We had it on our list of supplies to get when we went to the settlement next month, remember?"

I groaned. Given enough time, I could have broken up some pewter plates and melted them down to cast new musket balls. But because pewter has a much higher melting temperature than lead, the process would take hours..

We didn't have that kind of time.

As if to punctuate that thought, several musket balls slammed into the cabin's shutters, and I ran to the window and returned fire. By the time we'd beaten back that attack, just barely, there was only one round left.

We sat on the floor with our backs against the wall while I rolled the single remaining shot in the palm of my hand.

After a long spell of silence, I spoke what we both knew. "They'll overrun us with the next attack."

She nodded and closed my hand around the ball. "You use it."

"Are you mad, Abby? You have no idea what they do to women captives. I've seen it."

"You forget. So have I, many times."

"I don't care. I won't let you go through that." I primed and loaded the pistol. We were silent for a moment. Finally she said, "But what will you do?"

I looked around the room. "We have no more shot, but there's almost a full keg of powder." I grinned. "I'll take some of them with me."

She didn't berate me but gave me instead a wry smile. "Yes, Joshua. You're well-named in this life. You still are a warrior."

The one remaining shot went into my pistol and we settled back to wait. We didn't have long. Out the window I saw them massing at the edge of the woods. We stood up. They began to run toward the house.

I got the keg of powder and placed it beside us, then put my arms around her. They were approaching fast now. I pulled back the hammer on the pistol. "I love you, Abby."

"And I you. We shall be together again."

My words were thick in my throat. "I know."

She pressed her lips against mine—they tasted of cinnamon and honey—and closed her eyes. I closed mine and gently pressed the muzzle of the pistol against her breast.

I pulled the trigger.

She slumped in my arms, and I laid her tenderly on the floor. The war band had thrown themselves on the ground when they heard the pistol shot, but when it wasn't followed by another, they came on. A moment later they were battering at the door. As I saw the hinges bend, I took the now-empty pistol and cocked it again. There were no more bullets, but the spark from the flint would work just fine for the welcome I was planning. I knelt down next to the open powder keg and placed the pistol on the twenty pounds of raw black gunpowder.

The door crashed open. I grinned at their surprised faces and pulled the trigger.

Chapter 7

I awoke with a start. I'd heard something. Wait, there it was again . . . the sound of a branch breaking and then . . . "Shit! Fuckin' branches!"

"God damn it, Paulie! Shut the fuck up, you moron. He's gonna hear you comin' a mile away."

"Fuck you, Frankie. He's miles away by now. And anyway, it's too fuckin' dark to see a thing. I could fuckin' trip over his ass and not even see him in these shit-hole woods."

There was silence for a moment, then I heard Clarisse stir beside me. I clamped my hand over her mouth. She started to squirm, and I could feel her trying to cuss me out and felt her teeth grip my palm.

"Shut up," I hissed. "They're almost on top of us."

She stopped struggling and lay quietly. Just then, a flashlight went on and we both froze. I could see them through the pine branches, no more than fifteen feet away. If they turned and shone the beam in our direction . . . I quietly pulled the Desert Eagle from my bag, recalling the dream and thinking what wonderful inventions automatic pistols with multi-shot magazines were. We waited.

For a full five minutes they stood there arguing, cursing and blaming the woods, the trees, their employer, the majority of the human race and me. Especially me. They never mentioned Clarisse, and that interested me. At least enough to keep her on the top of my list of people, places and things to be suspicious of.

At one point she glanced up at me as if she knew what I was thinking, but the circumstance didn't lend itself to long introspective discussions, so we kept our respective thoughts to ourselves.

I must confess my thoughts ran to whether or not I should kill them then and there, but consideration stayed my hand. Meaning I considered the possibility that there might be more of them in the woods than the two I had in my sights.

Eventually they left. I could hear their progress as they retreated, bouncing off every tree and branch on the way and punctuating their passage with, "Fuck! God Damn it! Son-ofa-bitch!" and so on.

As the sound of their profanity-laced blundering faded away I slipped the Desert Eagle back into the bag and whispered to Clarisse, "We're home free, let's go."

She stood up, took two steps and stepped into a gopher hole.

"God damn son-of-a-bitch!"

The sound of snapping branches and heavy footsteps that had almost faded away suddenly stopped. "Hey, Paulie, dija hear that? Go get Carlo and Tommy."

I head more sounds of breaking branches which I assumed was the indicated Paulie doing as he'd been told. Sure enough a few minutes later a distant voice yelled, "Hey Carlo, Tommy, c'mon! This way. We just heard some bitch yellin'. I think we got 'em."

Oh, perfect.

For a moment I debated leaving her. Then I debated shooting them. Then I debated shooting her.

In the end, I grabbed her hand and pulled her through the underbrush, snarling, "If you decide to step in any more holes, please make sure you break your neck."

"Go fuck yourself."

Did I mention that she was a brilliant conversationalist?

For the next half a mile we crashed through underbrush and scrambled down gullies until finally we came to a chain-link fence topped with rusted razor wire. I checked my compass then took off my shirt and threw it to her.

"Make yourself useful. Tear off the cuff."

"Huh?"

"Oh forget it." I grabbed it back and ripped the fabric. Then I tossed the shirt cuff onto the top of the razor wire, hoping they'd see it and assume that this was where we'd crossed.

"Huh?" she said again.

Like I said, a great conversationalist.

I put my jacket back on and pulled her along the perimeter of the fence. We followed it west for a quarter mile until we came to my crossing spot. I pulled away a fallen oak tree and a tangle of branches that concealed a hole just big enough to crawl through.

When I pushed her toward the hole, she shook off my arm and turned on me. "No way I'm crawling through that shit-hole."

The muzzle of the Desert Eagle to her forehead changed her mind, though she swatted it away with her hand. "You won't do it. They'll hear you."

"You've got a point there, Clarisse." Removing the silencer from my gym bag, I slowly screwed it into the muzzle. "Now they won't."

She gave me a dirty look but got down on her hands and knees and crawled into the hole.

I followed, pulling the brush back in place behind us. Once on the other side, I took another compass reading and headed northwest. Just before dawn we emerged from the woods in back of a small rest area where another non-descript GM car was parked. I slid my hand under the front bumper and retrieved a small magnetic case containing the key. Clarisse climbed into the passenger seat, curled up and promptly fell asleep. I started the car, put it gear and headed to Montreal.

A few hours later when we got to Montreal I checked us into a small pensioner hotel I knew of in *Vieux-Montreal*—the Old City. The hotel was small enough to be unobtrusive but had a second floor room that provided a good view of the narrow, cobblestoned street. In addition, it was only two blocks from a wonderful little bistro that served the best

French onion soup this side of Paris, and this was where I took the still grumpy Clarisse as soon as we settled in.

When I told her to try the onion soup, she informed me she didn't like soup, citing the scintillating bit of reasoning that when she was in high school only the "dorks and losers" ever had it.

I glanced up at her from my steaming crock of fragrant onion soup covered in a crust of lightly toasted cheese. "Has anyone ever accused you of being complex, Clarisse?"

For once she didn't tell me to go fuck myself, but contented herself with sticking out her tongue at me and flipping me the bird.

I paused with the spoon halfway to my mouth. "Do you have any other forms of expression besides the colorful but quickly-becoming-tedious, 'Fuck you' and the single digit salute?"

She leaned back in the chair, folded her arms, cocked her head and stared at me for several moments. "I know men. Lots of them, and all kinds. Smart, dumb, big shots and bastards. But there's something about you that doesn't add up."

I raised my eyebrows. "Do go on. Have I perhaps missed one of your hidden talents in addition to *entertaining* men for a price? Are you also a psychoanalyst on the side?"

She ignored my sarcasm and continued to stare at me. "You come across as a stone-cold killer. And I've watched you in action, so I'm not saying you aren't. But then there are times when you get, like, real thoughtful. And you got this big vocabulary, and I never knew a killer who used all the ten-dollar words you do when you want to."

I scooped out the last spoonful of soup and tore off a chunk of warm French bread. "Glad my command of the English language impresses you."

I didn't tell her that I knew at least three dozen more, some of which were functionally now extinct. She cut a slice of the bread and slathered it with butter. "Careful darlin'," I said mockingly, "you don't want to ruin that girlish figure." She laughed and ran her hand slowly down her breasts to her right thigh. "Don't worry about me, sugar. I know how to take care of Clarisse's little money maker." For some reason that truth depressed me, but I didn't know why.

She leaned back once more. "Tell me about you. What's the deal?"

"Deal? What deal?"

"You know, like who are you, where you grew up, why you became a killer. Do you have a wife, kids, girlfriend, dog, goldfish?"

"Planning to write a book, are you?"

"A girl likes to know this stuff about who she's going out with."

"Forgive me. I wasn't aware we were going out. Should I make our date for the prom now?"

She snorted and folded her arms. "Okay, then if we're not dating, this is business. And just remember, I don't fuck fossils for free."

"Ouch! I wasn't aware I was that decrepit."

"You're not." She gave me an appraising look. "In fact, you're actually pretty damned ripped for a dude your age."

"Yeah, and what age is that?" As she continued to let her gaze travel over my body, I asked, "Would you like to examine my teeth?"

"Huh? Why on earth would I want to do that? That's weird."

"It is now, but that's the way they used to examine slaves before they purchased them."

"Yeah? Where?"

"All over the world. In the Deep South before the Civil War and in ancient Rome for almost a thousand years." I knew, because that's what had happened to me when I stood on the auction block during the reign of the mad Emperor Nero almost two thousand years before.

Her brow furrowed in puzzlement. "You are definitely weird. A badass when you want to be, but cute, kinda' sexy and weird. But something else, too."

The waiter brought a nice, velvet-smooth estate-bottled Bordeaux. I poured her a glass. She downed the wine in one long swallow then held out the glass for a refill. Settling back, she smiled. "So, okay, give. What's the deal with you? Fill Lil' Clarisse in on all the cute stuff. You know, the tree-lined street you grew up on with Mommy, Daddy and your pooch, Spot."

Even if that had been true I wasn't ready to talk her about it yet, if ever. So I shook my head. "Uh, uh. You first. But you can leave out the part about dear old Spot."

She laughed, but it wasn't a happy laugh. "That would have probably been the one good part. Except for my sister." Pulling out a cigarette, she lit it. "Me and my sister grew up in West Virginia in a nowhere town with not much to do except mine coal, pump gas or cook up Meth in the basement. Our mom was kind of ditzy and apparently had been pretty hot when she was young. But too much booze, Meth and screwing around pretty much wore her out by the time we were entering our teens. Not coincidentally, that was about the time the Old Man took off. It was no loss 'cause he really didn't pay a whole lot of attention to me and Catherine when he was there."

"Catherine?"

"My sister. Anyway, when he hit the road, dear old Mom went to work in the diner and did a little hooking on the side." She gave me a bitter look. "I know, like mother like daughter."

I didn't say anything.

She angrily stabbed the cigarette out then shrugged. "After that? Same old story. Got through high school and had all the boys chasing my tail and bitching at me to put out. But, believe it or not, I didn't."

She shot me a challenging look as if waiting for me to dispute her. I didn't.

"My grades in high school were in fact not bad. Of course nothing like Catherine's straight A's, but even if I wasn't some big brain, one thing I did know was that I was not gonna get knocked up in the back seat of some guy's car, pop out a couple of kids and live with some bastard who'd screw me next to the fridge so he could get a beer while he did it. No way. If all I had was my looks and one hot ass, then I was gonna make 'em pay. So I hitched a ride to Jersey with a trucker, paid him off with a BJ and took the train into NYC."

She took another swig of the Bordeaux and looked across the table at me. "You want to know who I gave up my cherry to?"

I almost gave her a smartass answer, but for some reason held back.

She stared at me a moment. "He was a fat old greasy fuck, about sixty. He burped a lot and smelled like garlic and old cheese." She paused. "But he paid me twenty grand. And with that dough I rented a nice place, bought some bitchin' clothes and set myself up in business at two grand a pop." She poured herself another glass. "Wanna know how much I got socked away in Barclays' Bank?"

"Millions."

This look said she didn't know if I was being sarcastic or serious. "Yeah, I just bet you'd like to know." She was getting slightly tipsy. No, make that a lot tipsy. "Well, let's just say it's a nice pile. A very nice pile for a very nice retirement. I'm gonna buy a villa on some island, you know."

She polished off her glass. The bottle was getting low.

"I'm sure you will, Clarisse. You've got the looks to do it."

"Awww . . . That's sweet. Hey, you wanna go back to the room and fuck? I can't keep giving you freebies, but I'll do you for half price 'cause you're being nice now."

"I'll take a rain check."

She sat back and slammed her glass down. "Oh, I get it. You don't wanna do me 'cause I'm a hooker."

I shook my head. "Nope, not even close. I've just got some things I have to do."

She finished the bottle. "Yeah, sure. Don't mind me, I'm just a hooker." She looked thoughtful. "Hooker. I never thought about it, but that's a strange name for a whore isn't it? Where do you suppose it came from?"

Without thinking I answered, "It came from the Civil War. It was a derisive term for the women who followed the Union general Joe Hooker's army. But it was an unfair term because most of them were women whose husbands were serving in the army, or laundresses and seamstresses who did washing and sewing for the troops. And still others . . . "

"Hummm? Still others? What others?" she asked muzzily, swaying in her chair.

But I wasn't listening. I was remembering a dusty Virginia road on a warm spring day a hundred and fifty years before.

Chapter 8

*May 5th 1863 — Spotsylvania County, near Chancellorsville
Virginia*

We had done it again. Our Brigade under Major General Lafayette McLaws had whipped more than twice our number of General Hooker's men, and now ol' Fighting Joe, as the Blue-bellies called him, was hightailing it back across the Rappahannock. And in his haste to skedaddle, Fighting Joe had left most of the baggage and all of his camp-followers to fend for themselves.

Thus the roads were a tangled mess of wagons, mules, discarded equipment, wounded men and all manner of females—young, old and in-between. When the captain called for a ten-minute break to let our artillery train clear the road ahead, we fell out next to a buggy with a broken axel filled with several women and a couple of wounded Union soldiers.

Two of the women were young and one was pretty, so some of the boys started to tease them, asking if they were maybe some of them "sportin' women," reputed to be traveling with Joe Hooker's army.

I sat down under a willow tree, prepared to close my eyes for a bit, but after a few minutes I noticed the teasing had begun to turn nasty. Most of our boys hadn't been near a woman for the better part of a year, and there were one or two who didn't know how to take "No" for an answer. So as their corporal, I reluctantly got up and walked over to the buggy.

There were three women and two men. The two youngest females were seated on the driver's seat while the third, a woman in her late twenties, sat on the rear seat cradling the bandaged head of a wounded lieutenant. She had long, chestnut hair and big blue eyes, and she was the one who'd drawn my woman-starved men like bees to honey. She looked just that sweet. But she was also distraught and terrified.

As I approached, the boys were standing around the buggy gawking like kids in a candy store. One big dumb private—the youngest son of our town blacksmith who we'd nick-named Ox—kept pushing his face under the buggy's fringed top and trying unsuccessfully to tip his cap. Each time he did he'd say, "Howdy missy," then bump his thick skull on the buggy's canopy, mumble "ouch" and repeat the process.

Albert Winch, a weasel-faced little ferret who shared the corporal duties with me, kept running his fingertips over the soft fabric covering her arm. She quite obviously didn't like it. So, that's when I got involved.

"Winch, leave her alone. And the rest of y'all simmer down and let these ladies be."

"Ladies?" said a lanky, tow-headed private who was no more than sixteen. "Corporal Winch done tole us that these'uns was jest a bunch of them camp followers what tags along after 'ol Joe's army. The ones they call, hookers."

"Hmm . . . Is that so? Well maybe Corporal Winch will share the benefit of his wisdom with me." I walked over to where Winch stood next to the woman and tipped my hat to her. "Is our resident pole-cat here botherin' you, ma'am?"

She gazed up at me, her big, beautiful eyes searching mine. We knew it instantly. But of course she was married. I could tell that from the ring on her finger. And she was also in love with her husband. I could tell that from the way she tenderly cradled the head of the wounded lieutenant in her lap.

Turning those beautiful, deep eyes on me, she implored, "Please help us, Corporal. We're trying to get to the landing to cross the river. My husband took a ball in the leg, and another struck his head during the battle yesterday. I fear that without a surgeon's attention the leg will mortify and he may lose it. Or worse."

All through the long ages I have been helpless to resist what I saw behind those eyes, so I nodded. "Okay boys, let's show the nice lady how strong we grow our Southern boys. Ox, why don't you lift up the end of the buggy while a couple of you others slide underneath and re-brace that axle."

They nodded and began to move, but Winch held up his hand. "Now jest you hold up a minute, Luke. I'm a corporal of this here unit, too, and I say let them wounded Yankees go to hell where they belong, and we'll take their women with us." He put his hands on his hips and stared belligerently at me. "So why shouldn't the boys follow my orders?"

I moved to stand nose to nose with him. "Because if they do, Corporal Winch, I'm gonna kick your scrawny ass all the way over to the river and drown you." He took a step back. "But the choice is yours." I glanced over to the men. "Boys, I gave you an order." I looked Winch up and down. "Unless Corporal Winch here is of a mind to dispute it. Well are you, Corporal?"

His mouth opened several times as if he was going to say something. Then he tugged down the brim of his forage cap and stalked off.

I felt a gentle hand on my shoulder. "Thank you, Corporal." Her smile in that moment almost made up for the fact that I knew I'd never have her in this life. And before she drove away fifteen minutes later in their repaired buggy she called back to me, "God bless you, Corporal. We will meet again. I am certain of it."

"**H**ey . . . Hello? Earth to Cody! Yoo-hoo, anybody home?"

I saw a hand waving in front of my face and blinked.

"Yo, sugar. You know, lots of guys pay lots of money just to look at me. And here you are, zoning out like I don't even exist. Where were you, anyway?"

I shrugged. "Long ago and far away."

"Did I tell you you're weird?"

"Several times now."

"Well, if all you're gonna do is stare through me like I'm an open window, then I think we should blow this cheese-and-onion stand."

I nodded. "Yeah. Okay, we'll go back to the room."

"What? No way. I'm not going back to that crappy little shithole."

I stood up. "Shut up and let's go." I pulled on her elbow, but she pushed me away.

"Hands off." Angry now, she folded her arms and shook her head. "And so we're gonna go back to the room and do what? Watch TV? Or no, what a minute . . . Oh yeah, I can always watch you sitting in front of the window watching the street. Wow, there's big fun, huh?"

She put on her jacket. "I'm gonna go find some club or something. I feel like dancing. Hey, you wanna dance?"

"No. And you're not, either."

"What are you, my fucking father all of a sudden?"

I grabbed her arm and held on tight as I propelled her out the front door. Loud scenes in little restaurants were not good in my profession.

In a low voice I said, "Who I am is the guy who's gonna kick your pretty little ass all the way back to the hotel if you don't move your feet and shut your mouth."

And so we returned to the room, and I went into the bathroom to take a shower while Clarisse sulked in front of the TV.

I could hear the TV blaring even in the shower, so I assumed she was pouting along with some brainless star on Jay Leno or Conan. But when I come out of the bathroom toweling my dripping hair, it took me all of two seconds to realize she was gone. Figures.

When she returned several hours later she was smiling and happy, so I wasn't surprised when she told me where she'd been. "I found this really bitchin' club downtown, did some dancing and picked up a little fast cash."

"Should I ask how?"

She flipped her blonde hair back. "How do you think?"

"I thought you were trying to cut back."

"Hey, a girl's gotta . . ."

I held up my hand. "Yeah, I know. Spare me the sad life of a working girl. I just hope you were discrete."

"Discretion is my middle name, lover. And do you know what I got?"

"No, but I'm sure you'll tell me."

She tilted her head up. "Twelve hundred for fifteen minutes of work."

I clucked my tongue. "I thought you told me you charged two grand. Are you slipping?"

She put her hands on her hips. "That twelve hundred was for a hand job."

"Now that *is* impressive. How did you get him to agree to that?"

"Well, he didn't actually agree to it. By the time we got back to his hotel room he was pretty drunk, and after I finished he sort of passed out. Soooo . . .

"You just helped yourself to his wallet."

"Hey, I earned it!"

"You are a piece of work, Clarisse." I sighed. "Well then, you can go downstairs and pick me up a couple of packs of smokes."

"'Fraid not."

"Why? Are you too cheap to part with a few bucks of your ill-gotten gains?"

"No. It's just that I, well, I don't have it any more."

Now it was my turn to be surprised. "What, you found an all-night poker game on your way back or dropped it into a Salvation Army pot?"

"Nope," she said, adding proudly, "I wired it all to my bank."

I stopped cold. "You what?"

"On the way back, I stopped at an all-night check cashing place and had it wired to my bank in New York."

I grabbed her by both shoulders and shook her like a rag doll. "You ignorant little slut! Don't you know that wire transfers can be traced? Tony Bags has probably got people monitoring your accounts just waiting for you to do something stupid. Like you just did."

I almost hit her. I felt like doing it and thought she had it coming, but for some reason when I saw the look on her face—part fear, part defiance and part resignation—I couldn't.

Instead I pushed her away in disgust. "Get packed. We're leaving. And as soon as we get far enough away from here, I gonna dump you at the first bus station I find."

But I didn't. Dump her, that is. Oh I wanted to, and I should have, but I didn't.

And once again I wasn't sure why. Maybe I was getting used to her or was developing a soft spot for duplicitous little sluts. Or maybe I was just plain nuts after too many years of living constantly on the edge. For whatever reason, despite her steady stream of muttered complaints about everything from my crappy choice of hotels, cars and places to dine right down to what I could do anatomically to myself (which showed a certain degree of creativity though a shocking lack of practical application), I kept her with me.

Perhaps it had something to do with a half-remembered fragment of the one life I couldn't recall. The life that seemed more like a dream than the dreams did. The image of sad, caring eyes searching mine for a spark of compassion and humanity that wasn't there and a soft voice forgiving the unforgivable. A gentle hand reaching out to one that was stained with blood and calloused with indifference. A voice already fading with the approach of death, trying with her last breath to bring understanding to a man clutching a bloody sword who was puzzled by her quiet strength and dignity. A man who would continue to hear those words echo down through the long dark ages of his existence . . .

. . . "Some day, be kind to someone who does not deserve your kindness."

Chapter 9

Once again I felt safer waiting until the morning rush hour to leave the city. Even if they were following, Montreal's bumper-to-bumper traffic insured that unless they were right behind us they couldn't manage a tail. And I made sure of that by taking a quick left-to-right exit across three lanes of traffic onto a feeder road and into a small strip mall. I parked and went into an electronics store whose sign I'd spotted from the highway, purchased a GPS unit and programmed it for the fastest, most direct route to Ottawa, several hours away.

We ditched the car in a downtown Ottawa garage and caught a cab to the airport. On the way, I stuffed the GPS down between the cab's seats and left it there. We got out at Departures then walked downstairs to Arrivals and caught another cab back to the city.

My hope was that Tony would have people tracking GPS signals high-tailing it out of Montreal via the highway, and that his goons would spend a fruitless and hopefully frustrating afternoon tracking a Pakistani cab driver around Ottawa.

I told the cabby to let us off across from Parliament, and we walked to the nearest Hertz office. Just for a change of pace, I rented an SUV, and since I didn't want one with their "Never Lost" GPS system, it was an older model. The clerk asked our destination and how long we'd have the car. I told him we were driving to Montreal for a two-week vacation, which meant that by the time they figured out the car wasn't coming back, we'd be long gone from Canada. At least that was the plan for the moment.

As soon as we got into the car I threw the cheap rental company map away and stopped at the first bookstore we passed and bought a detailed map book of every tiny town and hamlet in eastern Canada. Because that's where we were going.

Well before dark, I pulled off the highway and began taking secondary roads, doubling back occasionally to make sure no one was following us. No one was. Late in the afternoon, I spotted a reasonably out of the way and slightly decrepit, off-brand inn of the type frequented by fighting couples, parents with screaming kids, and salesmen who worked for companies with very stingy Travel and Expense budgets. We checked in to a corner room on the second floor which offered a view of the two-lane blacktop and the parking lot. As soon as I kicked the door closed behind us, Clarisse turned on me.

"Okay, what's the deal here?"

"Deal? What deal?"

"With us."

"There is no *us*, Clarisse. There's you and there's me. And as the poet said, 'Never the twain shall meet.'"

She raised her eyebrows. "Really? Then what do you call what we did in bed that first night in Boston? That sure as hell seems like meeting to me."

"Score one for the little lady with the blonde hair." I smiled.

"Wow. You actually *can* smile. I didn't think you had it in you, although I'm not quite sure if it makes you look nice or just plain spooky. Maybe a little of both."

"Should I stop?"

She walked around and looked at me from the other side. "Nah, it beats your usual expression."

"Which is?"

"The kind a wolf must get just before it chows down on one of them bunny rabbits."

"Grrrrr," I said, and this time she laughed, and it was actually kind of cute.

Later on we walked across the street to a little place called *The Pit Master*, which the motel desk clerk had assured us served the best barbecue around. Apparently the words "best" and "around" must have had variable meanings because what we got was a piece of tough chicken and greasy pork covered in catsup.

"What do you think?" Clarisse asked, suspiciously poking her fork at the chicken. I took a mouthful of gristly pork and chewed. "Well, it can't hold a candle to what

Cookie used to make us back when I was herding longhorns on the Chisholm Trail."

"Oh yeah?" She glanced up. "When did you do that?"

I thought telling her the truth might raise more questions than it answered, so instead of replying, "Eighteen Eighty–Six," I merely said, "A while ago."

She looked at me thoughtfully and I wondered, not for the first time, if she was quite a dumb as she appeared. Or perhaps pretended to be.

After dinner I bought two six packs of Molson and we went back to the room and watched *The Maltese Falcon*, one of my favorite old Bogey movies. Since I'd been doing very unpleasant things as a soldier in the *Waffen SS* when the movie came out, I hadn't had a chance to see it until I watched it on a tiny, fuzzy black and white TV as a kid growing up in 1950s Ohio. But from that first viewing, I knew I wanted to be a detective like Bogey's Sam Spade. So it made sense that I would start off by becoming a cop. And of course the cops told me I should serve a hitch in the Army first. I did, and wound up catching a 7.62-mm round in the back from an AK-47 in Vietnam. So much for my dreams of Bogey's detective cool.

By the time the movie ended, Clarisse was already curled up next to me in one of my tee shirts—snuggling up to the pillow like it was a teddy bear or a long-lost love. She looked so innocent while she slept. But I was under no allusions. She was totally selfish and ruthless when it came to taking care of herself. It might be understandable considering her childhood. On the other hand, I knew thousands of relatively decent people who'd had horrible childhoods. Hell, I'd lived several of mine as a slave, a blacksmith's apprentice and a Viking shield bearer. Now those were rough.

No, there was something else that had induced her to hone her looks and sex into a weapon as beautiful and sharp as a scalpel. She was calculating and self-centered, but perhaps that hid something softer underneath. Perhaps.

All the same, when I turned off the TV and got into bed, I had my wallet and the Desert Eagle under my pillow.

It should have come as no surprise that after recalling some of the most unpleasant childhoods of my previous incarnations, when I fell asleep I dreamed of one of the worst.

Rome—71 A.D.—Under the Emperor Vespasian, founder of the Flavian Dynasty

The first full memory I can clearly recall is that of a slave boy in ancient Rome. Although in truth I can recall very little of the first ten to twelve years there except for being almost always hungry or being cuffed by the overseer when I moved too slowly.

For a slave on a large *Latifundia*, parents are a casual thing. I seldom saw the woman who'd given birth to me. And as for a father, I doubted if she even knew who he was.

From the first, I could remember duties that required long hours of drudgery centered around toiling in the vast fields of the estate. In the spring I would walk behind the women sowing the seeds, picking out those seeds that hadn't fallen directly into the furrows and placing them there. In the fall it was binding the shocks of grain and winnowing. The rest of my time was generally engaged in fetching things for the road and building gangs.

I was ragged, dirty and seldom satiated, but I learned how to stay one step ahead of the overseer's lash. Usually.

On the day which changed that life forever, I was still managing to stay just beyond the reach of serious trouble and, quite honestly, I can't even recall the infraction the supervisor decided to beat me for. But first he had to catch me, and that wasn't easy. I may have been thin, but I was quick and wiry. On that day, the son of the senator who owned me was riding through the fields when he saw me weaving and bobbing as I dodged the foreman's staff. The foreman had worked up a fine sweat trying to run me down but thus far had been unsuccessful. Then I tripped. In the next moment he had hauled me up by the scruff of the neck.

I silently resigned myself to being beaten black and blue as had happened so many times.

But before I received the first stroke, Publius, the senator's youngest son, called out, "Hold there. The lad is both spirited and quick. He might make a good addition to the *coffle* I'm sending to the *Lanista* in Pompeii."

He clicked to his horse to move, and the surprised overseer could only bow and answer, "Yes my lord."

As the young master turned and rode away, he called back over his shoulder, "He's filthy. Feed him and clean him up, then send him to me this afternoon."

Later that day when I went to see him, wearing the first new tunic and pair of sandals I'd ever owned, Senator Ruffio had joined his son as they sat sipping wine in the *peristyle*. None too gently, the overseer pushed me into the room, with the hissed admonition that I'd better guard my tongue as to what I said about him or risk having it cut out. But I didn't respond because I was too awed by my surroundings to understand what was happening.

As a slave boy I had never approached within a half mile of the senator's great house and, compared to the one-room shed where I slept on a dirt-and-straw floor with a hundred other slaves, all I could think was that I must have died and been transported to the paradise of the Elysian Fields.

There were vibrant tapestries and painted frescos. Floor mosaics showed a stately scene of Neptune seated on his watery throne. And then there was the food. Mounds of fruit and trays piled high with all manner of meats and pastries. The senator, his son, and a girl of about fourteen reclined on low couches, wine cups held out carelessly for serving slaves to keep replenished.

As I stood in the center of the room gawking, young Publius said, "Ah, Father, this is the one I was telling you about. Just a boy from the fields, but he seems remarkably agile. I felt he'd make a good addition to the group the *lanistia* will assess for skills enough to do us honor at the games."

The senator stroked his chin. "Somewhat scrawny, isn't he?"

"True, Father, but he is quick."

"Is he now? Well, let's find out. Bandar!" At the senator's call, the curtains parted revealing the largest and most frightening man I had ever seen. He strode into the room like a stalking lion and bowed to the senator and his children.

The senator's daughter—Lavinia I learned later was her name—coolly appraised him and smiled. "I hope you're not sending the poor little minnow to spar with one of our champions, Father."

The senator shrugged. "Better to find out now than to waste *sesterces* on his training, only to have his guts strewn all over the first arena he's sent to." He called for more wine, turned and looked around the room, then irritated, said to his daughter, "Where is your sister?"

Lavinia yawned. "I told her to come, but you know how she is when she gets with those boring Greek philosophers she insisted on for tutors."

"Well, send a slave to fetch her. It's bad enough that your mother's abed with the chills without my children lollygagging when they should be at the family meal."

"No need for that, Father. I am here."

Everyone turned toward the sound of the voice. A tall, willowy girl with a long neck and pale, delicate features stood in the doorway. Her hair was carefully but simply done in a style which left the back of her shoulders bare.

"Ah, Drusilla. Finally." Her father motioned her to the couch next to his.

"My apologies, Father. I was so deep into discussion with Aristophanes about the stoic philosophy that I quite lost track of the hour."

Her father only responded with, "*Hurumph,*" but then brightened. "You've always been a good judge of character—

what would you say about the chances of this young scarecrow making it successfully through the *lanistia* training at Pompeii?"

"He is so young, Father."

"The best time to start them. If not, then it's back to the fields with him and a short life grubbing in the mud."

I pricked up my ears. I didn't know who or what a *lanistia* was, but it certainly sounded preferable to a short life grubbing in the mud. I stood up straighter.

When Drusilla didn't answer, the senator said, "All right then, let's see how he moves. Strip off that tunic, Boy."

I was embarrassed but obeyed.

"He's nothing but skin and bones, Father," the beautiful Lavinia said from her couch. "And dirty besides."

"I am not. They scrubbed me down good before I came here!"

They laughed. All except Lavinia, who shot me a look of pure poison.

Oops.

The senator smiled. "Well his tongue is quick enough. Let's see if his feet can match it." He motioned to the big man still standing in the doorway. "Bandar, attack."

A split-second later, a Roman short sword streaked toward my head. Only unconscious reflexes and years spent dodging kicks and cuffs saved me from a swift, sharp end to my first incarnation.

"Ha! Look at the little scamp move." The Senator chuckled with delight.

"See, Father, I told you," his son remarked, obviously pleased with his own ability to judge slave flesh.

The giant barbarian, Bandar, wasn't pleased, though. He came at me again, feinting right and then swinging the sword back in the other direction in a flashing arc. This time I ducked and rolled forward between his legs, and his next stroke chipped the mosaic tiles as he slashed it downward.

The senator's family applauded. All but Lavinia. And as I grinned back at them, I felt a hand clasp around my neck. I was lifted from the floor and held close to Bandar's grinning face. one.

He howled and dropped me, and then I fastened both hands around his ankle and bit that, too. The entire family was now roaring with laughter and applauding, even Lavinia. And to put on even more of a show, I scampered around the room making faces at Bandar and mocking his howls.

During those early incarnations one of my worst failings was supreme overconfidence. Showing off before the senator's family, I somersaulted then bowed with a sweeping flourish. And that's when I felt the point of a sword in my back. Bandar, enraged at being humiliated, was about to slice me from backbone to gizzard. The tip of the sword momentarily left my back, but I guessed that was only because the angry barbarian was drawing it back to sever my spinal cord.

A voice screamed, "No! Father, make him stop!"

The tall, thin daughter had risen to her feet and was holding out both hands to the senator. He in turn raised his palm in my direction, and I could sense Bandar, standing behind me, quivering with frustration.

"And why should I stay Bandar's hand, my darling daughter? The sprat is too dirty and ignorant to make any sort of an attendant for you, and right now I've got an abundance of field slaves. So, unless this little one can fight, I hardly think he's worth feeding."

"But, Father, he is a person. Not a thing that should be discarded like a broken jug." The senator rose. "Do not take that tone with me, Drusilla. You are still a daughter under my roof and, as such, subject to my laws. Should I wish it, the ancient law of *pater familius* gives me the right, nay the duty, to slay you on the spot if I so deem it."

She took two steps forward and tilted her head up. "Then do your duty as you see fit, Father, for I shall not sit here and let a child be slain before my eyes."

The senator hesitated. I could tell he cared for his daughter and did not want to harm her in any way. He slowly nodded, but before he could turn back and tell the giant to release me, Livinia made a slashing motion with her thumb and snapped, "Finish him, Bandar! For me."

I twisted out of the way and felt the swish of the motion of his sword, but he was on me again in an instant. I backed up until I hit the wall. He grinned now, showing all his teeth. Now at the moment of the kill, I could see that the senator wanted to watch the finale more than he wanted to please Drusilla.

So out of sheer desperation, I called to Publius a few feet away, "Please. Your sword . . . Give me your sword."

It was resting on the couch beside him. With a laugh of delight, he tossed it to me just as Bandar's blade fell.

I have never in my life had such a sensation of gratification as I felt the moment the sword's hilt touched my hand. Though almost too big for my grasp, it felt like a part of me. I knew in that instant that somehow, somewhere, before being born an ignorant, fatherless slave boy, I had wielded a sword in combat. The barbarian's blade continued toward my head. I pulled Publius' blade from its sheath and, crossing them into an X, twisted the descending blade around in a quick corkscrew motion until it slipped out of Bandar's sweaty hand.

He gave a roar of outrage and, blind with fury, rushed at me. I was not sure I'd be able to stop his charge even with my weapon.

"Enough!" the senator called out before Bandar could reach me, and this time his voice was sure and certain. "This boy has proved himself beyond a doubt. If there has even been a more natural talent for battle, I have yet to see it." He stood up. "Bandar, you may go." The barbarian would have loved nothing so much as to rip me limb from limb, but he, like most slaves of Rome, were trained to obey. And they did if they wanted to continue living. So, he bowed and backed out of the room. But not before exchanging a look with the pouting Lavinia that went unseen by all but me.

The Senator clapped his son on the back and praised him for the keenness of his eye and judgment in discovering me. And from the grin he flashed me, I could tell that in young Publius I had made a friend for life. Just like for some as of yet unfathomable reason, I'd made an implacable enemy of Lavinia.

Her father stood before me now, a stern but proper Father of Rome. "What is your name young man?"

"Lucius, sir."

"An auspicious name. Then young man, swear that you will follow the instructions of your trainers at the *ludus* and bring honor to me and my house."

"I swear it with all my heart, lord."

"Excellent. Then you leave in the morning."

But it was what the tall, stately young woman with the kind eyes said to me as I walked out that was to sustain me over the next seven years—"I will be thinking of you. And I will also be praying for you."

And that was how I left the house of Rufieo to become one of the best and deadliest gladiators that ever strode the bloody arena sands of Rome.

I heard the sounds of sobbing. Who was crying and what could they be weeping for? There was no crying in the arena, only the roar of the Plebs howling for blood, the triumphal shout of the victor, and the agonized scream of the vanquished as he spilled out his blood onto the sand. But never tears. Yet those sounds filled my ears. Soft, feminine, brokenhearted sobs. Sounds of longing, sadness and regret.

But it wasn't in my dream. The back of my shirt was wet. I opened my eyes. Clarisse was curled up next to me in a tiny ball like a kitten, softly weeping as if her heart would break. She was mumbling in her sleep. I put my ear close to her lips.

"I'm sorry Catherine . . . Oh, so sorry."

Catherine? Who was that? Wasn't that her sister's name? I wanted to go back and finish the dream, search it for details of that first recalled incarnation. Perhaps find important clues as to who I was then but, more importantly, who—or what—I'd been before that. In the first life. The one where it all started.

But right now there was a woman—a sarcastic, selfish, deceitful and conniving, but somehow strangely vulnerable woman—lying curled up next to me sobbing her heart out. Even though I could already picture the big neon "Sucker" sign printed on my forehead, I rolled over, took her in my arms and kissed her.

I never did get back to the dream that night. Maybe I didn't want to relive those next seven years of pain and brutal training, though truth be told, as I turned out to be what today's psychiatric professionals would call a natural born killer, I suppose I'd actually rather enjoyed most of it.

No, that wasn't it. It was that as I closed my eyes again, feeling the up 'til then tough and cynical little blonde sniffling into the back of my tee shirt, I drifted off into a restful and, amazingly, dreamless sleep. The next morning, over coffee in the motel breakfast bar, she was uncharacteristically quiet. I stared at her while helping myself to another cup of the strong, black, almost-palatable coffee.

After a few moments, as I knew she would, she said, "What?"

I took a sip of coffee before answering. "Last night?"

She stared down at the tabletop, drawing little designs in the spilled sugar with her plastic spoon. I sipped more coffee. Finally she shrugged. "What, you mean when I was tossing around?"

"No, I mean when you were crying, talking, and holding on to me for dear life."

"Bullshit! I was just sniffling a lot. I think maybe I'm coming down with a cold or something."

When I didn't say anything, she leaned back in the cheap plastic-and-steel chair and thrust out her jaw belligerently. "Okay tough guy, I was crying. So what? I bet you left lots of 'em bawling with your Bruce Willis tough guy, 'I'm so frigging cool' attitude."

Her glare suggested she might have gone through that scenario a time or two herself and, if that was right, then it was still a raw wound. What she said next confirmed it.

"Yeah, big, rugged–looking, cold-hearted bastards that get a girl feelin' all soft and gooey inside. And before they even realize what's happened they're cleaning up all the empty beer cans from the living room, scrubbing down the filthy bathroom and washing out your stinky socks!"

"Speaking from experience, are we?"

"Fuck you, Cody! I'm going back up to the room."

"Be my guest. My wallet, my gun and the car key are all down here with me, so knock yourself out."

That wasn't entirely true. I had more than two-hundred grand in cash, gold and negotiable securities in the false bottom of my bag and sewn into the lining of my scuffed leather jacket, but I still didn't trust her very far. At least no farther than I could throw her. Right now, that was about as far as the end of the counter. And that was also about where my trust in the lovely Clarisse ended.

The thought struck me that I wasn't entirely comfortable with her out of my sight under any circumstances, so as she started to the exit I threw a ten down on the table and followed her.

I stepped into the elevator just before it closed, and she glared at me with annoyance. "What, now you don't trust me all of a sudden?"

"There's nothing sudden about it. I actually never trusted you." She hit me then— surprisingly hard for such a small girl. "That makes twice you sucker-punched me. You may have heard that third time's the charm, and in this case it is. Because the next time you do that, I'm gonna forget what a kind and gentle soul I am. And I'm going to smack you up alongside the head so hard you'll probably never get those pretty green eyes uncrossed."

She eyed me with contempt. "And you're probably just enough of a prick to do it, aren't you? Well go ahead. I've been slapped around by bigger and meaner bastards than you."

I turned the key in the lock and gently pushed her into the room ahead of me. "I don't know whether to take that as a compliment on my self-control or a criticism on my failings as a brute."

"Well, if you really wanna know what I think . . . "

But I never got a chance to find out her no-doubt insightful thoughts on the matter, because in the next moment a noise came from the bathroom. I made a sharp chopping motion with my hand followed by placing my fingertip to her lips.

"There's someone in there," I mouthed.

I pulled the Desert Eagle from the detachable shoulder holster in my jacked, inserted a fresh clip and twisted the silencer into place. Pulling back the slide to chamber a round, I thumbed the hammer back to full cock. Motioning for Clarisse to stand behind the door, I yanked it open. The oriental maid scrubbing the tub and humming an atonal tune screamed and tipped her tray of cleaning supplies into the tub.

She waved her hands over her head squealing, "I sorry—I think you check out—go. Not know you still in room. "Eyeing the gun, she carefully backed around me and out the door. "I go now. You and Missy stay long as want in room. Have lots of happy time. Okay?"

The terrified Asian closed the door, and we heard the sound of sneakers running down the hallway as fast as they could go.

I looked at Clarisse and she at me, and we collapsed together on the bed in helpless laughter.

Once we were back on the road, time seemed to suspend itself. I chose mostly two-lane blacktops that had just enough traffic to make it easy to spot a tail but not so little that any passing car might be remembered. Most of the roads led through backwater towns that had never made it to small city size. Some had, but their industry had collapsed or become outmoded, so they'd fallen into decay. These for the most part I avoided. People with nothing to do and all day to do it in tend to remember anything out of the usual no matter how insignificant. They also are happy to talk about it—to anyone—and for free. So rather that visit the local diner or restaurant, I chose convenience stores or Gas & Groceries. Even then I had Clarisse stay in the car, because while you might remember me if you were unlucky enough to see me just before I turned out your lights for good, if you saw Clarisse you were not likely to forget her.

By this time she had acquired a pair of those skinny jeans—the ones with the little button pockets on the butt that fit her so well that, on our way out of the store, some grizzled old goat in a Dodge pickup had whistled at her and cracked, "Hey there, Missy! How do you get into them jeans?"

And instead of giving him the tired old response of, "Well, you can start by buying me a drink," to that particularly tired old joke, she tossed her long blonde hair over her shoulder and snapped back, "With a lot more money than you have, Gramps."

See what I mean?

Unfortunately old Gramps—or Charlie or Wally or whatever his name was—would remember the hot little blonde in the skintight jeans and her sexy, cool response. And it would probably be the chief knee slapper down at the coffee shop for the next week.

So, after hustling Clarisse back into the car and leaving Gramps far behind wishing he did have enough money for a girl like her, I told her, "That's it. From now on you stay in the car, and I'll go in and get us whatever we need."

"Really? And how about when I have to pee? Are you gonna do that for me, too?"

"I'll find you a nice quiet bush somewhere along the road."

"Yeah? Well, I got news for you, pal. There's some times when a girl's gotta have something more than a few leaves and a couple of pine cones. And when that time comes, you'll get the hell outta my way if you know what's good for you."

I didn't answer, but I smiled and we drove on.

That night we stayed in an old-fashioned motor court with individual one-bedroom cabins. It was not what I wanted, and Clarisse's first response was, "Oh great, we're back to the log cabin with outhouse."

I pushed open the door and scanned the place. "No, it has a bathroom."

She stepped inside and looked around, and when she got to the tiny bathroom with the rusted metal shower she sniffed. "You know, maybe I might prefer the woods at that."

"Your choice. There's plenty of them around here. Just watch out for copperhead snakes and black bears."

She glanced up to see if I was kidding, but I kept my face expressionless, and after a few moments she sighed and went into the bathroom.

That night after a supper of canned Hormel Chile and hot dogs cooked in a single pot on a two-burner propane gas stove, we played a few hands of poker. She won. The fact that she was either a very good player or a very good cheat, and I suspect it was a bit of both, reminded me once more that I was not on a romantic vacation with Little Miss Muffet, and that it was still a good idea to keep both my wallet and Desert Eagle within grabbing distance.

And because something had been puzzling me since the start of my *Travels with Clarisse* reality show, I decided to perform a bit of an experiment.

When she climbed into the old, broken-springs double bed and remarked indignantly, "Well, are you coming? It's frickin' freezing in here," I answered, "In a while. I've got a few things to do first." Which was a lie.

Instead what I did was find a ratty old wool blanket and bed down on the couch. I wanted to see if I would go back to the beginning, to that earliest recalled life. The one where even today I can still hear the roar of blood lust from one hundred thousand citizens of the most powerful empire the world had ever seen, and smell the sharp, coppery stench of the rivers of blood that gladiators like me spilled for their entertainment on the sand of a hundred arenas.

Rome—80 AD under the rule of the Emperor Titus, son of Vespasian
The first 100 days of games to celebrate the opening of the Flavian Amphitheatre laterknown as The Colosseum

I had finally hit what vaudevillians would call nineteen centuries later The Big Time. After almost three years of hacking at condemned criminals, toothless old lions and motheaten bears in the hot, dusty backwaters of the known world, I was going to get to fight some real professionals in the great capital city of the empire. Rome.

Exciting!

And hard earned. From that day nine years past when I left the senator's estate, I trained and sweated until I couldn't move. Then they doused me with cold water and kicked me back to consciousness. I was forced to carry a hundred-pound beam around the training field until I learned that for a gladiator to fall down is death.

But I'd learned that lesson, as well as a hundred others needed for survival. How to shift my weight onto the balls of my feet. How to duck, parry and counterstroke. Where to stand in the arena at a particular time of day to make sure the sun shone in my opponent's eyes and not in mine. What weapons were best against which fighter. Spear against sword. Thracian dagger against trident. The brutal and efficient Roman *gladius* against the barbarian long-sword. I learned them all, and I learned them by hard use and harder knocks.

I had been cut, punched, stabbed, slashed, brained, clubbed and gouged, but I had survived. With every battle, skirmish, victory and defeat, I became stronger. Most of the young warriors that had been sold, sent or sentenced to the *Ludus* had been crippled, maimed or killed during the nine years I'd trained. But a handful, like me, had survived. And those who had were good, very good indeed. Among them all, they told me I was the best.

And now I had finally been given a chance to prove it in the greatest display of gladiatorial prowess and wholesale slaughter the world had ever seen. I was going to fight in the grand games to celebrate the opening of the new Flavian Amphitheatre. Its construction had been started by the Emperor Vespasian, who'd died before he could see its completion. But his son, the new Emperor Titus—and his mad brother, Domitian—would see to it that rivers of blood would flow to honor their father's spirit and christen the pristine white sand a deep dark crimson.

That was where I and my fellow gladiators came in. We were going to provide the screaming mob with the entertainment so dear to a Roman's heart—spectacular, brutal and numerous deaths presented in the most dramatic and inventive ways. Some of us would fight beasts. Others would slaughter condemned prisoners. The best of us would fight each other. I was one of those.

So now I waited under the arena floor's thick support beams. Even through the massive brick walls I could hear the roar and rumble of the screaming mob, like a howling wave against a distant shore.

I was excited and nervous but concentrated on keeping calm by reviewing once again who of the many possibilities would wind up being my final opponent. Because I had no doubt that I would make it to the afternoon paired matches, which was where the winners of the morning's melee would end up.

In a few minutes the wooden doors at the top of the stairs would be thrown open and, dressed as Roman Legionnaires, my band of gladiators would emerge onto the hot sands to meet another group of gladiators dressed and armed as the soldiers of Rome's greatest historical enemy, Hannibal.

Suddenly there was a great cheer from the mob. It was time. I drew my sword, and we flooded out into the arena. Keeping to our role as Legionnaires, we locked shields and advanced in step. Their first wave crashed into us and broke upon our shield wall. Then it was every man for himself, and the massacre began.

I dispatched the first opponent with an economical backhanded slash that allowed me to sever the hand of another with the return stroke. The crowd loved it. After that, it was merely a matter of pleasing the crowd with the drama of my kills. And I knew how to do that.

Feigning a wound, I listened to the crowd moan, thinking me a dead man for certain, as did my opponent. I sank to one knee as though powerless to stand. Playing to the crowd, my opponent strutted up to me and raised his hands in victory. Fool.

That was when I sprang forward and skewered him like a gaffed fish. The crowd was ecstatic. By the end of the mock battle there were but a dozen men left standing out of the fourscore who had entered the arena. But I was one of them.

As the games paused while former sailors and slaves manned the ropes of the huge sailcloth awnings that protected the crowd from the noonday sun, I rested and ate in the cool dark basement rooms, then changed into my armor for the matched-pair combat.

We weren't supposed to know who we'd be facing until the fight, but I had bribed one of the guards and learned I'd be matched against a giant blonde barbarian from Germania. That was good. He'd be strong but slow, and I was strong and quick. Very quick.

I was proved right when I faced him that afternoon. We fought until we were the last pair still in combat, and that was the way I wanted it. Why? Because I wanted to make a name for myself. I wanted to be seen by all, from the lowest plebe in the stands to the great Emperor Titus himself. And now I was.

I risked a glance at the Imperial box as the big German rushed me again, and I easily sidestepped him. Yes! Titus and his brother were watching. My time had come. The huge German was tiring himself out by putting too much effort into swinging his long, heavy sword. We both knew that if one of his blows connected he would take off a limb. Or my head. But it required far less effort to sidestep or deflect those heavy cuts, and thus I was still breathing in steady, measured breaths while he panted and gasped like an old hearth bellows.

One more glance. A senator rose and started toward the emperor. In another moment, Titus's attention would be diverted. It was now or never.

I opened my guard and baited the barbarian into rushing me with a mighty swing. Catching his long blade in mine with a corkscrewing motion, I twisted it from his sweaty grip and opened up his stomach with a single slashing strike. He bellowed in pain and dropped to his knees. Then I performed the trick I'd spent years perfecting—I twirled my weapon, tossed it end over end in the air, caught it by the hilt in my right hand and slashed. I twirled it again, caught it in my left hand and slashed. The barbarian howled as a perfect X appeared on his chest, spurting blood. I turned to the emperor and crashed my sword hilt against my chest plate and bowed.

The crowd went wild.

Titus let the shouts build before smiling at me and making the slashing gesture that meant death. I bowed again and turned to the luckless German bleeding to death on the sand.

"May the goddess Fortuna treat you better in the next life, Brother." My blade moved once in a circle, and I decapitated him with a single stoke.

The crowds' screams seemed to make the very sand and stone vibrate and rumble. After a few more moments, I bowed again to Titus and began to walk toward the stairway. That's when I noticed his brother, Domitian, whispering in his ear. Titus nodded, and a Praetorian guard was sent running out to me.

"The Emperor commands your presence in the Imperial box."

I had done it.

When I reached the emperor I went down on one knee, but he bade me stand.

"I understand you were Senator Ruffio's slave before he sent you to the *Ludus*."

"Yes, Majesty."

"And that he sold you five years ago to pay his debts."

"That is also true, Great One."

Titus and his brother exchanged a look. "Then it seems most appropriate that you perform one last service for your former master."

"Of course, Emperor. I am yours to command."

"Excellent. You see, the good Senator and all his family stand accused of treason. In fact, were it not for his daughter Lavinia coming forward and convincing me that only one of them was responsible for the treachery, the entire family would now be entering the arena in chains to await execution." He turned and nodded to a woman reclining on the other side of his brother. She slowly looked up and smiled at me with triumphant spite. Lavinia!

I must have looked confused, because he sighed. "Yes, I don't doubt that a gladiator confines himself to thoughts of combat rather than politics, but an emperor must be constantly vigilant against all forms of subversion. And one of the most insidious is the seditious new cult of the Christians." He shook his head in disgust. "As my brother correctly points out, they consider that Hebrew criminal executed almost fifty years ago to be their true king. That is treason!"

All I could do was nod and wonder what all of this had to do with me.

He told me.

"It's bad enough when slaves and plebs are seduced by this cult, but when members of the nobility, a child of one of the Fathers of Rome, is guilty of practicing this treason . . . Well, it leaves me no choice." He looked me up and down. "And that's where you come in. You can do a service for your

Emperor and your former master as well. Senator Ruffio assures me he is loyal and has submitted his daughter to our justice. As our champion of today's games, it shall be your honor to execute this criminal."

He nodded, and I heard the massive arena gates swing open behind me. I turned.

While the emperor had been talking, a stake had been erected in the center of the arena and walking towards it, slowed by the weight of heavy chains, was a pale, thin girl with a long, aristocratic neck and delicate, sensitive features. The only person who had ever shown me kindness.

Drusilla.

As I watched, remembering her defense and compassion shown to a ragged slave boy who would have been slaughtered without her intervention, I felt an unfamiliar sensation of concern and affection. She'd offered a soft word, a gentle touch, a concern for me no one else had ever shown. But most of all, I recalled the way she had looked at me that day with tenderness in her beautiful dark eyes. And in the years of brutal training that followed, that memory had sustained me and given me hope. Hope that I would one day be something more than a slave—and now I was. I was champion of all Rome and the only person I had ever cared about was being chained to a stake in the middle of the arena before 50,000 cruel and bloodthirsty animals who were howling for her death. And I was expected to provide it.

I turned back to the Emperor. "Majesty—please, I know this woman. She is good and kind and no traitor. She . . ."

"Silence!" Domitian stood before me, face dark with fury. "Do you presume to tell the Emperor who is and is not a traitor? You will do as you're commanded or join her at the stake!"

He turned to the captain of the Praetorians. "Escort him to the stake and see he does his duty."

Two burly Centurions fell in on either side of me, and I descended back onto the arena sands. In a walking daze, I tried desperately to think of a way to save the only thing in the world I'd ever cared for.

She saw me coming, and when I was a dozen steps away—in spite of the manacles around her wrists that cruelly stretched her arms over her head, almost suspending her—she broke into a beatific smile.

"Lucius? Is it really you? I had heard of your fame even in my cloistered circles. I always feared for you, but was glad you had found a path that could free you from a life of slavery." She gazed around the arena and then at the sword at my side. She smiled sadly. "And now you have found the way, for at the conclusion of these games, the Emporer will surely present you with the *rudis,* the wooden sword of freedom."

I felt my face redden with shame. "I am sorry, Lady. I do not wish to harm you. Tell me what to do to save you. My sword is yours to command. But say the word, and I will cut down all who come to slay you."

She shook her head. "You cannot fight all of Rome. I have been condemned by my own family."

"Lavinia!" I spat the word.

"Do not hate her. She is a product of her world. I have tried to bring her and my brother into mine, but could not. My brother was puzzled by my faith, and Lavinia despised what she could not understand. Because of that faith, I'm not afraid to die."

"Yes, in the barracks I heard of your cult. They say you all expect to go to some sort of paradise where the shade of your nailed-dead carpenter will welcome you to the Elysian Fields."

She smiled. "Something like that, but so very much more."

"And so you believe that with your death here today you will enter this paradise?"

"No, it is not my time yet. I am charged with continuing on. With you."

"With me? I don't understand. Then you wish me to fight for you here, to rescue you and escape? Then I am yours to command, Lady." I drew my weapon. Thinking me about to kill her with it, the crowd cheered. I leaned close to her ear. "When the first of the guards approaches, I'll kill him quickly with a single thrust, then use his spear to bend out the links connecting your manacles. And then "

"No. You misunderstand me. I don't want to see you kill or be killed, so you must do as commanded. But do not worry, we will meet again."

The crowd had become restless. Some had begun to boo while others called on the guards to dispatch her. I saw them look to the emperor. He was frowning.

"You're not making sense. Meet again? How? I do not believe in your crucified god, so how will we meet again?"

"In another time and another place. Just as we have before. Look into my eyes, Lucius. Do you remember?" I stared into those dark eyes as they locked onto mine. "What do you see?"

My throat had gone dry. My mind filled with a confused jumble of images. "I, I see a girl. A young woman in a ragged brown dress. She is reaching out to me. Pleading. But I have my orders, so I close my ears. She is crying. I have a sword in my hand. She begs me not to use it, but I . . . No!" My heart was pounding so hard I couldn't breathe. I whispered, "I killed you."

"And I forgave you."

"Gladiator!"

I spun around. Domitian stood in the Imperial box pointing at me. "Carry out your orders this instant!"

All I could do was shake my head.

He whispered to his brother then turned and faced the crowd, spreading his arms wide. "Citizens of Rome. It seems our champion has so worn himself out with his earlier battles that apparently his sword arm has not enough strength left to sever the neck of one thin woman."

The crowd laughed and jeered at me.

Domitian raised his arms for silence. "Therefore our noble emperor, my brother, has decided to send him some help." He waved his hand. "Release them."

A section of the arena floor dropped, and from the elevators operating below there came a gut-chilling roar. Moments later the floor rose again, only this time it was covered with ravenous lions.

Earlier, the guards had told me that the lions had not been fed for three days before the games so they would instantly charge any living thing and tear it to pieces.

And that's exactly what they did.

Four or five of them bounded across the sands, and I barely had time to draw myself into a fighter's stance a few feet in front of Drusilla before the first two were on me. I dispatched one with a thrust straight into his ribcage and through the heart, then whirled just barely in time to catch the second as he leaped. I stabbed straight up and caught him in the throat as he came down. He roared. I twisted the sword and he went limp.

The crowd was yelling again, but this time it was for me. The third, a lioness, tried to sneak in from the side. I saw her out of the corner of my eye and rolled toward her, slashing her belly open with a two-handed gash. Her blood and intestines spilled onto the sand, and the other two pounced on her and began tearing away hunks of living flesh.

I stopped them. I had won. The crowd cheered themselves hoarse. The air shuddered with clapping hands and stamping feet.

I turned back to Drusilla. "You are saved, Lady. They must set you free now."

Fool.

Domitian was not through yet. I saw his hand dip again, heard the rumble of the elevator and more great cats. Lions, now followed by leopards and striped tigers from the Orient, came pouring forth.

I cut and slashed and stabbed until I was dripping with blood to the elbows. And that's when the now-slippery hilt of the sword turned in my hand. I felt a great claw rip my shoulder open, and I scrabbled for my sword as the spotted cat savaged my left arm. At last my palm closed on the hilt, but it was too late.

A gasp from the crowd, and I turned my head to see a huge male lion with a bristling dark mane rear up on his hind legs and sink his fangs into Drusilla's long, aristocratic neck.

In the instant before her eyes rolled back in her head they caught mine with a look that seemed to pierce my soul. And then she was gone in a great gout of blood as the lion tore into her.

I screamed, hacked at the cat on top of me and half severed his head. Still screaming, I stumbled forward, charging the lion savaging Drusilla's body, stabbing him over and over as I felt the other cats sink their fangs and claws into my flesh. I stabbed and screamed until the world turned into red mist, and all I could see were her eyes.

I felt their claws on my shoulder and scrabbled for my sword. I couldn't find it, so I grabbed the lion by its long golden mane and pulled, prepared to rip out its throat with my teeth if that's what was necessary to keep it away from Drusilla.

"Shit!" The lion screamed. "What the fuck is the matter with you!"

The lion screamed . . . "Shit" . . . ?

I blinked and released the mane. Because it wasn't a mane and it wasn't a lion. It was the long blonde hair of a very pissed Clarisse.

"God Damn you, Cody, I climb out of a warm bed to try to help you, and you almost fuckin' kill me!"

I got up and walked into the bathroom, splashed cold water on my face, then came back and sat on the edge of the bed next to her. "I'm sorry."

"Well you should be, you bastard." She rubbed her throat. "Damn, you are fuckin' weird. What were you dreaming about? You were crying and screaming and thrashing around, waving your arm like you were stabbing something."

"I was."

"Huh? What is it with you and these dreams? It's like you're really there or something."

"I am."

She sighed and lay back down, touching my hand lightly. "Okay baby, do you wanna talk about it?"

"No." I lay down on the bed next to her, rolled over and closed my eyes.

Chapter 10

I wasn't sure if my half-assed experiment had been a success or a failure, but either way I didn't dream any more that night. And, for some unfathomable reason, I was beginning to think that it might have something to do with Clarisse.

While alone on the couch I had relived my first incarnation, at least the first one I could remember clearly, and perhaps most painful of the many lives I'd lived. But I knew that while my life as a gladiator who killed to amuse the bloodthirsty mobs of Imperial Rome was the first one of many seared into my mind, it was not the beginning. My true first life was the only one I could not call to memory. All I had were nightmare snatches of blood and darkness, and two great dark eyes gazing at me with unbearable sadness. I shook my head angrily and got up. I moved to the bed and lay down next to her. And for some reason with the little blonde curled up close beside me, there was nothing, just blessedly peaceful sleep. A coincidence? Over two millennia I had learned not to believe in them.

When I awoke the next morning after a rare, dream free sleep, I looked down at the conniving, double-dealing little hooker next to me who looked like an angel and cussed like a sailor. But there was something more to her than the sexy package of deceit and desire showing on the surface, and I decided to watch her more carefully until I figured out what it was.

The following afternoon we arrived in Toronto. I took the 401 Highway west, got off in the northern suburb of Yorkville and turned onto Bloor Street.

This time I had decided on something different in case we were still being followed. . So far we'd stayed in small, city hotels or tiny, out-of-the-way motels. If they were on to us, that's what they would be expecting. So I did the opposite. I booked us a plush room in the Four Seasons on Avenue Road in the swankiest section of the most upscale neighborhood in Toronto.

"Well this is more like it." Clarisse's eyes lit with dollar signs as she took in the luxurious lobby and suave guys in suits with expressions that almost begged to be taken for a sucker's ride. And my little blonde tart was just the girl to drive them there.

The desk clerk was too well-trained to ask if we could afford the rate, but rather than show him we could, I was careful not to flash too much of my roll. Instead, I pulled out a billfold I kept for just such an occasion and counted out enough to cover the tab in advance for two nights. Once again we'd only be staying one.

The bellman asked awkwardly if he could take my bag. My gym bag.

"No, but thanks, anyway." I picked it up as I looked around for Clarisse.

She was already lining up her future scores. I had to cut her off quick before she called too much more attention to herself. If that was possible.

"Come on, Darlin'," I said in the tone any guy with a girl who looked like Clarisse gets used to using when it's time to drag her away from the cluster of guys she inevitably attracts.

"What the hell do you think you're doing? You're . . ."

I squeezed a pressure point at the joint of her right elbow that if done correctly can cause momentary loss of motor functions. I had learned it almost a thousand years prior from a Chinese monk. He had taught me well. I saw her knees wobble and her eyes roll back.

Snaking my arm around her waist just before she fell, I winked at the two guys who gaped at me as I rained on their parade. "She had a little too much on the flight in from Chicago." It never hurts to muddy the trail.

By the time I got her up to the room the dizziness had passed and she was back to being pissed. But before she could build up a full head of steam, she noticed the room. The angry pout quickly morphed into a smile. "All right Cody! For once you didn't book us into a shithole." She fell back onto the king-size bed and stretched out her arms. "Come here, Hon. Clarisse has got a little sugar for you."

I put my gym bag on the desk and checked the Desert Eagle's magazine. I was going to have to break it down tonight and ship it ahead of me to our destination. Tomorrow I was going to board a flight to San Francisco, and I still hadn't made up my mind if I'd be alone or not. But first I had a phone call to make. Grabbing another throwaway phone, I slid it into my jacket pocket then turned to Clarisse.

"I'm going out for a while. The room has a nice Jacuzzi tub and a whole bunch of scented soaps. Have yourself a bubble bath." She started to open her mouth, but I slipped the Desert Eagle into my jacket holster and walked over to her. "Enjoy your bath, Clarisse. But if you leave this room for any reason, I will find out and I will kill you."

I turned and left, shutting the door quietly behind me.

When I returned, before sliding the plastic key into the lock, I checked the small square of transparent tape I'd left between the door and the jamb. Broken. The door had been opened. If she wasn't there, I'd find her. And this time I would kill her.

But she was there.

The sound of the Jacuzzi accompanied her surprisingly sweet, sultry singing. But had she been out? I checked her shoes, but the tiny grains of table salt I'd sprinkled in them hadn't been disturbed. So she hadn't left the room. But someone had entered. I drew the Desert Eagle and eased open the bathroom door.

She lay in the tub up to her neck in bubbles, a champagne flute dangling from one hand.

"Don't you ever get tired of playing with that gun?" She took a sip and poured herself another glass from the half-empty bottle sitting in an ice bucket on the floor. "Room service," she said taking another sip. "Did you know I did three semesters of psych at City College? Very useful in my profession, by the way. They always talked about things men use as substitutes for having a good package. You know things like cars, boats, fancy clothes. Guns."

She looked me up and down. "But you puzzle me, dude. I've seen you in action, and you've got no problem there. So what's your kink? I mean what is it with you and that cannon?" She did a theatrical little pout. "It's enough to make a girl feel inadequate."

I couldn't help it. I smiled. It actually felt kind of good. "Get dressed, Clarisse. I'm taking you out to dinner."

And that's where we were spotted.

I didn't know it then, but a busboy who ran coke on the side heard from a friend of a friend, etc., that anyone who spotted a hard-looking guy with a hot blonde was to get in touch with the guys from NY. And he did. But like I said, I didn't know that then.

That night we were just a guy and girl out to dinner. That is if you ignored the fact that the guy was carrying a .50-cal with a silencer, and the girl, who looked like a movie star, would probably roll you for a quick hundred.

But the food was good, and the Merlot was even better. And for once I felt like talking. That's always a mistake.

"So tell me all about Cody" She tore off a hunk of French bread and slathered it with butter and about half of the very expensive *pâté fois gras* I had sprung for as an appetizer. I had become quite fond of it while serving under Napoleon. She wolfed it down and licked her fingers. "Mummm. Nice." She picked up the menu. "Hey, is this petite filet one of those super-tender little Philly steaks?"

"You mean a filet mignon?"

"Yeah, that's the one. Hey, you mind if I finish up that meat paste stuff?" She tore another chunk of bread and without waiting for my answer polished off the rest of the *pâté*. "May I ask you a question, Clarisse?"

"Shoot," she answered around a mouth full of bread and *pâté*.

"How do you stay so . . . ? I mean, you've got a smokin' hot body for a girl who eats like an NFL linebacker on steroids."

"Don't know, Cody. Maybe good genes or nervous energy, or I secretly barf it all up when I get home. Take your pick."

I leaned back and smiled. Damn. This was beginning to be a habit, and not one I was used to or particularly wanted.

"But anyway, you're dodging my question. C'mon, what makes Cody tick, outside of blowing guys away?

"I also like kitty cats, long walks on the beach and cleaning my gun."

"C'mon, dude, don't be such a shit. I told you all about me. Give me something. Like where did you grow up? Did you have nice parents? A brother? Sister? Dog?"

I started to laugh, then realized I couldn't even remember their faces. Which ones were they? The nice suburban Ward and June Cleaver ones I had growing up in the 'burbs during the Fifties? Or my old man who used to beat me with a leather razor strap? No, it was neither of those, but for some strange reason I told her.

"Not much to tell. I grew up in LA. My parents were ex-Flower Children who made the transition from the Free Love Sixties to the Paid Love Seventies via the porn industry. So I sort of grew up on my own until my teen years when I got jumped one afternoon coming home from school. It was a Hispanic gang, but there were only five of them. When we were finished, two had broken arms and one—according to the doctor's report—will be unlikely to father any future gang members."

"So you were a badass from day one, huh?" She cut off a big bite of her filet mignon. "Ummm. Okay, so then what? Did you go to college. Have a girl friend?"

"What, you writing a book?" I took a sip of wine and sighed. "Anything else?"

"Yeah. When did you start killing people?"

I took my steak, sliced the remaining loaf of bread in half, then put the meat into it and took a bite. Old habits from a hundred armies die hard.

"Wow, and you think my style of eating is weird!" She shook her head. "Anyway, you were telling me . . . ?

"Actually I wasn't, but the short version is that because I had a talent for fighting and was very good at it, the gangs actually started paying me to take down rivals. I was eighteen when I went up before the judge and he gave me a choice, the Army, or three-to-five. I don't like confined spaces or playing peek-a-boo in the shower with guys named Butch, so I chose the Army. And I was very good at that, too." I took a long drink of wine. "I always have been."

"Huh, what is that supposed to mean?"

"Nothing. I think that's enough chit-chat for one night. C'mon, you've finished your steak. Let's go." I started to get up.

"No way. I haven't even had desert yet. Do you think they've got any of that chocolate mouse stuff?"

I started to tell her it was *mousse* not mouse, then stopped myself and smiled. "I think so. Hey, waiter, bring us both a big serving of chocolate mousse."

It was on the way back to the hotel that I felt that odd prickly sensation which always warned me when I'd picked up a tail. I kept stopping to let Clarisse look into store windows and, while she rattled on about the clothes or jewels, I scanned the reflections for anyone following us. I couldn't see anyone, but I knew they were there.

When we got back to the hotel Clarisse polished off the remains of the champagne then bounced down on the bed. "C'mon killer, champagne always makes me frisky."

She was gorgeous, sexy and hot, and I enjoyed it very much. And most importantly, afterwards she curled up in my arms and went to sleep. I slept, too, and it seemed as though my theory was proving correct because I didn't dream. For some reason, when Clarisse was close to me I didn't dream.

And that was a good thing because, unencumbered by my violent, thrashing dream-induced memories, I was able to come instantly awake when I heard the door lock click open at 4:11 AM.

I was out of bed in an instant, slipping behind the door just as it swung open. I let the killer enter and take three steps toward the bed to make sure he didn't have anyone with him, then kicked the door shut with my foot and was on him before he could swing his 9- millimeter around.

Snapping his wrist with a quick turn, I then released the catch on the five-inch, carbon steel blade of my OTF combat knife. It opened with a deadly *snick,* the tip halting a millimeter from his right eyeball.

"Damn," I said. "Missed. Would you like me to try it again?"

He shook his head.

"Good answer. Now let's sit down and get to know one another."

Chapter 11

I didn't like the first answer he gave me, so I broke one of his fingers just to let him know that he needed to try a little harder. Only one, because Clarisse, now awake, was watching me. And oddly that made me uncomfortable. Not that she said anything or expressed any emotion— she didn't—and maybe that's what made me uncomfortable.

It's been my experience that women have one of two reactions to violence. They hate it or they love it.

Don't believe me about the love part? Just watch the women who go to boxing or wrestling matches and look at their faces. They're getting turned on watching a couple of guys pounding the crap out of one another. In fact, a dance-hall girl in San Francisco back in 1891 told me after watching Gentleman Jim Corbett fight Peter "Black Prince" Jackson that the fisticuffs made her feel, "all warm and squishy" inside. Ah, the gentle flutterings of the fair sex. Yeah, right.

But Clarisse was the first woman I'd ever met who expressed no emotion at all about violence. She didn't approve. She didn't condemn. She merely observed.

That made me uncomfortable.

She sat cross-legged in the middle of the bed, elbows on her knees, chin resting on her hands. I did my best to ignore her, but I kept having this feeling that there was more going on behind those pretty green eyes than I was picking up on.

Fortunately, after the hit man tried out his first half-true story and after I broke one more of his fingers to demonstrate what was going to happen every time he lied to me, he caved and told me we'd been made by the busboy at the restaurant. He'd gotten the call and the contract because he was local talent and on the spot. He also told me while I cleaned my fingernails with the sharply tapered point of the OTF knife—I always try my best to provide an atmosphere that encourages honesty—that he was to take me alive if possible. Because three of Tony Bags' boys would be in Toronto by morning, and Big T especially wanted home movies he could watch in prison of me being dissected. Slowly.

When he was through he asked me if I was going to kill him. Stupid question. I asked him how many people he'd killed. He shrugged. "Enough."

I nodded. "Then you know that assassins don't die in bed." He didn't say anything but he knew. "Ever do any women or kids?"

"Not when I can help it."

"Good man," I said. "Then I'll make it quick."

I was about to tell Clarisse to go into the bathroom and then recalled how she'd watched me blow away Little T without so much as a gasp. Still, I don't like an audience. But he was a killer and a loose end, and I don't like loose ends either.

The silencer quickly attached, I went around behind him and pressed the barrel to his skull just behind his ear. Still she watched, head cocked to one side like a quizzical owl. Oh, what the hell. I drew back the barrel and smacked it across the back of his head.

He pitched forward.

"Take that sheet off the bed and bring it to me," I snapped at Clarisse. I glanced up. She was grinning. "What?" I snarled.

She pulled the sheet off, walked over to hand it to me. "Here ya go, tough guy."

"You know this sheet is big enough to hold two, Clarisse."

She stuck her tongue out.

I sighed. "Okay, get me a washcloth to gag him with and help me roll him up.. Then I'll put him in the closet. I've got the room for two days, so we'll put the Do Not Disturb sign on the door, and hopefully they won't find him for at least a day. By that time, we'll either be long gone or dead. Now get some clothes on. We're leaving"

As usual we avoided the lobby and the front desk by going down the back steps. I told Clarisse to walk down one block then turn right and hail a cab. Surprisingly, that's just what she did. I half expected her to take off as soon as she was out of my sight, but apparently she'd decided I was a good meal ticket and was content to ride along. Until I got killed or something better came along.

For my part I still hadn't decided if I was going to dump her at the airport, but I had a hunch that when whatever dust we were about to stir up settled, we'd be riding the big 757 to San Francisco together. Or we'd be dead.

The cab pulled up next to the corner of the hotel. I scanned the street one last time before I got in. So far so good.

On the ride to the airport I kept looking at the cars around us for any potential tail. Just before we pulled up to the departure terminal, I spotted it. A big black Escalade with windows tinted so dark they were almost black. I couldn't see who it contained, but knew it was them.

Once we pulled off the exit ramp to international flights, the size, newness and blacked-out windows of the SUV made it stand out like a nun at a bachelor party. I waited until we pulled into the chaotic mash of taxis, limos and buses. Once fairly certain we'd been lost in the jumble of vehicles disgorging passengers, I told the driver I'd made a mistake and that we were picking up, not departing.

The driver, who spoke very little English to begin with, merely shrugged and spun the cab down the ramp

A few minutes later we were down at Arrivals in front of the baggage terminal. We went up the stairs to Departures and, almost without thinking, I bought two business-class tickets to San Francisco. I handed one to Clarisse, who raised one eyebrow and gave me a look somewhere between a question and a smirk.

"I know," I sighed. "I'm as surprised as you are."

Now all we had to do was stay alive until boarding. Worst of all, I was soon going to be unarmed. I had broken down the Desert Eagle and sent it along with the OTF switchblade to my Post Office box in San Fran. I still had a 9-millimeter Ruger, but I was going to have to ditch it before we went through Security. In the meantime, I needed to find us a place where we could see without being seen.

"Clarisse, get us a couple of burgers and bring them over there." I pointed toward the window to a table almost obscured by a potted palm. She nodded and held out her hand. "Jesus, can't you even spring for a couple of lousy burgers?"

"Hey, a girl's gotta—"

"Spare me." I pulled out a twenty. "Just go get the food."

I watched her walk away. I'd bought her a raincoat in one of the airport shops in hopes of making her very attractive figure a little less conspicuous. It wasn't working. The swing of her hips still turned heads, even covered by an extra yard of fabric. If the bad guys had worked their way to this terminal, it wouldn't take long for them to spot her.

But our luck seemed to be holding. Clarisse made it back with the burgers, and we settled in to wait behind the potted palm. As I kept scanning the terminal I thought I spotted one of them on the upper concourse checking out the shops. But I was spared making any decisions to move because the loudspeaker called our flight for pre-boarding. I'd delayed as long as I could. We had to get through Security as quickly as possible.

I gave the Ruger a quick wipe down then dug my hand down as far as I could into the palm's roots and slid the gun under them. When and if it was ever found there was no way it could be traced to me. And most importantly, we'd be long gone before they could lock down the terminal and bring in the gun-sniffing dogs. That was the good part. The bad part was that I was now unarmed, and they weren't. I took Clarisse by the arm and joined a mass of people heading into the security line. I'd already selected the passport I was going to use.

We were only one row away from passing through screening when they made us.

Our three pursuers were the same three who'd tracked us all the way from New York, and they didn't try to pretend to be anything else. They were here to kill us. The big fat one— I remembered his name, Paulie—smiled at me. Making his forefinger into the little gun symbol, he mouthed, "Bang."

They didn't try to pass through security. They couldn't, they were all armed to the teeth.

We put on our shoes, grabbed our carry-ons and hurried toward the gate. I kept glancing around.

"Hey, lighten up," Clarisse said, gasping for breath as I pulled her along. "Tony's punks can't do anything now. They can't even get through security."

"I'm not worried about them," I said while my eyes never stopped moving. "I think they've got someone on the inside."

We got to the line where the last of a dozen or so passengers were shuffling through the gateway.

"I don't know what you're talking about. There's no one behind us except the cleaning crew."

Cleaning crew! She was right. Less than a dozen feet behind us, a swarthy, heavyset Pakistani was reaching into his cleaning cart.

I hissed in Clarisse's ear, "Keep them distracted for a few minutes."

She didn't say anything, but when I dropped back a step and bent over as if searching for a dropped object, I heard her say, "Ummmm, hey, do you think I can change my seat?"

As the two gate attendants tried to navigate through her tortured logic, I continued to search the floor. As I did I watched the cleaner's black shoes move closer. I saw his hand slide under the cart and knew it would emerge with a silenced automatic.

With my back still toward him, I stood up, proclaiming loudly, "Ah, there you are," and held up a gold-plated pen as if to show the entire world.

He moved in behind me, intending to put the shot right in my spine, paralyzing me and sending me into an ambulance that would no doubt be driven by Tony's boys. So just as he started to draw his gun, I stepped forward, clicked the button of the pen, and through the hypodermic I'd replaced the ball point with injected him with twenty-five cc's of sodium pentathol. He immediately became disoriented, and I left him hanging on to his cart while I joined Clarisse at the gate. We boarded the plane. and the captain has turned off the seat belt sign. So you may move about the cabin, but . . ."

Blah, Blah, Blah. It went on and on, droning in the background. I stared out the window at the tiny dots that were houses and farms, and the tinier ones that were cars and trucks. No people. People were invisible from up here, and that was fine with me.

Next to me I heard Clarisse's seatbelt click open.

"Finally," she grumbled. "I gotta go pee." She got up and moved toward the rear of the plane.

I leaned back in the seat and again stared out the window. We flew above a bank of hazy gray clouds, and the sky and the land seemed to blend together into a featureless pattern with no horizon, no beginning and no end. I felt the gentle rocking back and forth, up and down—like a ship at sea. I rested my head against the cool of the bulkhead and closed my eyes.

The northeast coast of England—813 AD

The sky was cold and gray, the sea colder and grayer still. An equally cold gray wave burst over the prow of *The Raven*, Guthrum Skull Splitter's longship. It drenched me and my friend, Egill, but neither of us shivered or even bothered to wipe away the salt spray that froze in our beards. After ten days of running before the winter north wind, we barely felt the cold.

For most of the voyage from our Norse coast we had not had much to do with the oars except help the steersman keep the slender, single-masted ship on a southwestern course.

Now, however, every warrior except Guthrum himself had been called to man the oars. Every ounce of strength was needed to steer the ship due west toward the murky smudge of darker gray that the more experienced Viking raiders had assured us first voyagers was land. Although we only totaled sixty men, there were two other longships off to ourright. As we pulled for the ever-closer slash of rocky shoreline, we made it a contest to see which ship could claim the honor of first ashore.

Honor. It was honor that had brought me to the rocky coast of Northumbria. The honor of conquest and the honor of taking riches in battle. But above all was the importance of establishing my honor as a warrior and making my name. Unlike the weak and womanish Christian god, our god, Odin, demanded a man make himself a name as a warrior that would live after him.

When slaves and women and farmers died, they simply ceased to exist and were quickly forgotten. But the name of a warrior of great deeds and many battles would be sung in mead halls for all time. And those who were the greatest of warriors and died in battle with sword in hand would be taken by the Valkyries to Valhalla. That was what I wanted.

Oh, I wanted riches and slaves from my viking voyages, but most of all I wanted glory.

I had been a beardless stripling when a sword cut to the leg ended my own father's raiding. I had sworn to him that I would uphold our family honor and take his place in the longship. Besides, I did not want to end up a farmer or a smith with a small *steading* and one fat, plain wife. Not when my father had built himself a fine hall from the gold chalices and silver plate he'd taken in the great raid on Lindisfarne twenty years earlier.

I also wanted to bring a woman or two back with me. After all, my father had taken many slaves and wives before his injury forced him to make do with the four he had left. Yes, I had much to live up to, and my uncle, Sokki Bone

Crusher, who commanded our second ship would make sure that I did.

"'Ware rocks!"

The steersman pulled the long sweep over hard, and we narrowly missed being smashed to pieces on an immense jagged clump of rocks that seemed to rear up out of the crashing sea foam. I clutched my hammer amulet and murmured thanks to Thor the Thunderer for his aid. Then I heard the sound of gravel scraping under the hull, and the longship came to a shuddering stop.

Our crew cheered at being first to ground our keel against a rocky shore ripe for plunder. Within moments the other two ships slid in beside us. My uncle jumped from the prow of his ship, *Shadow Chaser*, and drew his battle-ax.

"Come, come my pretty blood-letters, the timid priests and fat Saxon lords wait for the kiss of your swords. And their wives and daughters wait for the kisses of your salt-crusted lips and your unused cocks!"

We laughed and cheered and beat our shields with the pommels of our swords.

In less than an hour's time we'd formed up and moved inland, my uncle and Guthrum at our head along with their chosen shield warriors. Until we were able to prove ourselves, we newlings were relegated to the end of the column, and both Egill and I chafed to show what we could do.

As things fell out, we didn't have long to wait.

After marching several miles we came to the first village—a poor place filled with farmers and fishermen. We had no horses, and though most of us wore rivet-linked armor of thick boiled leather except for the shield warriors who wore mail, none had heavy armor or breastplates. Thus, we made little noise in passing. Before they knew it we were on them. Within minutes we had slaughtered all the men, taken what little plunder there was and set fire to their hovels. There was little raping. The women, all of surpassing ugliness and stinking of fish, weren't worth it. No self-respecting Viking would have insulted his woman at home by bringing her such a poor specimen, even for a slave.

Laughing, the older warriors threw the few teenage girls to us young ones. "Here, you boys can practice on these."

Egill took one frightened, dull-eyed slattern, but when I saw their cringing, stringy-haired countenances, I turned away in disgust. When I'd taken my first girl at fourteen, she had been a fine, strapping, blue-eyed Norse girl with hair like ripe barley. I would not sully myself with one of these pathetic creatures and told Egill so.

He laughed as he casually cut the throat of the one he'd just finished with. "You're too fussy, Sveinn. I think I may have to start calling you Dainty Cock from now on."

I grabbed him by the hair and pulled his head back, pressing my dagger to his throat. "And I may have to start calling you Egill No Neck when I sever your head from it."

His eyes blazed, but only for a moment. He'd seen my blood rages before. He let his hands go limp, and I released him.

"Odin's blood, Sveinn! You are ever the hothead. It was but a jest."

"As was mine, Egill." I smiled.

But we both knew it wasn't.

We cleared the next hill and left the smoke and blood of the burning village behind. A mile later we halted by the side of a small stream, and as we knelt to drink I could hear my uncle Sokki and Guthrum arguing. Sokki was berating Guthrum for killing everyone in the village.

"I told you to take some prisoners," he complained.

"They would only have slowed us down," Guthrum snarled.

"Aye, but they could have at least pointed out the richest monasteries and towns before we killed them."

This was my chance. I ran forward. "Uncle, as we entered the village I heard one of the women scream to her children to run to the monks in the hill chapel."

"Which way?" Guthrum asked.

"That way, Lord," I pointed to a low rise of hazy hills several miles off.

My uncle grinned and Guthrum clapped me on the back. "Perhaps your scrawny nephew might have the makings of a warrior, Sokki. Come Sveinn, you march with me."

"Cody."

I opened my eyes.

Clarisse pointed to the flight attendant leaning toward me. "Excuse me sir, would you like anything to drink?"

I rubbed my hand over the back of my neck. "Grey Goose, rocks, twist." She nodded and glanced at Clarisse. "And you, ma'am?"

Clarisse ordered a Chardonnay and I paid. Of course.

"So what were you dreaming about? You were making these kinda grunting noises. Was it sex?"

I sipped my drink. "Not that time."

She put the plastic wine glass to her lips then put it back down on her tray table. "Where do you go when you dream? I know it's not normal places like normal people do. I mean, I know everyone has weird dreams, but I think your dreams are weirder than most." Her gaze was inscrutable as she ran her fingertip lightly over the back of my hand. "What do you dream about, Cody?" she whispered.

I drained the plastic cup and let the cold, fiery liquid slide down my throat. I answered almost without thinking. "Back. I go back to all those other lives, other times, other places. I looked different, spoke different languages and fought different wars in different lands, but it was almost always the same result. Blood and death. And in each life, in each time, I have one chance, one way out. But I never know it until it's too late. I suppose that's part of the curse, too. No matter what I do or how hard I try, the result is always the same—failure, blood and death. Always death but never release. Never oblivion."

I closed my eyes. When I opened them again, she was still looking at me with that same unreadable expression. I couldn't believe I'd told her. I'd never told anyone except Her—The Girl—and she always knew anyway because she was always waiting for me.

Clarisse rested her palm on the back of my hand, opening her mouth to speak, but I pulled my hand away and stared at her. "If you ever tell this to anyone or ever mention it again, I'll kill you."

I closed my eyes again, but this time I didn't dream. The plane flew on into the setting sun and I slept. Just slept.

Chapter 12

When we arrived in San Francisco I made Clarisse accompany me on the bus in to the city. She didn't like it and bitched all the way.

"Shit. What are we, some kind of half-assed tourists now? Doncha know taking the bus puts you one step above the bums and bag ladies? Where are we staying? You got a nice cardboard box picked out for us down in Union Square?"

I did my best to ignore her. We needed to remain as anonymous as possible, and if she didn't like the bus she probably wouldn't like my choice of which area of the city to stay in.

Tough. I had to keep our shadows off balance. Since I'd used cheesy out-of-the-way motels and a swanky luxury hotel in the most exclusive part of Toronto, this time I'd chosen a funky but cool little hotel smack dab in the middle of the biggest tourist destination in San Francisco—Fisherman's Wharf. The area shifted hourly between campy and tacky, depending on who was on the streets, the tourists or the freaks. For my purposes that was just what I wanted. Most of the time the streets were so crowded it was all but impossible to walk, thus easy to slip through crowds and into doorways and through crowed shops or restaurants.

The hotel I'd chosen was right on the main drag of Jefferson, one block from Ghirardelli Square. It was called the Argonaut, and I'd used it a few times a dozen years ago when I'd been meeting members of my team in San Fran prior to mercenary gigs in Asia. It was good cover and had the added benefit of having a great wine-tasting bar with a side entrance right off the hotel lobby. Perfect for slipping in and out. Which turned out to be a damn good thing, as it was the only thing that finally put an end to Clarisse's interminable grousing.

I paid for my usual two nights in advance, but before I could even get into the elevator Clarisse was pulling me into the wine bar.

"Come on, buy a girl a drink, for Christ's sake."

When she saw my expression she made a little-girl pouty face. "Aw, c'mon, Big Guy. Who knows? You might get lucky tonight."

"I doubt it. I'm running low on cash," I grumbled but let her lead me into the dark, cherry-wood paneled bar where we took seats at the end nearest the wall.

Two *fume blanc's* later, and Clarisse was all cuddles and smiles.

"You know, Cody," she purred, running her fingers over my thigh, "I think you're beginning to grow on me." When I didn't answer, she followed up with, "Am I beginning to grow on you, too?"

I probably shouldn't have answered, "Yeah, like a case of herpes." But I did. And that ended any possibility of a freebie. At least for that night.

"You know something, Cody? You can be a real jerk sometimes. No, wait. Make that most of the time."

She swept her half-full wine glass off the bar and stormed out.

I paid, naturally, and followed her out. Not to apologize, but because she didn't have a key. And the last thing I wanted was to have her make a scene at the desk. So I gave her one of the plastic key cards and kept the other.

"Go get changed, and we'll grab some dinner."

"Where are you going?" she asked suspiciously.

"I have to make a call. I'll be up in a few minutes." I didn't bother to add what would happen if she went anywhere else but the room. I think we'd pretty well come to an understanding about that.

As soon as the elevator doors closed I made a call to my guy and got the phone number of the lawyer who'd told my friend he wanted to hire me. I dialed the number and conversed for thirty seconds with a prim, mature-sounding secretary before a man with a well-modulated but elderly voice came on the line. We settled on ten AM , and he gave me instructions on where to meet. Then he told me he'd be wiring the first payment of fifty thousand to one of my numbered accounts in the Grand Caymans and agreed to give me another twenty thousand in 'walking around' cash when we met the next day.

I needed it. Being with Clarisse was like having an exotic pet or an expensive hobby.

By the time I got back up to the room the lady in question was over her snit. With the help of a bottle of *Moet Chandon* just to get my room service bill off to a flying start.

She had on a short, black leather mini-skirt with matching faux biker jacket and struck a sexy pose as I walked in.

"Like it?"

"I'd have to be dead or gay not to, and I'm neither. But I must have missed something—did you make us dinner reservations at a biker bar? Because that's about the only place where we're not going to stand out like a ballerina at a rodeo."

She sighed, then motioned me over to the window. She pointed to the teeming street. "Look down there. Do you really think I'm going to stand out in *that* crowd?"

She had a point.

So when we went out to dinner that night I chose a touristy but good Italian/Seafood restaurant on the pier. I had my favorite—tiny bay shrimp to start followed by a plate of white clam sauce on linguini. Clarisse had a sautéed piece of red snapper. An extra fifty dollars secured us a corner table where I could cover my back and watch both street and pier at the same time. Lots of people passed by, but none who looked like the wanted to kill us. Perhaps mug us, panhandle us or annoy us, but not kill us. At least for the time being.

For the moment it seemed as though we'd eluded them. I knew it was only temporary. Tomorrow I'd take care of my business in the City by the Bay and then get the hell out.

Clarisse knocked back the last of her wine, then rose to go to the ladies room. Since I was staring out the open window at the dark waters of the bay, I barely saw her leave the table. I heard the lap of waves against the pier and the cawing of sea birds unseen in the night sky.

They cawed that night, too. A thousand years before, in another time and place where the only thing that mattered to me was to prove myself in battle.

If only it had really been that simple.

Northumbria—the northeast coast of England—813 AD

We saw the monastery just before nightfall of the first day. Some of the men wanted to set up camp. Eat, drink and rest for the night, then attack in the morning. But my uncle and Guthrum squashed that notion and belittled those who'd made it, calling them cowards, weaklings and women. The fact that none of them flew into a Berserker rage and demanded to fight them for the insult proved their assessment was correct.

Guthrum turned to me. "What of you, young Sveinn? Do you think we should attack or spend the night warming our arses before the fires?"

I knew what he wanted me to say, but I must confess— even had it not been what our warlord wished to hear from me, I'd have said it anyway. "Attack! Attack, my lord. Batter down the monastery doors and spill the fat monks' guts upon their altars while we loot their gold crosses and silver chalices and rip their chanting tongues from their heads!"

Suddenly, I realized I'd been screaming at our war captain, who now stood before me, open mouthed and staring.

"You carry strong opinions, Boy," Guthrum said, expression unreadable.

I had gone too far. I dropped to my knee. "Forgive me, Lord," I stammered. "I . . . I am sorry for raising my voice to you."

"The young pup has spirit, Sokki. Shall we see how much?" Guthrum's eyes narrowed. "Do you have enough sand in your belly to lead the attack, Boy?"

Even had I not, the only response a young man out to make his reputation could have lived with was, "I would be honored, my lord."

But as I said it I also meant it. That was how very green I was.

Guthrum nodded, though whether he was pleased with my fighting spirit or was just looking for a fool to spit himself on the monastery portcullis was hard to tell. But my uncle's eyes shone with pride.

Had I been the meekest of cowards I still could not have done less that grip my sword and smash it against my shield. "I await your command, Lord."

And ten minutes later it came.

He allowed me to pick a dozen men, but the rest he chose himself. And though I didn't realize it at the time, his choice affirmed his belief that given proper support I could, despite my untried youth, take the walled monastery.

We stood on the edge of the wood in a straight line fifty men wide and watched the orange red ball of the sun sink behind the crenellations of the monastery walls. As soon as the light faded from our eyes I shifted mine towards Guthrum, and he nodded. I slashed my long-sword down sharply, and the fifty men on either side of me trotted forward.

They were waiting for us—the monks. They'd been warned, most likely by the squalling brats I'd seen running from the village. However, we felt their resistance showed the favor of Odin. For after all, what glory is there in fighting men who'll not fight back or wresting gold from those who'll not protect it?

But in the end it made no difference—no difference at all.

Although the monastery had walls, the monks had no means to defend them. They had neither bows, ballistas or even shields with which to deny us entry. We flowed through the main gates like shit through a goose, cutting them down in their flapping robes while they waved rusty swords gleaned from some ancient armory.

The only place where their resolve seemed to stiffen was when we got to their chapel. There, the spirit of their nailed god rested along with the moldering bones of some long-forgotten local saint. It took us only a short time to batter down the heavy oak doors. The chapel was rich, but not nearly as rich as we'd hoped. Still the men began ripping gold-threaded tapestries off the walls and crushing silver cups under foot to make them easier to transport.

As we approached the altar where the gold cups and jeweled reliquary rested, our way was barred by an enormous monk wielding the gold altar cross like a battle-ax. He resembled some brown, wool-covered mountain come to life and, though unskilled, his great size almost made up for it. Almost.

Three of our shield men surrounded him, but none could break through the wild arc he made swinging the great cross around his head. I saw them hanging back and knew this was my chance to begin building my reputation.

I called for them to stand back, then advanced toward him with my long-sword at the ready. He swung clumsily. I dodged easily and slapped him across the rump with the flat of my sword. The men roared with laughter and pounded on their shields.

We continued this dance for several minutes, until I glanced up and noticed that my uncle and Guthrum had arrived. Guthrum watched for a moment or two then gestured impatiently for me to finish it. We had other more lucrative fish to fry. So, on the giant's next frenzied pass I swung to one side and slashed the back of his calves, hamstringing him. As he crumpled, I thrust my sword through his throat. Guthrum nodded and strode over to the corpse. He pried the gold cross from the dead monk's hands then, reaching over the body, plucked up the golden chalice from the bloodstained altar and tossed it to me.

"Well done, Sveinn, Kettil's son."

I was on my way.

By the time we'd sacked and burned everything, the night was half gone, so Guthrum ordered us to set up camp next to a stream that ran through the monastery's fruit orchard. Using the light of the burning buildings we ate the monks' bread and drank their ale. Most of the men feel asleep immediately, content to let their leaders plan the next day's attacks. But I wanted to know more, so using my newfound stature as a promising young warrior, I drifted over to Guthrum's fire and stood on the outskirts as he planned with my uncle.

My uncle Sokki pointed to the burning abbey. "All hope of further surprise is now gone."

"Aye," Guthrum nodded. "The thanes and lords will have seen the flames and even now will be barring gates and pulling up drawbridges."

He leaned over to punch my uncle's arm. "But when has that ever stopped us, eh Sokki?" Grinning, Sokki nodded. "Then it's settled, we attack at daybreak." Guthrum stood.

It was then he saw me standing awkwardly at the edge of the circle of battle leaders and seasoned warriors. He motioned me forward.

"And what care we for walls and gates and drawbridges when we've got young fire-eaters like Sveinn here? Tell me, boy, how many Saxon Ceorls do you intend to kill tomorrow?"

"All of them, Lord. All of them."

That night in the hotel room we made love. Clarisse didn't call it a freebie, and neither did I.

But afterward I noticed she used the words, "us" and "we" a lot, and even though part of me kind of liked the way it sounded, the cold-blooded warrior in me warned that I needed to cut off any entanglements. Especially with a girl who was used to selling her favors to the highest bidder. There's always someone willing to pay more. And she already knew more about me than was good for either of us.

So I said what I shouldn't have said. "There is no *us*, Clarisse, there's only two people who do things to others for money. I kill 'em and you fuck 'em."

She stared back at me, and I saw tears in her eyes. I wanted to believe they were tears of rage, but I don't think they were.

Glaring at me, she rubbed angrily at her eyes with the back of her hand. "You know, Cody, I don't think you've ever loved a woman. And that's probably a good thing because a woman would probably break her heart trying to find yours. And yes, I know there's something inside you. Way down deep. Something from long ago that's eating at you from the inside out. Pretty soon it won't just be bad dreams. It'll be all the time, waking and sleeping. It won't make any difference how many people you kill or how much money they pay you to do it, because all the things you've done will be with you. Not just every night, but every day, too."

"They already are," I whispered, but I doubt she heard me.

She shook her head. "If I didn't hate you so much, I'd feel sorry for you."

And with that she moved over as far from me as she could in the king-size bed and curled herself up into a little ball of hurt and anger.

I watched her. I should have moved over next to her, told her I was sorry and asked her to hold me and keep me from the part of the dream memory that I knew was coming next—the part I didn't want to relive. Instead, I let her lie there wrapped in her hurt and defenses, surrounded by the stone walls she'd built around her heart. Just like the walls that had loomed up before us on that crisp, bright morning so long ago.

In the early morning light, sitting atop the bare, windswept hill, the fortress looked larger than it probably was. But, then again, I was still a youth and this was the first time I'd ever seen a castle.

The outer walls were made of timber reinforced with earth, but the twin towers guarding the gate were of rough-dressed stone. As was the great Keep that loomed up at the highest point of the complex like the cold, skeletal finger of a frost giant, promising death to all who entered.

I could see apprehension on some of the younger warriors' faces, but there was none on Guthrum Skull Splitter's. His was alight with anticipation of blood and plunder.

"Do you remember the fortress at Iona, Sokki?"

My uncle stroked his beard and nodded slowly. "Aye, the rolling trunk, fire and grappling hooks."

"Set the men to work on it. We'll feast this night in their stone hall with the corpses of their men for our footstools and their women to warm our beds."

But before my uncle could give the order there was a trumpet blast from the walls, and the drawbridge came down.

As we watched in puzzlement, a troop of several dozen mounted Saxons in chain mail and steel helmets came clattering across the drawbridge led by a richly-dressed lord in a gold-chased breastplate.

But that wasn't what kept me staring open-mouthed as they rode up and halted before us. It was the figure who rode beside the lord. It was a woman. Not just any woman. A goddess.

She was clothed in a cloak trimmed with white fox and a dress of forest-green velvet with cuffs of ermine bedecked with silver-threaded ribbons that fluttered in the morning breeze.

But all that was a mere frame for the greatest jewel of all. Her face

I overheard my uncle whispering to Guthrum, "I've heard tales of this one. The Thane's daughter, Bronwyn. It is said that her mother was a princess of Efland or queen of the water sprites. And whether a myth or no, her father encourages the tale and has her by his side constantly to enhance his own power as one who sired a princess from the unseen world."

For once Guthrum had nothing to say, and I could understand why. Her beauty transfixed us all. And I think most of us believed at that moment that she was indeed the offspring of some goddess from Asgard.

Her fair hair shone silver in the early morning sunlight. Her high, delicate cheekbones were offset by almond cat's eyes of sparkling gold. The moment her gaze touched mine, an electric thrill went through my body, leaving me so stunned I almost dropped my sword. It was *The Girl*!

Each of my past lives came rushing back to me all at once. By Odin's blood, it was the woman I'd been searching for over the past eight centuries. Now here she was, and in the form of a goddess. I wanted nothing more than to fall to my knees and worship her. Kiss the hem of her robe if only she would turn that golden gaze upon me.

The lord of the Keep, her father, began to speak. "I know who you are, Guthrum Skull Splitter. I have heard of your deeds, your godless blasphemies in destroying the monastery, defiling holy relics and shedding the innocent blood of holy men."

That made Guthrum grin.

"I'm glad my reputation has reached your hall. Then you will know what I can do and realize the only way to save yourself from death is to throw open your gates and lay your treasure before us. Do this, and we may let you keep your life and a few of your ugliest wives."

The Saxon gritted his teeth and glared back at Guthrum. "Pagan dog! Followers of Christ have but one wife, and the richest of our treasures we give to God's Holy Church."

"And that is why you will scream in vain to your weak god for mercy as you writhe under our swords."

The Thane's face turned red as he tried to control his rage. "Do you think we are not prepared for you? Know this well, Heathen. As soon as we saw the burning abbey we dispatched riders to the King of Northumbria. He is even now riding to our aid with a thousand men."

Guthrum leaned on his ax. "And why should he care what happens to one insignificant noble on the edge of his kingdom?"

The lord grinned triumphantly. "Because the great King is betrothed to the Lady Bronwyn, my daughter!"

Guthrum spat on the ground and laughed. "Then he will pay a handsome ransom to get her back."

The Thane sneered. "Your choice is to stay and be crushed between my Keep and the soldiers of the King, or to leave now and sail your dragon ships back to your ice-bound pigsties."

Guthrum crashed his battle-ax against his shield. "And yours is to hand over your gold and your daughter, or be spitted on the door to your Keep just like your nailed god!"

The Thane tugged savagely on his horse's bridle as his troop formed a protective circle around him and his daughter. Turning, they all galloped back to the fortress.

Guthrum turned to my uncle and grinned. "I shall have that pale-hired piece in his own bed this night."

My heart turned cold. *Over my lifeless corpse, Guthrum Skull Splitter.*

I opened my eyes. The memory remained, but the stark reality of the dream was gone.

Something soft and silky brushed against my skin. Long blonde hair. Clarisse had rolled over and lay sleeping beside me. I didn't know if I was glad or disappointed because all I could see etched in my mind was a pale, ethereal face and golden eyes.

Before I left for the meeting with the lawyer, I sat Clarisse down in the chair next to the window overlooking the bay.

"Okay, Clarisse, here's the deal. I've got a meeting this morning, and when I come back I'm going to be leaving. Alone. So from now on, you're on your own. But I gotta admit that, aside from trying to rob me a couple of times and braining me with a lamp, you've been a pretty good kid. So if you want to stick around for a few hours, I'm gonna give you ten grand when I get my pocket money. That should allow you to go wherever you wanna go and get yourself set up in whatever you wanna do."

I didn't add that I hoped it wouldn't be hooking.

"That's very generous, Cody. You pay well. I'm just not sure if I'll be here when you get back." between Nob and Russian hills.

When I got there a woman who looked like she'd had her heyday back in Sixty-two when Tony Bennett was crooning about leaving his heart in San Francisco ushered me into a walnut-paneled office and asked me if I'd like some coffee or tea.

"Tea—green. Japanese Sencha if you've got it." And what do you know? She did. About the same time my tea arrived so did the lawyer.

He must have been well into his eighties but was still trim and firm, except for a slight limp which he compensated for with an ebony walking stick boasting a ruby-eyed golden dragon for a handle. I recognized it immediately because I'd had a similar one made for me in Hong Kong. I gestured toward the cane. "Chinatown?"

He smiled. "Very good. Yes, from a very small but exclusive shop. It's an antique."

"I know." I pointed to an intricate swirl of filigree about three inches below the handle. "And I'm sure the shop owner told you to add a drop or two of very fine watchmaker's oil to that release catch on a regular basis. They do tend to stick sometimes. And then, just when you need it most, all you're left with is a cane."

His smile grew as he pressed the gold filigree with a click and drew a twenty-eight-inch length of gleaming—and from the look of it, razor-sharp—steel.

"I'm impressed, Mister . . . Ah . . . " He looked at the piece of paper on his desk. "Smith." And now the smile twisted up at one end with amusement. "Not terribly original."

I shrugged. "People don't hire me for originality. They hire me to do things. Usually things they don't want to do themselves."

He nodded. "Well, I am impressed with your knowledge of antique weapons. I can see my client picked the right man for the job."

"I've seen my share." I didn't add that I'd fought deadly battles with most of them, too.

I took a sip of tea. It was quite good.

"Thanks, but before we go any further I need to get a bit more information. For instance, exactly who is your client and why did he or she ask specifically for me?"

He shook his head. "Just like your own name, Mr. Smith, my client's name is likewise confidential."

"Then thanks for the tea and have a pleasant day." I got up and moved toward the door.

"Wait. Please, sit back down. I can't tell you her name."

"So, it's a woman."

"Yes. And I can also tell you she's an artist, a poet and a museum researcher. She lives a very quiet, almost reclusive life in New England, studying local artifacts and writing poetry."

"So how'd she come to ask you to contact me and, more importantly, how'd she come to hear about me? Generally, the only people who do are those who've done bad things to other bad people."

"I can say quite truthfully that I have no idea why she specified you. But she described you quite accurately, and when I put out the word—very discreetly, of course—through the contacts it's taken a lifetime to develop, one reference led to another. They finally brought me to your friend, who contacted you."

I didn't like that. If my description could be run down, even anonymously, then my security was weak. I'd have to take care of the problem.

"My client is willing to pay very handsomely to have you deliver a certain item to her."

"The figure you mentioned was a quarter of a million. That's a lot of money for some museum bookworm, even for a painter like Picasso. It doesn't make sense that some starving artist probably living in the New England woods would pay a quarter mil just to have her own personal UPS man. Why don't you just use Fed Ex, or a bonded courier?"

"Because there is a degree of risk, even danger, involved with this item. According to my client, there are many very ruthless men who would think nothing of killing to get their hands on the item in question."

Hmm, death, danger—those I understood.

"Okay, then, second question. What is this item?"

He walked over to an intricately carved Chinese cabinet and stood in a way that shielded his hands from me, but I heard a click and then a thump from inside. He opened the doors and took out a steel case—the kind spies and couriers carry—and brought it over to the desk to open.

Inside was a wooden box. What kind of wood I couldn't tell, but it was very dark and very old. Somewhere back in my far-distant past I'd seen similar boxes when they were new. It would also have a hidden catch.

"Open it." He shook his head. Again, I started to get up. "Then we're through here." He sighed. "Very well. But I must have your word that once you leave here with the box you will make no attempt to open it until you deliver it to my client."

"I get paid the big bucks because I always do exactly what I'm contracted to do." He took the box off the desk. I could see his elbows twitch, indicating that his hands were working some combination, probably similar to a Chinese puzzle box.

He put the box back on the desk and lifted the lid.

Inside lay a dirty piece of brown cloth about the same consistency of an old burlap bag. Old, wrinkled and filthy, with smudges of dirt and spots of black tar, it covered something else. I reached out, but the old man closed the box with a snap. I heard a hidden catch slide into place.

"I have done as you asked, Mr. Smith. Now, I must ask you to keep your end of the bargain and promise you will make no further attempt to view the box's contents."

I stared back at him. "I may break a lot of things, but my word isn't one of them."

He nodded. "That is what I had heard. Now that I've met you, it is my feeling also." He pushed a small leather case about the size of a book across the desk. "Here is your retainer and expense money. The pouch also contains detailed instructions on how to find my client. I have full faith that you will take all precautions to assure you are not followed."

"That I can guarantee."

He stood up and extended his hand. "Then I shall wish you good luck and God speed, Mr. "Smith."

"Just a moment. Where did this case come from? How did it come into your hands, and why is it in San Francisco and not New England where this woman lives?"

"I fail to see why that has any relevancy to the task at hand."

"It's got lots. In order to know who might be coming after me to get it back, I need to know if the box is stolen or was swindled away from someone."

"I can assure you it's nothing like that. Mrs. Charlotte Hopkins, one of my firm's oldest and most respected clients, has possessed it for many years."

"Yeah, like how many?"

He thought for a moment. "Why, I believe about eighty."

"So, you're telling me some old lady has been holding this for that long? Then why's she sending it to some artsy babe on the other side of the continent?"

"Because on her deathbed Mrs. Hopkins told me I was to send the box back to its original owner. The woman she had been holding it for all these years. Her sister."

"Sister? Christ, how old is she, a hundred?"

"I don't know. The truth is, up until I got the call summoning me to Mrs. Hopkins' bedside, I was not aware that she had a sister. No one is entirely sure of what happened, but some time back around 1930, there was a murder in the big house on Nob Hill. Rumor and newspaper accounts of the time claimed that one of the two daughters, presumably old Mrs. Hopkins' sister, had been brutally murdered. But obviously there must have been another sister or the reports were wrong since Mrs. Hopkins' will stipulated quite emphatically that the box in question be delivered to a woman whom the document clearly stated is her one and only sister."

I stared at him a full minute. I didn't like mysteries, especially when they involved me, but he said nothing more. Finally, I nodded, took money and the box and left.

On my walk back to the waterfront, I stopped into a funky urban outdoor supplies store and bought a backpack into which I put the steel briefcase and leather case containing my cash. As I did I thought about the irony of one of the best mercenaries and assassins playing delivery boy to some old lady artist. Well, a quarter mil was easy money, and I had to keep on the move anyway.

Back at the hotel I got into the elevator and punched the button for four. On the way up I counted out the ten thousand I planned to give Clarisse. I actually found myself glad to do it, and on impulse added twenty additional hundred-dollar bills to the wad.

I opened the door and slung the backpack onto the bed. "Clarisse?"

No answer, so I checked the bathroom. Empty. I opened the closet. Her clothes and suitcase weren't there.

She was gone.

Chapter 13

I told the cabbie to take me to SFO but just as we got to the *Embarcadaro* I caught sight of a black Beemer i-Series in his side mirror. As we slowed at the light I risked a glance back. Although the windows were dark, I could make out two forms in the bright San Francisco sunlight sitting in the front seat.

They'd found me.

"Turn right at the next light and head up to Union Square."

"Thought you want go airport," the driver said in a thick Russian accent made thicker by disappointment.

"Now it's Union Square. Head straight for the center."

"This time day? Lots of traffic. You miss flight."

"Yeah, well, life's full of problems isn't it?" But that was just what I wanted—lots of traffic.

And I wasn't disappointed. The crowded square was packed with pedestrians, shoppers, gawkers, tourists, street vendors, bums, crazies and cars. Lots of cars. In fact, the converging streets were almost gridlocked. Perfect.

As we slowed to a crawl I shot a quick look back at the Beemer one light behind us and then slipped the cabbie a twenty for the fare and another to assuage his disappointment. I waited until the crosswalk was jammed with people before slipping out of the cab and joining them. As soon as I got to the curb I approached a panhandler in a filthy raincoat who was shoving a copy of the *Homeless News* into the face of each passerby and demanding money. I pressed a twenty into his hand.

"Here you go, I'll take 'em all. And here's two more for your coat. Buy a bottle of Thunderbird on me."

He grinned a rotted-teeth grin and shuffled off as I slipped into his coat and took the papers. I held one up to block my face and began mumbling, "Homeless News," in a slurred voice. I moved on down the sidewalk as people ignored me or sidestepped to avoid the bum in the dirty raincoat. As I approached the Beemer, I held the paper up in my left hand and slipped the Desert Eagle out of its shoulder holster with my right.

My cover was perfect. As I approached the driver's side they didn't even look up. "*Homeless News.* Hey pal, c'mon," I whined. "Don'tcha want the *Homeless News*?" They tried to ignore me, but I pounded on the window then slid my ring down the glass, leaving a long scratch.

The window went down.

"Hey!" the driver screamed at me. "Yuh dumb fuck, look what yuh did! Yuh scratched the fuckin' glass, yuh piece of shit. I'm gonna kill you!"

"Other way around." I leaned close to the open window and squeezed the trigger twice. The silencer made two little *pops* that were lost in the street noise, and I walked on. The whole thing had taken less than thirty seconds.

However I had two minutes at best before the light changed and the soon-to-behorrified drivers, after honking their horns in vain, discovered that the guys in the Beemer weren't asleep at the wheel, they were dead.

I kept walking at a normal pace, shedding the raincoat and discarding it and the papers in a trash can.

One block from the square I found what I was looking for—a college-age kid sitting on a motorcycle next to the curb talking to a pretty girl.

"Hey, kid." He looked over at me. "Is the bike for sale?"

"No. Why would it be?"

"I'm interested in it. How much would you take for it?"

He laughed. "Fifty grand."

I pulled out a bundle of bills. "How about fifteen?"

He stared, open mouthed, obviously thinking about it. That was twice what the motorcycle was worth.

"Here, tell ya what—I'll throw in another grand for the helmet."

Five minutes later, I was roaring through the Tenderloin District listening to the sounds of sirens converging on Union Square.

As soon as I'd noticed the tail I'd realized they'd have SFO covered and would likely be checking the airport at San Jose, too. So my plan was to bypass them both and run the bike all the way down US One to the small airport at Long Beach where Jet Blue had a nonstop flight to Boston. And just to make sure my pursuers were completely thrown off, I planned to hole up somewhere along the coast for a week or two. By that time they would have given up watching any airports and assume I'd taken a train, bus or car across the country.

It was a good plan. Almost perfect. Almost.

I rode mainly by night, on back roads and in some cases avoiding the two lane blacktops altogether and using roads that were little more that dirt trails. I didn't care about the extra time. That only worked in my favor. The longer it took me to get to Long Beach, the less likely they were to be checking the airport. By day I secreted the bike in some underbrush and slept in the woods. Not only was I used to it after spending hundreds of years roughing it in thousands of army bivouacs, I rather enjoyed it.

Three days later I found what I was looking for. A roadside sign read, "Big Sur Cabins and Campgrounds. Tents and cabins for rent by the day or week." I rented an eight by ten tent and chose the campsite farthest away from the others. I bought a blanket and some supplies at the campground store and settled in.

It was a beautiful spot, just twenty feet away from a cliff that fell down to a spray– splashed, rock-strewn beach. And while an old, twisted pine sheltered the tent, the site provided me with a clear view of anyone approaching. Aside from hikers down on the beach trail, no one did.

I decided to use the time to sharpen my martial arts skills and clear my mind, so I spent long hours running and meditating. Or trying to.

For some reason Clarisse kept intruding into my thoughts. I would be jogging along the beach or, worse yet, trying to clear my mind with techniques I'd learned fifteen centuries earlier when the little blonde with the pouty red lips and cynical smile would wink at me from the back of my mind.

Could I possibly be missing her? I'd never missed anyone over my hundreds of lifetimes except Her. But no matter how hard I tried, I could not make Clarisse's image go away.

Maybe that's why what happened next shouldn't have been surprising.

I'd taken the bike out and run up the coast to a town where I could get decent cell phone reception. I needed to check in with my contacts and see what the word was on the street about Tony Bags' two *goombahs*, the ones I'd clipped almost two weeks prior. But first I needed to tell my friend, Chuck, to get word to the lawyer that there'd been a temporary delay but the package was safe and would be delivered as promised. When I finally got through to him I could tell he was agitated.

"Shit, man, where've you been?" I told him. "So you haven't heard?"

"I've been communing with nature, getting in touch with my inner hit-man." Chuckles didn't laugh. Something bad was going down.

"Yeah, well speaking of hits . . . After you smoked Tony's boys, he got so bullshit that to get even with you he put out a contract on your little blonde squeeze. So I hope she's there with you now 'cause, if not, she's dead meat."

Ten minutes later, I was on the bike headed for L.A.

It had only taken five minutes to pack up the few items I was bringing with me and stuff them into the backpack which I tied on the back of the bike. All the rest I left. The tent was rented, and I left the blanket, food and other assorted camping gear in it. I planned to drive straight through to Long Beach Airport. Except my destination was no longer Boston. It was Lexington, Kentucky. According to Chuckles's latest bit of intelligence, my little blonde hustler had for some reason decided to become a coed at the University of Kentucky.

It wound up taking almost an entire day to get there, twenty-two hours to be exact. Jet Blue had no direct flights, so I had to follow a tortuous route that led me through Austin, Omaha, Chicago and Cincinnati. There I shouldered my pack and made my way to long-term parking where I settled in to wait. Fortunately I didn't wait long. Within fifteen minutes a young couple driving a beat up Honda Civic pulled into a space two rows away. They got out and, pulling two overstuffed suitcases and a tote bag each, took off at a stumbling jog for the exit, she berating him for not driving faster to the airport, and he retorting that if she had been ready on time, it wouldn't have been necessary to drive faster.

Young love.

I waited until their squabbling voices faded and then moved toward the car, slipping my auto B&E tools from my pack. Two minutes later, I was explaining to the parking attendant that I'd lost my ticket and—after ruefully paying for the entire week—exited the airport and headed south.

And that was why I hadn't tried to get a flight to Bluegrass Field in Lexington. It was much smaller than Cinci, and I couldn't count on getting a car.

It was one of my tried-and-true methods for obtaining transportation in a strange city. Find someone entering long-term parking who's loaded down for a week or two of vacation and borrow their car. Since it was unlikely such people would return to find their vehicle gone before I was done with it, I didn't worry about being pulled over for Grand Theft Auto. And, since I was such a thoughtful guy, I would leave the car—after wiping off my prints, of course—in a garage somewhere. It would eventually be found.

And people think I'm cold and unfeeling.

All the way to Lexington, I drove the Civic at just a couple miles over the limit.

Two hours later the directions Chuckles had wrangled from somewhere led me to the sprawling campus of the University of Kentucky where, according to his strange but usually correct information, Clarisse Fontain—formerly a high-priced NYC callgirl of NYC—had started classes two days before as a freshman in pursuit of a degree in psychology.

Good choice, I thought, turning the Civic onto a side street filled with stores and restaurants. She's enough of a whack-job in her own right to use her new skills on herself.

Perhaps even more of a surprise though was the other bit of intelligence Chuckles had uncovered. Not only was our little college girl attending class, but she was apparently set on working her way through–honestly. She'd taken a part time job as a sales clerk in a downtown Lexington jewelry store. Considering her background and the way she'd been used to getting her bling, I found it rather ironic and somewhat amusing that she was probably working for minimum wage selling earrings and bracelets to college kids when a month ago she could have walked into the place with one of her sugar daddies and had him buy out the store. I was also inexplicably proud of her.

I found the store easily enough and parked across the street.

From where I sat, I could see her blonde hair swaying back and forth as she got out various items from the jeweler's display case to show a young couple who were either pricing out the cost of making their cohabitation in sin legitimate, or the guy was trying to buy his way out of the dog-house or back into bed.

I watched her tilt her head back, watched her laugh and realized with a start that I'd actually sort of missed her in the two weeks we'd been apart.

She finished with the two customers and busied herself replacing the pieces she'd been showing back into the case.

I checked the rearview mirrors, took another look at the street and nearby buildings then slipped out of the Honda and walked across the street. She didn't look up when I entered, but somehow I think she sensed it was me.

There was an instant of surprise then, in quick succession, expectation, recognition and hope followed by suspicion, caution and calculation.

"You followed me," she said, halfway between appreciation and reproach.

I shrugged. "I think you might be in danger, and I think it might be my fault."

That was an understatement because she *was* in danger, deadly danger, and it was most definitely my fault. But I had enough guilt after two millennium of trying to figure out what the hell I'd done to be interested in taking on any more remorse, so I prevaricated.

"I hear you're back in college."

She nodded. "Not back. Going for the first time, unless you count those three semesters of psych I took at City College. Although that was more for something to do rather than watch the soaps or sleep all day. But I always kinda wanted to go to college. Remember, I went straight into *business* right after high school." She folded her arms and leaned against the counter. "Funny thing is, I actually took the college boards and did pretty good. In fact the guidance councilor actually thought I might be able to get a work/study scholarship to UWV but it never came through. Like I said, there were those courses in NYC. But for the most part all I wanted was to get some nice clothes, a nice apartment and keep as far away from home as possible." She gazed up at me defiantly. "And I did."

I shrugged again. "No argument there but who are you trying to convince—me or you?"

"I don't know, maybe that's why I decided to major in Psych . . . to get into my head." She cocked her head and gave me her little half smile. "And maybe when I'm done with that you'll let me poke around in yours to see what makes you tick."

"Trust me Clarisse, you really don't want to see what's crawling around in there. It would give you nightmares for a month."

She glanced up with a strange look. "You might be surprised."

"About what?" I asked, but she changed the subject.

"And speaking of Psych class, I gotta get going or I'm gonna be late." She locked the glass case and then called into the back room. "Bye Mr. Fletcher, see you tomorrow."

She shouldered a book bag and turned to me. "Come on, you can walk me to class."

"What am I—eighteen again?" But I followed her out.

We walked down Limestone, the main street to the University. The big linden trees shaded us, and I felt like I was in some sort of stupid college movie. The two students on campus—romance in academia.

She looked up at the trees and the sun gilding the brass railings on the steps leading up to the brick walk quadrangle and smiled. "This is what I wanted."

"What, long walks on crowded brick paths?"

"Yes, and everything that goes along with it. Trees, and classes and books. Buildings with ivy and ... Well, everything. The whole nine yards."

We passed a couple playing kissy-face under a big Linden tree, and she smiled again. But this time it was mixed with sadness.

"You know, even while I was making big bucks as a *working girl,* I always regretted not getting a shot at doing this. I guess that's why six months ago I finally sent in that application that had been gathering dust in my drawer all those years." She glanced over at me. "Believe it or not, just before you came into Little T's bedroom, I'd decided I'd had it with the life and was gonna leave New York and come down here. Then I got hooked up with you, and for a while I thought maybe . . ."

Her voice trailed off, and she gave her head a little shake as if shaking off a daydream. I got the feeling she wanted me to say something, but what I thought she wanted was something I couldn't say. She seemed to realize it too and changed the subject.

"So did you ever go to college, Rambo?"

"Yeah, graduated too." I didn't mention that it had been in the mid-Sixties, and I'd followed that up with Vietnam where I'd gotten my head blown off.

"Yeah? What did you major in?"

I put my hand on her shoulder and stopped her. "Look Clarisse, I didn't fly halfway across the country to take you to the malt shop for a soda."

"Then why did you come?"

"To keep your pretty little head from getting shot full of holes."

"Okay. Then thanks for the thought, and if you don't mind I'm late for class." She hurried on and I almost let her go but felt this tiny little mouse of conscience nibbling around the outskirts of my brain and caught up to her in a few strides.

"Screw the class–you need to come with me–now."

"Nope." She kept walking.

I thought about picking her up and carrying her back to the car, but there were too many people on the pretty tree-lined path crisscrossing the Quad, so to buy time as much as anything, I asked, "So when you bailed in San Fran, what made you come here?"

She didn't stop, but walked a little slower. "When I was seventeen, the guy I was dating went off to UK, and about a month after he'd started he invited me here for the weekend. I loved the campus and all the people and really wanted to go here. But of course when I asked Ma, she said we didn't have the money, and then she gave me some bullshit about getting another job and helping me out. But she started drinking more and doing Crystal Meth, and it all turned pretty much to crap. I tried saving up, but it was hopeless, and there weren't any scholarships available for trailer park trash, so I gave up. You know the rest. When you left me in the hotel that day I was gonna wait and get paid, and then–I dunno— something came over me, and I decided I was sick of fucking twisted creeps for money, and that I wanted to go back to the beginning. You know, start over. Keep that promise I made myself before I met you and try for a regular life. Maybe have the college years I never had. Study something interesting. Have a respectable job. Meet a nice, boring guy. Be normal."

She stopped, and there was a fierce determination in her eyes that I'd never noticed before–or maybe it was new.

"And I'm gonna do this Cody, and nobody's gonna stop me. Not you, not Tony Bags's hit men or the devil himself. So thanks for the thought and sorry you had a long trip for nothing."

She gazed up at me then touched my chest. "You know you might actually have a heart in there if you ever took the trouble to look." She leaned up and gave me a kiss. "And if you ever decide that you want to try, give me a call."

She turned and walked away and was soon lost in the milling throng of students hurrying to class.

I watched her until she disappeared and thought of a half dozen things to call after her, like, "Hey, I'm too old for this campus *Love Story* bullshit by many years–make that many hundreds of years . . . " But I didn't.

Instead, I walked back across campus toward the car. I should have been feeling relieved, but I wasn't. I felt vaguely dissatisfied and very uneasy. I knew if they hadn't found her yet they soon would. I tried to tell myself that I'd done my best, gone above and beyond, but the damned little conscience mouse kept taking bigger and bigger bites, and I knew it wouldn't let up until I checked.

So I drove about twenty-five miles out into the country to a good-ole-boy Chuckles had set me up with, and he outfitted me with a new Desert Eagle, a silenced .25-cal Berretta hide-out-gun, a pair of throwing knives, an ebony-handled butterfly knife from Thailand and a 7.62-mm sniper rifle with a 4x scope.

Then I drove back to town and picked up a small bottle of Grey Goose vodka and some smokes and walked back to the campus. I spent the rest of the day tailing Clarisse. It wasn't hard, it's what I do and she wasn't looking for me. For all she knew I was long gone. And I should have been, but that little bastard conscience can be a real bitch when it sinks its teeth into you.

Besides, I knew Tony's boys would be here soon, and it would be easier to stalk them while they were stalking Clarisse. I hadn't gone totally altruistic.

They didn't show up until late the next afternoon.

By this time, I'd gotten a copy of Clarisse's class schedule, her apartment address and work schedule. I'd been curious to see if she'd found any new sugar daddies to help with the bills, but aside from a couple of grad students who she met for a drink, her love life seemed pretty tame. Was she really out of the profession? And why should I care? I had only ever loved one woman, and Clarisse certainly wasn't her. But on the other hand, I couldn't deny that there was something about the little blonde. Maybe I recognized a kindred spirit with my same "fuck you" attitude to the world. But then why did it seem to please me to see her beginning to come to terms with that same world I'd been fighting for the past two millennium?

It was Clarisse's last class, and if she followed her same routine, I knew she'd drop in to one of the campus pubs on the way back to her apartment. So, I positioned myself at an oblique angle so I could see her when she left the building and shadow her from a distance. And that's when I spotted them.

There were four this time. They weren't taking any chances.

Two were sitting on stone benches across from each other, and the other two were loitering at either end of the building, so they could dog her no matter which way she turned. There were too many people to grab her right off the walkway, so I suspected they were going to tail her and grab her at whatever bar she went into. That meant there were one or two more waiting in a car somewhere, in constant touch by cell phone.

Sure enough, I spotted the little blue winking light of a Jabra Bluetooth earpiece in one of the guy's ears.

Suddenly, the doors to the building opened and students spilled out into the Quad. Clarisse came down the steps, flanked by two of the guys I'd seen her talking to yesterday. Dressed in jeans, boots and a fashion top, she fit right in. And if the guys didn't look too closely, they probably wouldn't notice that she had a good decade on both of them. Then again, with a body like hers they probably weren't spending much time looking for crow'sfeet.

As she passed by the two *goombahs* on the benches, I saw one nod to the other and say something into the earpiece of his Bluetooth. They both got up and began following her, staying a dozen feet back.

So I follow a dozen feet back from them.

The pub they went into was a noisy, crowded one with cheap pitchers for Happy Hour, so naturally it was jammed, and right away I saw that this would give them the perfect opportunity. They could walk up behind her, jab her with a needle filled with tranq then help her out like they were helping out a friend who'd had a little too much.

I also spotted a big black Suburban pulled up across the street, sitting with the motor idling. They didn't plan to wait long, so I couldn't either.

I crossed the street and pulled the blue Kentucky Wildcats baseball cap I'd picked up down low, shading my face. I walked up to the SUV and tapped on the passenger side window.

"Hey, 'scuse me–do you know where the administration building is?"

I had to say it twice before the driver rolled down the window to tell me to "fuck off," but before he could I shot him twice in the forehead with the silenced Beretta. Then I leaned in and took the keys. They might come in handy.

Checking to make sure I hadn't been spotted, I crossed the street and entered the pub. Right away I knew I'd made a mistake–a big one.

Soldiers in combat–those who survive—develop a sense when they're in danger, sort of a feeling that someone has you in their sights. That's what I got the minute I walked into that bar. I didn't know who or where they were, but I knew someone was watching me, and it wasn't because they wanted to buy me a beer.

At the same time I knew that Clarisse was in terrible danger.

I tried to pick out her slight form as I quickly scanned the sea of laughing, yelling, jabbering faces of college kids making the most of Happy Hour and cheap beer, but it was too crowded. I moved slowly forward into the center of the room muttering "Excuse me" and "Can I get through here?" But it was no good–there were too many people, and with her size I knew I'd need to practically stumble over her to find her.

Then miraculously I did.

But I was too late.

Just as one broad-shouldered jock turned to order another beer, I caught a flash of long blonde hair and saw her turn toward me with a smile—a dreamy vacant smile. The word "Cody" formed on her lips, but no sound came out. I saw her eyes roll back in her head and her body go limp as two big guys on either side grabbed her elbows.

I was too late. They'd drugged her.

I started toward them and that was when I made my second mistake–I didn't watch my back.

When you've been stabbed a hundred times, you know exactly what has happened the moment you feel that sharp, burning pain followed by a warm, throbbing wetness radiating from the spot, and you know that you have to react, and quickly.

That instinct saved me.

I whirled around and saw a thin, wiry guy with sun glasses and caught a glint of red stained metal, a stiletto. The noise of the bar had drowned out the tell tale *snick* that marked a switchblade opening, allowing him to stick me just above my right kidney while I was distracted by Clarisse. Now he was drawing his hand back to finish the job, but what he hadn't counted on was that he was dealing with a guy who'd been fighting with knives to the death long ages before he'd been born. As his hand jabbed upwards trying to slip the long, slender blade under my sternum, I slammed my right hand down into the crook of his arm and with my left turned the blade up and pushed it between his two uppermost ribs.

He looked at me with profound surprise, then his jaw went slack and I maneuvered him down into a corner booth and pushed my way toward the door. I was bleeding, but I could tell it wasn't bad. The thick leather of my jacket had prevented a deep cut. Most importantly, it wasn't bad enough to slow me down, and I pulled the Desert Eagle as I trotted to the SUV. They saw me coming, but I had their keys.

They had managed to push the dead driver into the back. As I approached, one of them was franticly going through his pockets in a fruitless search for the keys.

I walked up to the driver's side window and dangled them in front of one of the guy's I recognized from Little T's place in New York.

"Looking for these?" I pointed the Eagle at him. "Get out of the car, and bring Clarisse with you if you don't want your brains splattered all over the windshield."

"Now take that statement and apply it to your girlfriend."

I looked on the other side of the driver and saw that Clarisse was between him and the guy called Paulie–and he was holding 9-mm Glock to Clarisse's lolling head, and so was the guy in the back seat.

I pointed my gun at Paulie. "I could put one in your head before you could pull the trigger."

"And then Frankie back there would put one in your head, and Vinnie would cap the girl."

The bastard was right. He had me.

The driver held out his hand. "Keys, asshole."

I dropped them into his hand. "Now let her go." Though I knew they wouldn't. "Fuck you." The driver said and drove away leaving me standing helplessly in the road clutching the useless Desert Eagle and dripping blood onto the warm blacktop.

Chapter 14

But they forgot one thing.

Remember that old saying, *Two can play that game?*

Well Tony's boys forgot it.

What they had done to me in New York I did to them now. I had bugged their car.

After I popped the driver of the SUV, I had slipped a tracker under the rear bumper. I had also put a tiny microphone under the driver's side seat, so not only could I track them but I could hear everything they were saying. And that was not necessarily a good thing because what they were saying was turning my stomach.

Clarisse had come around, and they were taking great delight in describing what they were planning on doing to her, in great detail.

I had to hand it to her, she was one tough little babe. After they sneered about how they were gonna gang-bang her, she only laughed and snipped back, "And that's supposed to scare a hooker? What—did you forget? I've been screwed by Little T, and after that a gang-bang would seem like a day at the beach."

Good girl! I thought. *Keep 'em off balance.* But when they upped the ante and started talking about pliers and blow torches, I could hear the underlying fear in her voice hovering just beneath the bravado.

"Hey Paulie," she said with an obvious yawn, "you wanna shoot me up with another dose of those knock-out drops, or do you just want to keep talking until I pass out from boredom?"

Smack!

I could hear the sound of a big meaty fist striking flesh and her sharp intake of breath.

"Keep talking, bitch," I heard Paulie snarl, 'cause every smartass remark is gonna be another mark on your pretty little body, and we're gonna take all night 'cause Mr. T. wants to have a nice long session. You see we're gonna record the whole thing and send him a DVD so he can watch you scream every night."

And now Clarisse was silent. She was scared, and she had every right to be. I was scared for her.

Almost two hours later we passed a sign that read, "Entering Gravel Switch, Kentucky–Population 503." Fifteen minutes after that, the bug told me the SUV had turned off the blacktop.

I ditched the Civic about a quarter mile from where the blip had stopped and went the rest of the way on foot, Vietnam re-con style. The sun was beginning to set when I crawled up to a big oak about two-hundred-fifty yards from the farmhouse where they'd taken her.

They'd obviously chosen it not only for the remote location but because it was surrounded by clear fields for almost three-hundred yards except for the lone oak I was behind and a couple of scraggly bushes.

There was a rusted-out pickup truck parked near the farmhouse door, and a guy with a red baseball cap sitting on the front porch, a pump-action shotgun on his lap. I waited to see if they had hired more than one of the local talent to watch out for party poopers like me and, sure enough, after about ten minutes another guy came around from the back and took a beer from the pickup. After a few minutes of idle chatter, he ambled back around the side of the house and disappeared out back, most likely by the back porch.

I heard a short, sharp scream, and the guard on the porch opened the front door, looked in and stepped back out shaking his head.

They'd started, and I was running out of time.

I quickly assembled the sniper rifle and focused the scope. I didn't have time for sighting and calculation for wind and drift, so I set the crosshairs slightly up and to the left of the guard's chest and squeezed off a silenced round.

He toppled off the chair and rolled into the yard without making a sound. I picked up the rifle and the gym bag containing the rest of my arsenal and made my way around back. There I went through the same drill with the second guard, but at the moment I squeezed the trigger he swatted at a mosquito and the shot took him in the shoulder.

He dropped down behind the porch railing, denying me a clear shot.

"Shit!" I picked up my bag and ran toward the porch. As I approached at a dead run, I could see him fumbling to cock a deer rifle. I didn't have time for a rifle shot, so I pulled the Eagle and fired off three silenced rounds in quick succession. The third one did the job, and he staggered backwards and slumped down against the railing.

I started toward him to make sure he was dead, but another scream and then a moan followed by coarse laughter stopped me cold. I dropped the bag, inserted a fresh clip into the Eagle and opened the back door silently.

They were set up in the living room. Clarisse was tied to a straight-backed wooden chair, her blouse ripped half off and her face marked with welts and bruises. On the table next to her was a bag of tools and a hammer, nails, pliers and a blow torch all lined up and waiting. But it looked like they had just been softening her up with their fists first before they got down to the main event.

Paulie grinned. "That's just a little taste of what we're gonna do to you after we get through screwing your brains out." He motioned to the guy focusing the camera on a tripod. "Okay, Frankie, bend her over that table and let's have some fun." He sneered at Clarisse. "What, no smartass comments, bitch?"

She looked up. One eye was swollen half shut, but she still glared at him and spit a mouthful of blood down the front of his shirt. "Fuck you!"

Paulie reached into his pocket and pulled out a handkerchief. He stepped toward her, picked up the hammer and handed it to a brutal-looking man with a large purple scar bisecting his right cheek. "Show this bitch what we do to smartass little girls, Petey."

Petey grinned and grabbed Clarisse's left wrist, pinning her hand to the table.

Her face was pale, and I could tell she was trying not to let her terror show. But they were about to test her courage by smashing that beautiful little hand with a ball-peen hammer. Petey raised it over his head. I saw his bicep tighten in preparation for bringing it down. So I took my shot and blew his hand off.

He screamed as his mangled hand still holding the hammer splattered against the wall.

I stepped into the room and pointed the gun at Frankie and Paulie.

Clarisse looked up and said, "Cody!" But it wasn't in relief—it was . . .

I spun around a half second too late. A rifle butt clipped the side of my head, and I went down. I had made another mistake. There had been three men in the truck—not two.

I felt woozy, but I was still on my knees. The man I'd shot clutched his bloody stump and screamed, "Kill him! Kill the bastard!"

Frankie drew his Glock and yelled, "Drop it!" and I let the Eagle fall to the floor.The man with the rifle came around from behind me and put me in his sights. By now, Petey had wrapped a dishtowel around his stump and snarled, "Tie him to a chair and then bring me the blowtorch. You're gonna pay for this, fucker!"

That's when I flexed my arm under the leather jacket, snapping open the release catch on the throwing knife strapped there and with a quick snap of my arm, sent the perfectly-balanced blade straight into rifleman's throat. He clutched at it with a gargling sound, and I dove for my gun, but Frankie's first shot clipped me in the shoulder and his second in my left leg as I rolled over and scooped up the Eagle. This time I didn't try anything fancy. My adrenalin was flowing, and I emptied the magazine into him, each big .50-cal slug spinning and bouncing him back until he hit the wall where his mangled body teetered for a moment, dead eyes staring before he fell face first and lay still.

Suddenly, I heard the simultaneous *bang* of a pistol and the *thunk* of a bullet hitting the wall inches from my head. I glanced over and saw Paulie desperately tugging at the slide to his automatic, but fortunately it appeared to have jammed. I took two steps toward him just as he grunted, got it and raised the now-cleared Glock at me. But he was too late, and I was too close. I slammed the heavy frame of the Eagle into his face and heard the cartilage in his nose crackle like Rice Crispies. One more slam to the side of his head, and he slumped down, moaning.

Petey was desperately trying to get his gun out of his shoulder holster, but it was strapped to his left side, and I'd blown off his right hand, so he couldn't reach it. I walked up to him, grabbed him by the collar and pulled him over to the table with the tools.

"You were gonna use these on her?" I asked softly.

"No. No, we were just trying to scare her is all. We . . ."

"I heard everything," I said and smashed his face down into the mess of tools. He came up screaming, and I pushed him down on the floor. Then I flicked open the butterfly knife and cut the nylon cord holding Clarisse.

I had to catch her when she almost fell off the chair.

"Hi, cowboy." She grinned through bleeding lips. "just like in the movies, huh?" She pulled a sweaty tangle of hair back from her face. "Only next time, could you maybe get here ten minutes earlier?" She ran a hand over her bruised face. "This kind of stuff could ruin a girl's complexion."

Her knees started to wobble, and I helped her over to the couch. My own wounds were starting to throb, and I knew we should clear out quick and try to find a nice, discreet doctor who wouldn't say no to $500 to keep his mouth shut.

But I had one little thing to do first.

I pulled Petey to his feet and slammed him down on the chair recently vacated by Clarisse and looped the cord around him twice.

Then I stepped behind the camera.

"Now give us a nice smile, Petey. As you said, this is going straight up to Tony Bags in Upstate New York, and you wouldn't want to disappoint him by putting on a bad show, would you?"

I stepped around in front of the camera and stood next to him. "Hi, Tony. Sorry this isn't the video you were expecting, but I think you've seen by now that you're gonna need a whole new troop of scumballs because I've just about run through this crew. But I tell you what I'll do. I'll leave you a few just to make it interesting."

Petey looked up clutching his bloody stump and snarling from between pain-clenched teeth. "You better kill me now, dick-head, 'cause I'm gonna be coming after you."

I nodded. "I don't doubt that, but first I want you to show Tony in person what's gonna happen to every *goombah* he sends after me."

"Yeah, you think so? Me and Paulie will pull together another crew, and we'll be on you before you can even get outta the state."

"Then I guess I better slow you down," I said and shot him in the right kneecap. His high-pitched screams tore though the farmhouse.

I smiled into the camera. "I'll get this DVD right off to you, Tony. Happy viewing." I helped Clarisse up and we left.

Twenty miles north of Gravel Switch we found a discreet doctor. Lucky for us he was one of those old-fashioned docs whose office was in his home. He wasn't happy about being woken up, but when I laid a dozen fifties down on his examining table he grunted, stuffed the money into his pajama pocket and motioned for Clarisse to get up on the table.

He took a look at her bruises and then gave me a hard stare. "Did you do this?"

I shook my head. "Nope, but the guys who did gave me this." I pulled up my tee-shirt.

"And what did you give them in return?" he asked while dabbing antiseptic on Clarisse's face.

"You don't want to know."

We made it back to Lexington by midnight and, against my better judgment, I let Clarisse persuade me to stop by her apartment so she could pick up her things. Yeah, we were refuges together again. But funny thing was, I was getting used to it.

We drove to Bluegrass Field where I bought two one-way tickets on a six AM flight to Cincinnati and from there to Atlanta. That would take our new bloodhounds a while to run down. Then I swapped the Civic for a Jetta and, using one of the cell phone GPS's, found a still-active railroad freight yard. I had hopped many a freight in the Old West in the 1880s, and back then the yard bulls who guarded them would bash your head in and ask questions later. Now they relied mostly on sealed containers and locks, neither of which was an impediment to me.

I picked us out a nice boxcar filled with office furniture and as the train pulled out of the yard, headed northeast, we settled in to make ourselves comfy.

I flicked open the butterfly knife and slit the plastic wrap on several of the modules and pulled out a chrome-and-leather couch for Clarisse and matching executive desk chair for myself.

She stretched out, gingerly lowered her head down on a pillow and watched me for a while.

I finally raised my eyebrows. "Yes...?"

"You know that Tony will have Paulie put another crew together, and they'll be coming after you." I nodded. "You want them to!" she said incredulously.

I nodded again.

"Why?"

I shrugged. "Maybe I'm just getting tired of letting brutal, greedy men decide how I'm going to live *and* die."

She looked at me strangely. "That has happened to you before, hasn't it? In those dream nightmares you have?"

"Yeah."

"They're about war and killing, aren't they?" When I didn't answer, she asked quietly, "And there's a woman in those dreams, isn't there?"

"Yes."

"Was she beautiful?"

"She took many different sizes and forms—young, old, rich, poor, fair, dark—but she was always beautiful to me."

"Only to you?" she gently teased.

I thought for a moment. "No there were times when other men coveted her beauty. Once in particular–when her face and form were more than I have words to describe."

"And did you love her?"

Once more all I could whisper was, "Yes."

She got up and came over to stand beside me. "Tell me," she said softly.

But I wasn't listening any more. I stared out the half–open box car door and saw not dawn-touched cornfields but men with swords in chain mail standing before the battlements of a towering castle.

Northumbria—the northeast coast of England—SeaAxe Keep—813 AD

We had attacked the walls all morning, but each assault had been beaten back and the men were beginning to grumble. We Vikings didn't like waiting for our prey.

What was needed was a way to get over or through the walls, but we Vikings didn't like sieges, either. So my uncle and Guthrum had been huddled together for the past hour discussing and discarding plans they'd used in the past to breach walls. Finally they hit on one.

Guthrum saw me watching and called me over. "Seviin—come here boy." I hurried over. "Take a group of young warriors into the woods and cut me down the biggest tree you can find."

An hour later we were back, having commandeered a score of peasants to fell the tree and a team of oxen to drag it.

Guthrum quickly directed men to strip the wheels from two of the oxcarts and sharpen the end of the tree trunk to a point, and Olaf, our village smith turned Viking, hammered an iron shield boss over the point.

Then Guthrum ordered the terrified peasants to strip off their clothes. One protested but after Guthrum cut him down with a single blow from his ax, the rest couldn't get their garments off fast enough.

Finally he ordered the clothes to be wrapped around the sharpened tree trunk and soaked in oil.

I pointed to the huddled group of naked, trembling peasants. "What should we do with them?"

Guthrum walked slowly toward them, his broad axe dangling from his right hand. "I always like a good feed before battle. What say we roast a few?"

Our men roared with laughter and Guthrum grinned. He turned to me. "And you, my young wolf, are you feeling hungry?"

I looked at the pathetic collection of shaking bodies. "Nay lord, they are all too scrawny. Hardly more than a mouthful for a Viking shield-man."

Guthrum snorted with laughter and clapped me on the back. "Spoken like a true son of the North." He turned and growled at them like a wolf. "Go on, scatter like the sheep you are before I change my mind and chop you up for fish bait!"

They ran without looking back, and we turned and faced the castle.

Guthrum pulled on his helmet and hefted his ax. "Now let's give these Saxon bastards a knock on their door they won't soon forget!"

He clanged his axe on his shield, and our men formed a V-shaped line with the iron sheathed log at its apex.

"Torches!" he cried, and half a dozen burning brands were thrown onto the oil-soaked rags circling the massive trunk. Soon the first ten feet of the tree was a mass of flame, and the iron tip glowed red hot.

"Now," Guthrum called, "man the ropes and pull, you bastards, before the flames burn them through."

I grabbed one of the many trailing ropes tied around the tree and, along with twenty or thirty of our warriors, strained until the log started to move on the huge oxcart wheels.

"Pull, Pull–faster!" Guthrum screamed, and the log began to pick up momentum.

And the faster it went, the more it fanned the flames. I was in the front row of those on the ropes and soon could feel the flames scorching my face. I tried to pull my cloak across my nose and mouth, but it quickly began to smolder, and the fur trim burst into flames. I was about to drop the rope to rip it off when Guthrum trotted up behind me and tore it from my shoulders.

"You won't need this anymore, boy. In a few hours, you'll be dressed in some dead lord's ermine!"

By now we were running at full tilt, arrows from the castle battlements raining down on our ranks. But our own bowman were doing a good job of returning fire then keeping their heads down, so we lost no more than a half-dozen, including one who stumbled and was crushed beneath the wheels.

And then suddenly the great gate loomed up in front of us. We gave a final tug and jumped to the side as the enormous flaming battering ram smashed into the two-foot thick, iron-strapped wooden gate.

The iron tip of the ram burst through the portal, and the double doors quivered and groaned as they bent inward then stopped.

The door, reinforced by bands of wrought iron, had held. The ram had failed to batter it open.

A great cheer went up from the walls, and I could see the nobles and their men congratulating each other and caught a brief glimpse of the Thane hugging his daughter. In that instant I would have given up all future dreams of wealth and glory to change places with him for the moment of that embrace.

We fell back to just out of bowshot range as the Saxons on the wall jeered and called us cowards and women. The men were angry and began to grumble at Guthrum, but he and my uncle merely smiled and said, "Watch."

Then one by one we began to understand the cleverness of our warlord's plan.

He had known the door was too thick to be battered down, and that the iron bands crisscrossing it would make it impossible to shatter. That's why he had never intended the ram to do the job. It was the fire.

The red-hot tip of the ram had punched through the door, allowing a draft to fan the flames of the burning log and suck them into the hole. As the blaze burned hotter and hotter, the iron bands securing the door began to melt.

Soon the mood on the walls changed from one of joy to one of despair, and we could hear the concerned voices of the defenders and the wails of their women as orders were given to find whatever materials were at hand to throw in front of the burning, crumbling gate.

Guthrum straightened and yelled, "Shield wall!"

The moment had arrived.

He raised his axe, and six of our largest and strongest men ran forward carrying a ten-foot battering ram with a three-foot circle of wood on the front. This one didn't have to crash through anything, merely knock over burning, collapsing timbers. That it did very well.

With a tremendous shout we formed our shield wall—overlapping in the front rank and covering our heads against the arrows with the remainder of our shields. As we approached the now-smoldering gate, spears and stones joined the arrows raining down on us, but they didn't stop us. The men with the ram smashed it into the burning timbers once, twice . . . On the third stroke, the entire remaining structure of the gate collapsed inward in a great shower of sparks.

We were through and burst into the outer courtyard, howling like ravenous wolves maddened by blood lust.

There is a reason why all men fear the Vikings, and we set about reminding the defenders of that.

The men on the walls did their best. They ran down to meet us, and a score even formed their own shield wall and charged us. But it is hard to stand against Northmen whose blood is up and boiling for death and slaughter. Within a quarter hour we had struck down every man in the courtyard.

We spared not one of them. There was no point. They were all men at arms or house carls, so were worth nothing as ransom. And what little wealth they possessed they had on their person in the form of gold arm bands and weapons. Those we took when we killed them.

But the richest prizes of gold and silver and jewels remained locked in the high-walled round Keep that stood in the middle of the central courtyard. That was where the high lords were who had families and allies who would pay to ransom them.

That was also where the gold and silver object of my heart's desire lay. Bronwyn, the lord's daughter, The Girl.

"Cody?"

The world of the Ninth Century faded away, and I found Clarisse kneeling beside me waving her hand in front of my face.

I stared up at her, but images of smoke and flames and bloody swords still danced before my eyes. And above them all shimmered a face—the most beautiful face I have ever seen.

"Cody? Where were you? It was like you were in a trance. I couldn't even hear you breathing."

She looked worried then whispered, "Where'd you go? Where do you go? Where and . . . when?"

I shook my head. "I've got to go back."

"No—please, Cody. Tell me. You've got to tell someone. You can't see it, but it's eating you alive. Please."

"Maybe—later." My voice sounded hoarse, like I'd been yelling.

The face was drawing me back, like being sucked into the vortex of a whirlwind. I could hear Clarisse pleading with me for something, but her voice was growing fainter and fainter as the golden eyes and moonlight hair drew me back to the swirling smoke and crackling flames that turned the setting sun to a blood red orb of death and slaughter.

233

Chapter 15

The sun was low on the horizon, casting a sullen red glow on the outer courtyard, but it was hard to tell how much of the wavering red glow was from the setting sun and what was cast from the dozen small fires still smoldering from the guard huts and sheds.

All the bodies of the garrison had been stripped of mail and weapons, and I had been able to acquire my first chain-mail shirt. It was too big and rusty and had a large, jagged hole stained crimson where the tip of my spear had been able to punch through the ringmail and into the stomach of the big Saxon who had owned it up until an hour before. Now it was mine.

The fact that I had been able to drive my spear through the mail didn't dissuade me from wearing it. All warriors knew mail would not stop a well-thrust spear, but it would turn a sword cut, and in battle that might be just enough to keep a man alive. Besides, I had won it by killing its owner, and that alone meant I could sport it as a trophy of battle.

Guthrum noticed it, too, and commented on it. "Look, Sokki our wolf cub has grown sharp teeth and now covers himself with metal skin. Soon he will fancy himself invincible." He walked over to me. "Do you feel invincible, boy?"

In fact I did, so I answered, "Yes."

He nodded and grinned, and at that moment I knew I was in for trouble, but my blood was up and I felt ready for anything. What he said next made me doubly certain.

"I need a half dozen young men who can climb like mountain goats and soar like ravens. Can you do that?"

I nodded.

He pointed to group of our young warriors and motioned me toward it. When we got to them, Guthrum indicated a collection of ropes and grappling hooks. "I want five of you lads to scale these ropes while we keep the defenders heads down with arrow fire." Then he turned to me. "While they are occupied with you five, our Sveinn here will use his grapple and line to drop through the drawbridge slot and trip the mechanism. The moment that happens we will be in, and then the real fun will begin." He studied the expressions of the young men—some expectant, some apprehensive—and said calculatingly, "and your reward will be first choice of the spoils, weapons and women."

My heart raced with excitement. I was going to be the first into the keep, and I already knew what I was going to choose.

But my quest was almost finished before it began.

Oh, the first part of Guthrum's scheme went off just as planned, despite the fact that three of the five young warriors chosen to scale the wall were killed before they got halfway up–but Guthrum had only meant them to be a diversion, and their deaths did exactly that.

In the meantime, I scrambled up to the drawbridge slot and scaled down the rope that wound around the winding gear. I had sheathed my sword and was using both hands to tug the release lever when I felt something slam into my back that sent me sprawling. I rolled over and saw a house carl with a longsword drawing back for a second cut. The chain mail had saved me. But as I scrambled to my feet and blocked the second slash with my own sword, I saw another guard approaching from the left with a spear that would pierce the mail just as easily as I had done while acquiring it.

In desperation I jumped over the drum that held the winding gear and used it as a bulwark while they both came at me. It was *clang*, block a sword cut and *thud*, throw up my shield as the spear slammed into it.

I knew I couldn't hold the two of them off for long, so as they pressed in on me every time I blocked one of their thrusts, I slashed down on the rope holding the bridge cables to the winding drum.

It was massive and thick, and after three or four cuts I still wasn't through it. Thy saw what I was trying to do and pressed me all the harder. So, I took a gamble, and after their next thrusts I threw my shield at them and grasped my sword with both hands, putting everything I had into one great desperate stroke. With a tremendous *snap*, the rope parted.

The bridge smashed down with a resounding *crash*, and in the next moment scores of howling Vikings poured across.

As the garrison came thundering down the stairs to meet them, I was fighting my way up.

I had a prize to claim.

"Cody. Hey Cody, the train has stopped."

Clarisse was right. It had.

I shook my head to clear away the cobwebs of a memory I wasn't quite finished with yet. But castles and swords would have to wait. It was the here and now I had to deal with. Glancing over at Clarisse, I noticed the bruises had turned purple, but the swelling around her eye had gone down. The doc back in Kentucky had wiped off her smeared makeup and lipstick when he treated her, and somehow she actually looked better without it. Or maybe I was still thinking about the girl in the tower Keep. She had worn no makeup but, then again, what could modern cosmetics have done to improve pale white skin, blood-red lips and eyes as large and golden as some mythological cat's?

Clarisse's hand on my arm snapped me out of my reverie. Damn, these lapses were getting serious. For the first time in almost two thousand years I began to wonder if all the memories of all the lives were finally beginning to push me over the edge.

"Concentrate, Cody–fuckin' concentrate," I muttered

"What?"

I didn't realize I'd spoken aloud. "Nothing, just talking to myself."

"Well that's fine as long as you include me in your soliloquy."

"Soliloquy? My, my, two weeks of college, and you're talking like an intellectual." She did something I'd never seen her do. She blushed. "I'm not completely dim, you know. I told you I got good grades in high school, and I still read a lot."

"Really? Like what?"

"Stuff you probably never even picked up, tough guy, 'cause there's no guns or bimbo's in 'em."

"Enlighten me then. Such as . . . ?"

"Marcel Proust, James Joyce, F. Scott Fitzgerald, Jane Austen and Shakespeare. So there." She ended by triumphantly sticking her tongue out at me.

"I'm impressed—although I feel compelled to remind you that there's more blood, murder and bimbos in one of ol' Willy S's plays than in the average car chase, shoot 'em up at your local movie theatre."

"That's probably why I prefer Jane Austen." She sighed. "I especially like *Pride and Prejudice,* 'cause it's about some head-up-his-ass rich dude who learns that a girl doesn't have to be rich and put on stuck-up airs to be a good person."

"Humm, I'm not sure Jane would have put it that way, but I'll concede you the concept."

She looked at me funny. "And there's another thing I don't get. Most of the time *you* talk like you never finished third grade, or just grunt a word or two. But then all of a sudden you'll start using all these two-dollar words like you're some sort of professor or something. What gives? Or is it just another one of those secrets from the past you're never gonna let me in on?"

"We've all got our little secrets, Clarisse. Now we've got to . . ."

"Hold on—I've told you mine. Hell, I probably told you more than you want to hear, but I told you. You've told me nothing about yourself. It's like it's all dark and creepy or scary. Like when you dream, or zone out, like you did the whole train ride."

She took my hand and knelt down next to me where I sat in front of the open boxcar door, saying very softly, "Tell me Cody—please. I may seem like a dumb blonde, but I'm a good listener. And I think it might help you if you told someone."

"I have told someone."

I wasn't sure if I spoke or just thought it, but she asked, "Who?"

"The only person I've ever loved or trusted. The only person who can save me."

"And where is this person now?"

"I don't know."

"Is she your wife or girlfriend or lover?"

"She's been all three."

"I'll bet she's pretty. What does she look like?"

"I have no idea."

"I don't understand."

I turned and glanced at her. "No, you can't. No one but she can, and I don't know where she is or what she looks like—because I haven't found her yet."

Clarisse stared back at me. "She's the girl from your dreams, isn't she? And you've met her before. I know because you call out her name in your sleep. But it's always a different name." Her eyes searched my face. "I think I understand. It's like that Hindu thing, where they all get re . . . reincar . . . "

"Reincarnated."

"Yeah, that's it. And that's what's been happening to you. Am I right?"

"Yes," I whispered.

"Is it real? I mean maybe—" She took my other hand and covered both of them with her own in a gesture of concern that was nothing like a cynical New York call girl. "Maybe it's just something in your mind."

I felt a cold chill. Could that be it? Was it so simple that a little hooker from a hick town in West Virginia could figure out something that I hadn't for twenty centuries? Maybe I wasn't cursed. Maybe I was just crazy.

I laughed. "Oh, Clarisse—why couldn't I have met you a hundred lifetimes ago?"

"Maybe you did," she whispered.

I turned to her, but at that moment the train came to a jarring halt, and I heard the sputter of machinery and boxcar doors being opened. The time for navel gazing was over. "Come on, we've got to move."

I jumped down from the car and caught her as she jumped. We ducked around a stack of containers and headed toward a diner across the two-lane highway.

We went in and slid into a booth. "OK, so now what?"

"So now we order eggs and coffee. Lots of coffee." I held up two fingers, and a bored-looking waitress somewhere between fifty and eighty, with blue/grey hair like a shedding Brillo pad, lumbered over and said, "Yeah?"

I ordered bacon and eggs over easy. Clarisse wanted cantaloupe, but the waitress just laughed.

"We got stewed prunes if want 'em."

She settled for a large juice and scrambled eggs. "Where do you think we are?" I picked up the tattered menu. "Well, according to this we're in Harrisburg, Pennsylvania."

"Then, I repeat, so now what?"

"First we're going to eat our eggs." The waitress returned with our order and refilled my coffee cup. I waited until she shambled off, then said, "And next we borrow a car and continue on to New England."

"Continue on to New England? I'm not going to New England."

"Now you are."

This time I chose a four-year-old tan Ford Explorer and headed north to the turnpike. "So tell me again why *we* are going to New England?"

"It's for a job. I've signed on to play delivery boy and . . . " I stopped. Why the hell was I telling her? I'd spent too many lifetimes learning to keep my mouth shut to start changing now. Was this little blonde piece of fluff starting to get to me? I looked at her. No, that wasn't fair. She'd proved herself to be pretty damn strong and resilient. And yeah, when it came right down to it, she had a hell of a lot of guts, too.

I smiled.

"Wow. I don't see that expression very often. It's kinda' nice. Did I finally do something right?"

I smiled again. "You're all right, Clarisse."

She smiled back and for once didn't say anything.

That night we stayed in a small motel near Danbury, Connecticut and after a bag of greasy fast food burgers and fries, she asked me what I was delivering and where.

"I can't tell you the what, but I guess the where won't hurt, since you'll be going there, too." I glanced up to see if she reacted to that, but she knew as well as I what would happen to her if Tony Bags's crew caught up with us.

I leaned back against the cheap motel headboard and kicked off my sneakers. "We're going to some little town in Massachusetts." I reached over and grabbed the map that rested next to the sealed case in my backpack and unfolded it. "It looks like the town is on Cape Cod." I studied the map. "You know, I think Cape Cod is one of the few places I've never been."

"Cape Cod?" Clarisse brightened. "My sister lives there. She's the assistant curator of some little museum in a place called Sandwich."

"Sister? Yeah, I seem to recall you mentioned her once." Then I surprised myself by saying, "So tell me about her. You two sound kind of different. She's a museum curator in some back-road town?"

"Assistant, and yeah, we're really different, but she's the one person in the world who's never judged me."

"I take it she's your older sister. How much older is she?"

"Yes, she's a few years older, but—"

She looked distracted, somewhat uneasy. "But what?"

She shrugged. "She seems a lot older than me. No, that's not right. I guess more mature, thoughtful, cerebral would be a better way to say it."

She saw me looking at her and gave me a wry smile. "Yeah, I know, there I go again– cerebral. But see, I did tell you that I always liked to read and, well . . . I guess I always wanted to be more like her than me."

"Why, is she cute, too?"

"Hey, you actually gave me a compliment. Wow, I must really be doing something right. Or is it that tough guys only get turned on by brainy babes?"

"You tell me. But I was under the impression that you kind of grew up alone."

"No, not at first, anyway. When we were kids all we had was us, but that was okay because that was all we needed—at least up until high school."

She was looking at me, but she wasn't seeing me. I knew that look, knew that lately I'd been having it all too often— The Thousand-yard Stare we called it in 'Nam.

"We kinda went different ways in high school. I got wild, and she got quiet. I went for booze, weed, fast cars and faster boys. And Catherine, well she didn't date much—just studied and wound up getting a full scholarship to Dartmouth College. After that she got another scholarship to do post-grad in art history at Harvard and worked at the Peabody Museum until she got this job on Cape Cod a few years ago. Now she does that as well as lectures at Cape Cod Community College. And, oh yeah, if that's not enough, she's become a very accomplished poet and painter. You know, the artist type."

I glanced over at her. "Artist, huh?"

"Yeah, how 'bout that. And little ol' me? Well, you know the rest. She got a scholarship, and I got a one-way ticket out of town. She got her PhD in art history, and I got mine in . . . Well, I guess you know that too ."

She leaned back and laughed. A bit bitterly I thought.

"So how's that for *A Tale of Two Sisters*?"

I shrugged. "I've heard stranger."

She gave me that little crooked smile. "Yeah, I'll bet you have."

Clarisse picked up the lumpy motel pillow and plopped it under her chin. "OK, once again we've picked apart the sad life and times of Clarisse the girl gone wrong from West Virginia. And once again Mr. Cody the Killer is closed up tighter than a clam. In fact, it just dawned on me. I don't even know your last name."

"That's because I never told you."

"And my guess is that you never will. Am I right?"

I shrugged.

She sighed and rested her elbows on the pillow. "You really know how to make a girl feel special Mr. Cody Mysterious."

Clarisse began tracing small circles on the back of my hand. "You know, you need to tell somebody what you're all about some time. Why not me?"

I closed my eyes. "Give it a rest, Clarisse. I never did well at sharing feelings." She looked hurt, but I wasn't sure that it might not be an act. Though for what possible reason I couldn't imagine. I glanced over at her. Maybe I was being unfair. She seemed to be plying it pretty straight with me, but I'd spent a long, long time learning to trust only one person, and if old habits die hard, those ingrained over centuries die even harder.

But I was tired. I was tired of the modern world with electronic answers to everything, so I said, "Look, you're a good kid, Clarisse, but it's been a long, hard day. And they aren't likely to get any better, so let's get some sleep."

I switched off the light and a moment later felt her snuggling up against me, but I pushed her away as gently as I could. "Sorry, but you're a distraction to a good night's sleep. A very sweet distraction but we both need some rest." I heard her sigh in the dark, but she rolled over.

But that wasn't the reason. I couldn't have her touching me because I had places to go.

Northumbria — the northeast coast of England — SeaAxe Keep — 813 AD

I thrust upward with my sword into the belly of a guard at the top of the stairs and burst into the great hall on the second floor of the tower keep.

The Thane stood sword in hand surrounded by his house carls who were clutching spears and long axes. But I barely noticed them. I had eyes for only one thing in that room, the Lady Bronwyn.

For centuries after I would dream of her face and try to recall each instant of that moment when I saw her standing next to her father in the great stone keep, but mere words are inadequate to describe her. Make no mistake, in each of her many incarnations I found her beautiful, but in this one she was something more that beautiful. She was–otherworldly.

Even over the sea I had heard tales of her, and travelers spoke of her beauty in awed tones. The people in the surrounding villages had claimed she was only half mortal. The local legend asserted that her father had met and bedded the King of Elfland's daughter and that the child their union had produced was the lady Bronwyn. And at that moment I believed it.

Now seeing her more closely, I was even more enamored of her beauty. Her face was heart shaped, with high cheekbones, her ears so thin and delicate that I could almost believe she was part elf. Her wavy, waist-length hair was so blonde it appeared golden white. But the eyes–oh, the eyes. They were large and golden, and when she looked at me I felt as though I was falling into a deep well and almost dropped my sword. In fact, had the house carls not been clustered tightly around her and her father, they could have dismembered me while I stood dumbly staring at her.

Fortunately, before they could do that, Guthrum and a dozen of our men came howling up the stairs and clattered into the room. They swarmed in front of me, blotting out her face, and the spell was broken as I took a firm grip on my hilt and waded into the battle alongside them.

For the next ten minutes it was hot work as these were the Thane's handpicked warriors and fought well, taking down a number of our fighters with their long axes. But as the room filled up with ever more Vikings, their long axes became an impediment rather than an asset as they ran out of room to swing them. Soon our numbers overwhelmed them until there was only the Thane and his daughter standing beside his great, ornately-carved chair in the middle of the room.

Guthrum swaggered up to him grinning and gestured with his battle-ax. "Will you fight me, or do you beg my mercy?"

The lord of the keep stood up straight and said with what I thought was admirable dignity, "Were it not for my concern for my daughter's safety, I should be happy to run you through, Viking. But I fear that if I did win, your men would in revenge kill me and violate my daughter. So I yield."

Guthrum grinned. "A pretty speech for a coward, but you're right, I would expect no less of them. And since you haven't the balls to fight me—that's exactly what I intend to do." And with that he swept his axe in a blinding arc and took the thane's head off at the shoulders.

Our men shouted their approval and crashed their swords on their shields. Bronwyn gave a cry and staggered back, clutching the arm of her father's chair. I wanted to run to her, take her in my arms and tell her she would be safe, but I knew she wouldn't.

Guthrum kicked the Thane's still-bleeding corpse aside and grabbed Bronwyn's arm. He swung his axe in a short swipe and sank the blade into the arm of the great chair, then buried both his bear-like hands in her silver-gold hair and pulled her delicate face toward his rough-bearded one.

My heart felt like Guthrum's hands were squeezing out my own life. But it got worse. He kissed her savagely and then, still grinning, tore her long cloak from her shoulders and ripped her velvet dress down to her navel.

"No!" The words wrenched from my soul before I even had a chance to think. Guthrum turned and looked at me in puzzlement. "No? My young wolf dares to tell his chief no?"

I stepped forward, thinking desperately. "No, Skull Splitter, but did you not tell me that I would have my pick of both woman and spoils?" He nodded slowly, and I said in a rush, "Then I choose her, my chief."

He paused, thought a moment then shrugged. "All right. Just to show that Guthrum Skull Splitter is a man of his word, you may have her first." He pushed her toward me, laughing, and I caught her in my arms. The scent of her perfume would have made me dizzy had I not been so worried.

"Take her, young Seviin. And when you're done, I shall have her and then the rest of the men."

They cheered.

I started pulling her toward the curtained alcove that served as bedchambers, but he put his hand on my shoulder. "Where do you think you're going?"

"I was just looking for a private place, lord," I stammered trying to buy time, hoping that if I could get her out of sight they might become so absorbed in looting I could smuggle her out. But Guthrum was having none of it.

"What? Are you a Viking or some shy wedding-night virgin?"

The men laughed.

"But I–I . . ."

Suddenly, Guthrum's grin turned into a snarl. "Either throw her down on the floor and fuck her, boy, or I will."

"No, I can't—you can't. I won't let you."

In the next moment my head was bursting with pain, and I lay sprawled on the floor. Guthrum stood over me, wiping my blood off his axe handle. "You're out of time, boy."

Grabbing Bronwyn, he pushed her to the floor while tugging at the lacings of his truese.

I scrambled to my feet and without even thinking drew my sword

The great room of the tower Keep fell silent. Even the Skull-Splitter's shield men were stunned into silence. I glanced over at my uncle. Emotions warred on his face—horror for what I was doing and pride for my lack of caution to preserve my own skin.

We Vikings believed the worst end for a warrior was to die in bed, and my uncle Skokkii could see in that moment that a *skraaling's* death would never be mine. I would go to Valhalla as a warrior. Sword in my hand–most likely cut to ribbons by the fiercest war chief from our shores—but a Viking warrior whose fight to death with the Skull-Splitter would be sung of by the *skalds* around the mead hall fires for the next thousand years. And that was fine with me.   It was also fine with Gunther Skull-Splitter.

"You dare draw sword against me, boy? Your war chief?" He spat on the floor. "Do you see that spit, boy? In the next dozen heartbeats your guts will join my spit on the floor, and then I will use them to wipe my ass."

And then my uncle surprised me and gave me a feeling of gratitude I have never forgotten to this day.

He walked forward until he stood in front of Guthrum, the war leader he had sworn to obey. "Have care, Skull-Splitter. I am your shield man and will never betray my oath or leave your side, but I will not see you dishonor my brother's son."

Guthrum glared at him and gripped his axe tighter. "I could kill you where you stand, Sokki."

"That may be, Skull-Splitter. But it would not change the fact that before our war band, I bid you recall that my brother, the father of the lad you see before you, was the war leader of our Vikings when you were but a stripling. And had he not seen to watch over you in your first raids, you would not be war chief now. You would be food for Odin's swine."

It was then I thought Guthrum would strike my uncle down, and perhaps he would have liked to. But Vikings are not like those warriors who are bought-men for some Southern lord's gold. They follow strength, but they also follow their own code of rough justice. And right then, they were growling approval of my uncle's speech, for many remembered my father and his courage and leadership. And Guthrum, though brutal, hot-headed and cruel, was not stupid. He saw the mood of the band, and with a few moments' calculation realized that if he struck me down he would make a blood enemy of my uncle and most likely the better part of the war band.

So with as much grace as he could muster, he smiled through gritted teeth. "Very well boy–Seviin–nephew of my *loyal* Shield Man, Sokki, take the bitch. I give her to you, as a gift."

I drew in the breath I didn't realize I'd been holding and loosened my grip on the sword hilt that had by now grown slippery in my hand. Could it be possible that I was to be allowed to leave with the Keep with the Girl and my life?

I should have known better.

The Skull Splitter grinned. "But if you recall the stories that the skalds tell of the gods of Asgard, you will remember that all gifts carry a time limit and a price. And yours, Seviin, son of our former chief and nephew of my shield brother, is that you have but one day to enjoy your prize. After that . . . " He looked at me, but everyone in the room knew he was speaking to my uncle. "It is two candles past sunset, so look for me, young wolf, when the half moon has risen just before dusk in the evening sky tomorrow. For it is then that you will meet me or flee like a coward from the house of one of the greatest Norse heroes to command longships and give up all right to call yourself a Viking warrior."

He grinned. My uncle looked at me but shook his head– he could not help me with this. Guthrum had us neatly boxed in.

I took the hand of the Elf Princess, Bronwyn. She looked at me with more confidence and hope than I felt , but I smiled to give her the courage I wished I had.

All we could do was flee.

I felt a jolt like electricity roil through my body and sat up in bed with a gasp. Clarisse had her head on my shoulder.

I was furious and embarrassed. "What the fuck are you doing?"

"You woke me up. You're having another one of your dreams or spells or whatever it is. But I can't ignore this anymore. I'm not going to have someone sleeping next to me who's on a one-way trip to self destruction."

"It's none of your damn business." I pushed her hand off my shoulder. "Go back to sleep and leave me the fuck alone."

That's when she slapped me across the face.

"No."

I was too surprised to do anything but rub my cheek .

"No, Mr. Cody No-Name, I will not. Believe it or not, this little whore cares about you, though I can't at the moment think why–but I do."

I was confused. I'd spent hundreds of years having only one person in each lifetime to care for. And now here was someone telling me she cared, but she wasn't The Girl. How could that be?

My throat was constricted. I felt short of breath, blood pounding through my veins. "I–I can't talk about it, Clarisse. I have to go back. I can't explain it to you–about *Her*–who she was, what she still is to me. What she will be until the end of time. She–she is..."

Clarisse put her finger over my lips.

"I know. That's why you have to let me come with you."

"What do you mean?" My heart was pounding like a trip hammer

"I mean I want to go back with you to the place that you go and see what you see. Feel what you feel." She looked at me, and I realized I'd never really seen her before. Seen past the lipstick, powder, tight dresses and tough, bad girl manufactured persona to what lay beneath. And I couldn't have said for sure what it was, but it confused and fascinated me all at the same time. So I said the word I'd only said to one other person down through the long ages. "Yes."

She pressed her breasts against my chest and kissed each of my eyelids. "I'm with you now. Let go, I'm coming with you. Let go, Cody. Let go. Let—"

Chapter 16

Northumbria — the northeast coast of England — Thane's Wood — 813 AD

"Thank you, sir. I am forever in you debt."

I looked up from the small fire I was feeding branches and dry twigs into in the vain hope that we wouldn't make enough smoke to betray our position to the Skull Splitter. In a generous but calculated gesture, Guthrum had let us take two fine horses. I say calculated because he knew he could eventually ride us down, and having us on horseback would not only add to the sport but increase his reputation when he inevitably did. With or without mounts, he would find us soon, and we both knew it.

"Lady, I am—" my teenage voice cracked—some hero. I began again. "My lady, I am proud to be of service to you—to your beauty, to your charm, your grace and—" I lapsed into flustered silence.

She came around the small fire and sat beside me, taking my hand in hers. "But that's not the whole reason, is it brave Viking?"

I shook my head.

"You have seen me before—in another land, another time, another place. You remember it, don't you?"

I nodded.

She smiled, and my heart constricted with longing.

"Yes, I remember you—my paladin in ages long past. When you fought for me, bled for me and loved me."

"I will again, lady. You have my word as a Viking warrior. None will harm you while I draw breath, and each that I do is yours until I have no more to draw."

She smiled sadly. She was no more than a year or two older than I, but she had learned from the many lives she'd lived. I had not.

"I don't wish you to have no more breaths to draw. I would instead ask that you draw them close to me."

In that moment I could have—would have—fought a thousand Guthrum Skull Splitters. I dropped to my knees and covered her small, delicate hand in my rough one. "Lady, I am your man. In love, devotion and worship."

She laughed, a sound like water tinkling over pale pebbles in a brook. "No, my eternal champion, I do not require or wish worship or even devotion."

"But are you not the Queen of Elfland's daughter?"

"Is that what you think?"

"That is what I have heard."

She sighed. "Because that is what my father wished the folk to believe. It is quite useful to ask people to respect your word when your daughter is part divinity of the Old Gods. But the great irony is that, in private, my only devotion was and has always been to the one true God of the Christ Jesus."

"You worship the weakling nailed god?"

She squeezed my hand tighter. "He is not weak . . . Seviin, is it?" I nodded. "He is the only true King."

I pulled my hand away and strode to the other side of the fire. "Please, lady–I swore an oath to love and protect you as I know I have in past ages. I'm proud to do that. But I must insist you do not try to rob me of my manhood with your god of women and salves."

She looked at me, and the sadness in her eyes made me turn my head away, But when I glanced back, I saw she was still regarding me. "Oh, dear brave and foolish boy. When will I be able to reach you?"

"I don't understand this, lady. And please, if you have any regard for me do not vex me with this Christian talk."

"Yes. I'm sorry, noble warrior. I do wrong you. You have given up everything in your world for me—Gold, silver, slaves, reputation and your future." She got up, came around the fire and put her arms around me. "And what can I give you in return, my champion?"

I couldn't breathe. I had taken many women—slaves and girls of my village—but I had never dreamed of making love to the Queen of Elfland's daughter. I hardly dared think the thought, but she divined it anyway.

"Of course. Your reward should be the reward that a maiden should always give to a hero." She unsnapped the broach pin holding her torn velvet dress together and let it slide from her shoulders. Her pale hair shimmered silver in the moonlight, and her tiny, elfin face with the gold eyes regarded me solemnly. She stood before me naked. "Take me, my eternal love, and know that you are the first. The one for whom I have waited in this lifetime. You will always be the first in my heart. Until the end of time."

I took her arms, and time stopped as the stars fell from the sky and the earth stood still.

"Bronwyn!" The word wrenched from my soul. I was coming apart. I couldn't take this anymore. I knew now why I had wanted to go back to this memory. It was for this moment. Despite all those that came before or after, this was the one I wanted to bury my soul—with the beauty, grace and love of the Queen of Elfland's daughter.

I didn't want to go on through any more lives. I didn't want to go on to more meaningless, cold, brutal incarnations of killing and being killed. All I wanted was to beg the silver princess to wrap me in her arms forever and never let me go.

And so I did.

"Lady Bronwyn—Princess—hold me, love me. Wherever it is your kingdom lies, take me with you."

I looked at the tiny face, her delicate features shimmering in the silver moonlight, and tears that were not allowed for a Viking or a soldier or mercenary or assassin fell across her pale face. Her lips rose to mine, and we tasted the salt of each other's tears. She moved beneath me, and I felt as though I was drowning in a deep shimmering pool of ecstasy.

"Don't ever leave me, lady."

"I never will."

I gazed into the pixie face glistening in the moonlight. It wavered, and for a moment I saw a face close to mine, blonde hair spread like a golden curtain above me. *Clarisse?*

"I won't leave you, my only true love."

I didn't know who said it, but I blinked my eyes in confusion, and the silver-haired princess moved against me like liquid silk. I slipped back into the deep well of her beauty, and time ceased.

A thousand times a thousand years passed. The Earth ceased to turn, and one by one the stars winked out and still we made love. Only the cruel sun creeping into our woodland glade made us face the harsh reality that another day had dawned. And we both knew that neither of us would live to see the sun set.

But I had promised to protect her as long as my body drew breath, and a Viking's word and his glory were all he could take with him to Valhalla. And I had also made a vow to die with a sword in my hand. We Vikings believe that the Norns weave the threads our fate countless ages before we are born, and when they decide to cut those threads, no man can alter that fate. But that did not mean a man should passively accept death.

"Come, Lady Bronwyn. I know where our ships are beached, and I also know the secret of the loadstone that always points north. And with it I can steer one of our smaller craft to the land of the Sheiks of Islam, who will pay well for a Viking sword in their bodyguard."

She knew as well as I that Guthrum would never allow us to get that far–that even now he was closing in on us. And when he caught up he would . . . But she chose to participate in our dream fantasy, if only for a few hours.

And we had those sweet hours for most of the day as we rode through the cool woodland. Then just as the shadows were lengthening toward dusk, we topped a small rise and saw the sea.

For that brief moment I actually thought we could make it. Be free and happy together–free of endless ages and sorrow, loss and disappointment. I was naïve then. Another thousand years would teach me that the curse would not let me go that easily.

But for the moment my voice rose in joy and triumph. "There, lady. Do you see? Our ships. There on the far end is the one I helped my father build. *The Hammer*, named after Thor's magical weapon of power." I fingered the small silver hammer of the thunder god that hung around my neck and noticed her do the same to the gold cross of her nailed god that she wore.

But I was too happy to care about gods or curses. I should have.

We spurred our horses down from the ridge toward the beach a mile off and had covered a half the distance before we saw them. Guthrum and a dozen riders.

I put my horse between her and the approaching band. "Ride lady! And whatever happens, keep riding and don't look back until you reach the ships." I dug my heels into my horse's flanks. "If I am not right behind you when you get to the ships, then ride south to the King of Northumbria."

She pulled her pony to a halt. "No Seviin, I will not do that. I will not become a marriage pawn, a bride price for a king's alliance. I have, as you, searched down all of the long ages for you and having found you will not go back to a life that is no more than half alive." She stared up at me. "I will choose to die with you."

"No, lady! You cannot. You don't know what they would do if they captured you. Guthrum would rape you and then turn you into a slave whore. Odin's breath, I would sooner suffer my ribs and lungs to be torn from my body in the Blood Eagle than see you condemned to such a fate."

She pulled a long, gleaming silver dagger chased with gold and electrum from her cloak. "I will not allow them to take me."

And then they were on us. It really didn't matter. We could never have made it to my ship and launched it in time.

I slid off my horse, and Bronwyn came up and stood behind me. I drew my sword. Guthrum dismounted and walked toward me. "So we meet for the last time, my little wolf."

I gripped my sword tighter. "This wolf may be young, lord, but he has sharp teeth." And without warning I pivoted on my left foot, skidded down in a crouch and jabbed my sword upwards, sliding the blade across Guthrum's ribs.

He howled and fell back in shock. I saw the other warriors watching me with respect, and my uncle nodded.

And were it not for my uncle I know Guthrum would have sent his entire war band against me, but a Viking chief is only chief as long as he earns it. And despite his reputation, Guthrum knew that to make an enemy of his second in command would be to invite death, so he bared his teeth and charged me.

"Stay behind me," I hissed to Bronwyn, and she dropped back ten paces.

I beat back his first two rushes, but on his third attack my foot turned on a slick patch of mist-wet moss, and I went down.

A heartbeat later I felt the great axe Skull Splitter tear into my right shoulder, and my sword fell uselessly from numb hand.

I scrambled to my feet, beginning to feel light-headed from the fountains of blood gushing from my dangling right arm. I grasped my fallen sword awkwardly with my left hand. But I knew I was finished. So did Guthrum.

He laughed with triumph. "Go ahead, boy, kiss her one last time before I send you to the Valkeries, fuck your wench senseless and then give her to the lads for their plaything."

I turned to Bronwyn. She had tears in her eyes but managed to smile up at me. "Fare thee well, my love. Until we meet again."

She put one arm around me, pulling me close while with the other hand she drew the dagger. And as we embraced for the last time, she drove it into her breast.

Kissing her dying lips, I tasted her blood. It was sweet as wine.

I clutched her still body and turned to a stunned Guthrum, staring at us in disbelief. "Strike, Skull Splitter. I'll be waiting for you in Hell."

His axe blade flashed blood-red in the setting sun. The red turned to black and the world ceased to spin.

I awoke with pain, joy and regret all in equal amounts. My only thought was how I wished I could have held her in my arms forever. And suddenly I realized that my arms *were* still around her.

I opened my eyes and, yes, I was holding a girl with long, soft hair spread on my chest, but it was not the lost elf-princess Bronwyn. It was Clarisse.

The next morning we rode in silence until we stopped at a KFC just off the Mass
Pike.

We sat at a small outdoor table and ate in silence, until Clarisse finally threw a chicken bone into the bucket, turned to me and said, "What?"

"OK, you got me. What?"

"Why are you pissed at me?"

"I'm not."

"Well then, why are you giving me the silent treatment?"

"I'm not much of a conversationalist."

"Bullshit."

"Well, yes, I am that, too."

"Stop it Cody. I'm not gonna let you push me away again." She reached out and turned my face until I had to look directly at her. "Not after last night, Cody. Not after last night."

I grabbed her hand and pushed it away, but I continued to look at her and asked coldly, "What about last night?"

She didn't back down. "I was there. I went back with you. You know I did."

She was right, and I was shaken. How could she have done that? I stared into her eyes— concentrated—but I couldn't see anything. I couldn't see two thousand years of longing and struggling and losing and yet there was something there. . It was like looking into a window over which gauze curtains had been drawn. I knew there was something hovering just beyond my gaze, but I couldn't tell just what.

"Who are you, Clarisse? Who are you really?"

She shrugged, and for a moment tried to slip back into her smartass, tough-girl persona. "Just a little blonde with a nice ass from East Butt-fuck, West Virginia."

"No, you're not. You did something last night that no other person has been able to do except for the girl you saw in my dream memory. How did you do it? And more importantly, why?"

Suddenly the hard shell cracked, and all the defenses seemed to melt away. She looked years younger, small and shy and vulnerable. She sat quietly for a moment, twisting a white napkin with red lettering into little strips that fluttered in the light breeze.

"I don't exactly know. I just felt that I could. Like when me and Catherine were kids, we used to be able to get into each other's heads, and when we slept in the same room we even shared dreams."

Christ–was she another like me? Was she cursed, too? I almost didn't want to ask the question, but I had to know. "Can you remember your past lives, Clarisse?"

She smiled. "Most of the time, I can't even remember what I had for breakfast." But when she saw I wasn't laughing, she shook her head. "No, I don't think so. And if they were like yours, I don't think I'd really want to remember them."

"So then why did you want to come with me last night?"

"For you," she said quietly. "And I guess for me, too." She took my hand. "Cody, you're tough and self sufficient, and when we first met I thought you were just another brass-balled bastard. But I've seen you do things and be things that prove you're not and, believe it or not, I kinda like you."

I nodded. "Yeah, and just as surprising to both of us, I kinda like you, too."

"Then let me help you. You can't keep living a hundred lives all alone and all bottled up. It'll kill you."

"It usually does."

"Yes, but this time you've got someone who'd kinda like to keep you around in this life for a little while." She put both hands on my shoulders. "Will you let me help?"

I don't know what I would have answered, but at that moment one of those little alarms that I had honed over the centuries started tingling between my shoulders. I turned around and scanned the parking lot. Sure enough, there was an Audi Quatro with black-tinted windows and New York plates. I couldn't see who was inside, but I knew that we'd been spotted. They probably had sub-contracts all over the country, and now that I knew from what Chuckles had told me when I was hiding out in Big Sur they not only wanted me and Clarisse but the package I was carrying as well. I still didn't know why they wanted it, but I planned to find out the answer to that when I delivered it.

I knew I had to do three things in rapid succession. Lose the bastard in the Audi, get that package to its destination, then pick up two tickets to the most remote country on the far side of the world.

First, I had a call to make. I wasn't really sure I wanted to and even less sure that I should, but I had one of those uncomfortable, nagging feelings between my shoulder blades. And after two millennium, I'd learned to pay attention to them.

Chuckles answered on the first ring, so I knew I was right. Something bad was about to go down.

"Hope I'm wrong, but I think you may have an even bigger problem than you thought," he said by way of greeting.

It's always so nice talking with friends. "Well now you've peaked my interest, and here I thought I already had a big enough problem."

"Have you ever heard the name Dietrich?"

The little nagging feeling turned into a big nagging feeling.

"Yeah bits and pieces here and there. And that seemed to have been the way everyone who ever mentioned his name ended up. In bits and pieces."

"Christ," Chuckles swore. "Then I guess you won't be thrilled to hear that word has it he's supplying the bulk of the funds Tony Bags is spending to track you down."

My head began to hurt.

"Chuckles, I gotta tell you that I'm at a loss for this one. You were with me for over twenty years while we carried out our private little wars. In all that time, do you recall any tin pot dictator or paranoid, murderous thug we put an end to that had a connection with this guy Dietrich?"

"Shit, I don't know. From what little I've heard of him, the strings he pulls are long and remote. I mean for all I know, he could have been the guy propping up the people keeping those wars going."

"For all we know, he could have been the guy who started them." I took a breath, pulled up a vague recollection. "And now that I think back, I do remember hearing his name once. Remember that tribal warlord in Senegal—the one who used to take ears and noses of everyone who opposed him?"

"Yeah," Chuckles said immediately. "We got a million bucks to feed him to the crocodiles—in small pieces."

"Well, when we got paid off, the guy who handed me the money after we showed him the pics of war-lord-as-breakfast-for-the croc said, 'Dumb bastard never should have tried to double-cross Mr. Dietrich.'"

The line was quiet for a few moments, then Chuckles said softly, "You never told me about that."

"I didn't think it was important 'til now."

"Shit, Cody, then the rumors I heard about him must be true. They say the guy buys politicians like they were ten-dollar hookers, and even the Feds stay clear of him."

I saw Clarisse watching me from the car. She looked worried. She had a right to be. "Look, Chuckles, I need you to find out what the hell this guy Dietrich wants with me. What did I do to him? What did I take from him? What does he want that I've got?" But in the same moment I ended the call, snapped the cheap phone in half and threw it into the woods, I already knew the answer to that last question.

He wanted the box.

An hour later we were on the Borne Bridge crossing over the Cape Cod Canal, and that bothered me.

In 1922 when the Cape Cod Canal from Buzzards Bay to Plymouth Bay was completed, the elbow-shaped peninsula sticking like an arm with cocked fist from Massachusetts' Atlantic coast changed from a peninsula into an island. And since that day, the only way on or off the island, by land at least, has been by one of the only two bridges linking the Cape to the mainland—the Borne and Sagamore bridges.

That meant that someone watching those bridges could see anyone leaving or arriving on the Cape. That's what bothered me.

I suppose I could have driven to Buzzards Bay and rented a boat, but I was actually saving that for the very real possibility that the water might be our only way off. Besides, I had led the Audi through a few back roads in Milford before exiting onto Route 495 and back onto the Mass Pike toward Boston.

I was pretty sure the Audi was still following, but with some fancy driving that had Clarisse complaining and asking where the old KFC lunch bag was so she could throw up in it, I planned to leave our tail stuck on a four-lane highway with no way off until the next exit. I winked, and she squeezed her eyes shut as I cut in front of a honking semi and zipped off the Pike at Exit 12 in Framingham. I watched in the rearview mirror as twenty seconds later the Audi went screaming by in the passing lane. By the time they figured out what I'd done, all they'd be able to do would be to get off at exit 13 five miles away in Natick. And by then I'd be ten miles away and headed back down to the Cape.

Counting on some heated debate in the Audi about where I'd gone from Framingham, I was pretty sure that we'd make it onto the Cape before our tail did. However that didn't mean they hadn't called ahead to get people watching the bridges, so when we saw the Borne Bridge up ahead, I decided for the moment that speed trumped stealth and zipped up the scenic road hugging the eastern side of the canal and onto the two-lane blacktop known as the Mid-Cape Highway.

A few exits later Clarisse poked my arm and pointed at a sign up ahead. "This is it."

"This is what?"

"The exit for my sister."

I glanced over at her. The exit for her sister? OK, I could accept that. What I couldn't accept was that it just happened to be the exit that was written on the instructions I'd gotten with the briefcase.

The exit that was supposed to lead me to the mysterious person to whom I was to deliver that briefcase.

Chapter 17

"Slow down, Cody."

I pressed down on the brake pedal and watched as Clarisse leaned forward and squinted through the windshield.

"There." She pointed toward a faded, hand-lettered signboard half obscured by wild honeysuckle. It read, Beachplum Lane.

"Yeah, this is it." She nodded more to herself than me.

I turned, and a dozen yards later the blacktop gave way to a rutted, sandy track that seemed more potholes than road. The car swayed from side to side, and I had to slow to fifteen miles per hour to keep it from bottoming out. I glanced at the odometer—we'd come just over a mile. The instructions I carried said the drop was one-point-two miles. We had to be close, but there was nothing on either side of the narrow lane except scrub pine and the ubiquitous beach-plums that gave the winding road its name.

We topped a small rise and suddenly there it was. An old saltbox cottage with grey, weathered shingles nestled under an ancient elm overlooking a salt-marsh and, beyond that, the vast expanse of Cape Cod Bay.

I pulled the car up to a small, packed-earth parking area covered with crushed seashells and glanced over at Clarisse. She seemed both excited and apprehensive at the same time.

"This is where you're sister lives, isn't it?"

She nodded.

"You also know that this is where I've been instructed to bring the package."

She nodded again and began to say something but stopped herself.

I pulled the instructions that had come with the package out of my jacket pocket. "But it says here I'm to put the package into the hands of a woman by the name of Catherine Franklin. And you told me your name is Fontaine."

She shrugged. "Call that a stage name for my profession. My real name is Franklin, just like my sister's."

I parked the car next to an old VW Beatle and turned to her. "You know, it seems like a pretty big coincidence that my contact and your sister are one in the same. And I don't like coincidences, Clarisse. In fact, I think—"

But she was already out of the car and walking toward a brick walkway that led to the front door of the cottage. I sat there a moment. Had she set me up? It seemed like a long way to bring me here to kill me. She could have done that at almost any time while I was sleeping and simply taken the package. I took the Desert Eagle and checked the magazine. I had my own insurance for coincidences.

I slung my backpack containing the mysterious package over one shoulder and walked up the old brick path that led to the cottage's front door. The bricks were worn and cracked, with moss growing between them. There was a rickety picket fence that had probably been white when put up some time in the last century. Now the paint had for the most part peeled away, and the pickets lay sagging and askew. Wild primroses twisting trough them gave the place a wistfully nostalgic air of decaying gentility. I wouldn't have been surprised to see a little old lady in a high-collared black dress and cameo broach open the door and invite us in for tea.

Even so, I was a bit taken aback when the heavy front door swung open to Clarisse's strangely timid knock, and the little old lady of my imagination stood in the doorway. "Hello, Catherine," Clarisse smiled shyly with a sweet smile I'd never seen before. "Clarisse," the woman took both of her hands and hugged her. "I'm so happy to see you. Please come in. I've been expecting you."

I stopped cold. This was not good. How did she know? Had Clarisse called her, and if so who else might she have called? I reached into my jacket and fingered the butt of the Desert Eagle. I gave Clarisse a hard look, but she was already moving through the door. I put my hand on her shoulder, and she stopped just over the threshold.

"Oops . . . where are my manners. Catherine, this is my friend Cody."

Friend? What were we, high schoolers on a first date? Her sister walked up to me and extended her hand in a formal manner that made me wonder for a moment if I should bow or kiss it. I shook it.

"Very pleased to meet you, Mr. Cody. Forgive me—is that your first or last name?"

"It's my only name. And now if you don't mind, I've come a very long way to deliver a package to you. But before I do, I need to ask you some questions to confirm that you're who you say you are."

"I'll be happy to establish that I am indeed myself . . . " I think she gave me a wry smile, but it was hard to tell in the dim hallway. "But let's go into the living room and make ourselves comfortable."

I glanced at Clarisse, but she was already following her down the hallway like an eager puppy, so I went too. The living room was like the rest of the house—a relic from the Nineteenth Century. Dark heavy furniture, Hitchcock rockers in front of a huge brick fireplace with model sailing ships on the mantle and a brass sextant and compass placed carefully on a mahogany pedestal table softly glowing with generations of beeswax polish.

Catherine Franklin turned gracefully and pointed to one of the rockers. "Please have a seat, Mr. Cody. May I offer you some tea?"

Damn! There she was again, the little old lady with her tea. Although now that I could see her in the light I realized she was not an old lady—maybe ten or fifteen years older than Clarisse. But that didn't add up. Clarisse said her sister had left home for college while she was in high school, which meant Catherine would only have been four years older at the maximum. But she looked more like Clarisse's mother than her sister. I studied her a little more carefully.

Part of it was the dowdy way she dressed. She wore a shapeless grey cardigan, a tweed skirt and clunky, sensible shoes. Her face was pleasant enough, with Clarisse's same features but and unadorned by any makeup and with the beginning of age lines. Her eyes appeared to be a muddy hazel, but it was hard to tell because she wore bifocals with coke-bottle thick lenses. And where Clarisse's hair was long, blonde and silky, her sister's was a mousy brown pulled back in a severe bun. All in all, she presented an almost comical stereotypical picture of the old maid librarian. Or in her case, museum curator.

We made small talk for a few minutes, or rather Catherine spoke about Cape Cod, the weather and her work at the museum while Clarisse beamed and I tried not to yawn. But Clarisse fairly bubbled with enthusiasm at everything her sister said. And a moment later, I began to understand why.

"As I'm sure you know, Mr. Cody . . . "

"It's Cody, ma'am. Just Cody."

"Of course. Well as I was saying, I'm sure that you know all about Clarisse's acting career. In fact, forgive me if I'm prying, but is that where you and my sister met? Through one of her theatre groups? Or are you a thespian yourself, Mr. Cody—forgive me, I mean Cody."

This was a new one. I opened my mouth to laugh, but I saw Clarisse from across the room shaking her head and making desperate pleas with her eyes. She was begging me not to blow her cover. Obviously, this was someone whose good opinion mattered to her, and she didn't want the web of lies she'd woven torn down and her real occupation as a high-priced call girl laid bare before her older and almost maternal sister. So I played along.

"Yeah, you got it right out of the box. It was at a cast party a few months back."

I saw the relief on Clarisse's face and experienced a rare moment of feeling good about something I'd done. It was kind of nice. But as the two women prattled on, I kept glancing out the window at the white shell-speckled driveway and the packed sand-rutted road beyond. It was empty for now, but I did not expect it to stay that way. Someone would be coming, and I suspected it would be sooner rather than later.

So after a few more minutes, I interrupted. "Pardon me, ladies, but I think we need to get down to the business at hand."

They stopped speaking. Clarisse looked disappointed, but her sister nodded and folded her hands in her lap in a prim manner that reminded me more of the Nineteenth Century than the Twenty-first.

There was something odd about her I couldn't put my finger on, but she nodded once more. "Of course, forgive me. You must be anxious to conclude your business and be on your way."

It struck me that once I left this house by the sea I didn't have the slightest idea of what I was going to do next. I assumed Clarisse would be staying with her sister and, strangely, that thought bothered me as well. But I forced it down into the place where I pushed all things I didn't want to dwell on and instead reached into my backpack and pulled out the package I had lugged across a continent.

I handed it to Catherine, and as I did, I felt a tingle in my fingertips like a tiny electrical pulse. There we paused, each with one hand on the metallic case that contained I didn't know what, but at that moment I felt it was somehow very important I find out.

We sat that way for what seemed like hours but was only moments. Then I let my hand fall away, and she took the case set it on her lap. She looked at me and seemed to know what I was thinking.

"Would you like to see what you've traveled so far to bring me?"

I nodded.

She leaned forward and slid her thumb over the four tiny wheels that set the combination lock. When she released the catches, they opened with a click. Lifting the lid, she took out a package slightly smaller than the briefcase, wrapped in plain brown paper. She undid the twine and let the paper fall to the floor revealing, the antique, hand-carved wooden box I'd glimpsed in the San Francisco lawyer's office. I could tell the box was old—very old. The wood was dark, with a patina of age, and the lid was inscribed with writing I couldn't quite make out but felt I'd seen somewhere before, a very long time ago.

I waited for her to open the box and didn't realize that I was holding my breath. That's probably why I heard the sound from a long way off. It was faint at first. The deep rumble of an engine, barely audible over the wind blowing in from the ocean. But soon it became louder, and then I heard the sound of tires crunching on the crushed shells of the long driveway.

They had found us.

I got up quickly and moved toward the window, calling over my shoulder, "Get that box back in the case and hide it."

"I don't think that will do any good."

I stopped, turned and stared at Catherine. "Come again?"

She sat turning the box over in her hands, her eyes focused on something only she could see. I bent down in front of her.

"What did you mean, it won't do any good?" When she didn't respond I placed my hand on her shoulder. "Catherine, if there's something you know about this thing that's going to put us in deeper shit than we already are, I really need to know about it. Right now."

Slowly she dragged her eyes away from it and met mine. She shook her head suddenly, as if coming out of a trance. "I'm . . . I'm sorry. And yes, I need to tell you about what this contains, but I'm afraid it will take more time than we have under the present circumstances." We both heard the sound of car doors slamming. I pulled the Eagle and peeked out the window.

There was one car. The same one that had caught up with us at the KFC. There were two guys standing next to it, but they weren't moving toward the house. They seemed to be waiting for something or someone. Sure enough, a few moments later I heard the sound of another car approaching.

That tore it. There were too many to take out, even if I added the Sig Sauer in my knapsack to the Eagle's firepower. I'd still be outnumbered at least four to one, maybe more.

Definitely not good odds

I turned back to Catherine. "Is there a back way out of here?"

She put the box back into the briefcase and closed the catches. Then she stood up. "Yes there is, and it's much better than a mere back door, but before I show you I have to ask you one question."

"We don't have time for this." The other approaching car engine was louder now, so I checked the clips of both pistols and flipped off their safeties. She moved up beside me and put her hand gently on my right which held the massive Desert Eagle.

"If I can get you and my sister safely away from this house, will you promise me there will be no killing?"

I shook my head. "No, I can't promise you that."

She gazed back at me with a look so sad and stricken I almost wished I could make that promise.

"Please, Cody." I could see tears glistening in the corners of her eyes, magnified to twin pools of sorrow by the thick lenses of her bifocals .

"All right, then. Although I can't promise what I'll do if it comes down to them or us, I'll promise you this much. I won't be the one who fires the first shot."

She smiled and hugged me. "Thank you." Then she took my hand and Clarisse's and pulled us back into an old country kitchen complete with a butcher block table and dozens of bright copper pans hanging overhead.

Catherine opened a walk-in cupboard and moved two cans of tomato soup, then pushed the board behind them. There was a soft click, and a two-foot wide section of the back wall slid open. She motioned us forward.

"During the first half of the Nineteenth Century, this house was a stop on the Underground Railway. The owner had this built when he decided to hide runaway slaves from the bounty hunters that patrolled these waters." She took a flashlight down from a shelf and checked its beam. Not up to searchlight quality, but it would hopefully get us away from here.

I helped Clarisse through the doorway and grunted to Catherine. "So what was he, some kind of preacher or abolitionist?"

"Neither. He was a former sea captain who made his fortune and retired to this house."

"Okay, so a caring, sharing sea captain who helped the fleeing slaves by hiding them in his house and no doubt spent every evening sitting in front the fire with them roasting chestnuts and singing 'Kumbaya.'"

She turned to me. "Hardly. You see, the sea captain had made his fortune transporting human cargo. He was a slaver." She pushed the door shut, swung the flashlight beam around and started down a long, brick-lined tunnel before stopping, turning to me and saying something strange.

"Because, you see, it's never too late for redemption."

Chapter 18

The ancient brick and mortar tunnel ran on for at least fifty yards and was so dark I couldn't really see the walls surrounding me as much as I could sense their damp, moldy presence. Catherine held the only light, and the batteries must have been on their last legs as with every step we took the light got dimmer and dimmer. It finally got so dim I didn't see a turn in the wall and walked right in to it.

"That does it," I said. "Hold on, you two. I'm gonna hunt through my pack for my Zippo. It not the world's best torch, but it's sure as hell better than that flashlight."

"No need," Catherine called back from about ten feet farther up the tunnel. "We're here."

And so we were. A rusty set of iron rungs were set into the mortar and led to a crack of light I could just make out about eight feet above us.

"You two ladies should go first since I outweigh you by at least seventy-five pounds, and if this ladder crumbles under my weight, I'm gonna need you to toss me a rope."

They both nodded and scampered up the iron ladder. I followed a few seconds later, though much slower, testing my weight on each rung. Finally, I poked my head through a trap door and found myself in an old barn filled with rusted tools and rotting leather harnesses from another era.

The barn's floor and walls were checkered with rotting boards. In some places the wall planking had warped and fallen away, offering us some natural advantage. We could see out but our pursuers would have a much tougher time trying to spot us by gazing into the barn's interior, since the bright afternoon sunshine would make everything inside appear as one dark mass of mottled gloom.

I decided to make a quick tour of the perimeter to see if any of them were approaching the barn. I turned back to tell the women to stay put when I saw Catherine shifting something around in her big macramé purse. Whatever it was was too big for the bag, and the corner of it kept poking her in the ribs. *Oh, Christ.*

"Catherine, is that what I think it is inside your bag?"

"Yes."

"I told you to hide it, not bring it with you."

"There was no time to find a good spot. Besides, from what Clarisse has told me, it will be safer with you than anywhere I could hide it."

"Clarisse said that, huh?" I stared at her, and she looked down. "She must be a mighty fast talker, 'cause it didn't seem to me like you gals had any time for chitty-chat unless—"

"Please, Cody, don't blame Clarisse. I knew about you long before my sister became involved with you. I may be a mousy little bookworm, but I'm very good at research, and when it came to choosing someone who could get the box across the country, every criterion I used pointed to you as being the best."

"I suppose I should be flattered, but in my line of work we usually don't like to advertise our services to the general public. That's a way to get very dead very quickly."

"I can appreciate that. Very well then, let's just say I was pointed in your direction by word of mouth from a satisfied customer."

"And that doesn't make me want to jump for joy, either. In fact, I think I'm going to have to insist that you tell me exactly who it was who gave me such a glowing recommendation. Who knows, I may not even kill them."

She looked shocked, then uncertain as to whether I was joking or not. It was probably an appropriate expression as, at that moment, I couldn't have said whether I was either. But we never got the chance to find out because Clarisse came running over from the far wall and grabbed my arm.

"They're coming around the back of the house, and it looks like they're heading straight for the barn!"

Okay, this was it, the time when I was supposed to earn my pay. Take out the bad guys, save the good guys, or in this case gals, and stride off into the sunset John Wayne style. The only problem was as I peered through a three-inch chink in the barn wall, I counted five, no make that six, bad guys and only one of me. My total arsenal consisted of the Desert Eagle, a 9–mm Sig Sauer, and my hideout .25-cal Beretta in a leg holster. Now, I did have the sisters as backup shooters, but the little I'd seen of Catherine told me she was going to have a problem pulling the trigger on anyone, even the pond scum approaching the barn door with the obvious intention of putting out our lights.

And then there was the box. I was beginning to think maybe Tony Bags and revenge weren't the main event in this little circus. Especially given the addition of the name of the reclusive and sinister Mr. Dietrich to the equation. As I watched the first two goons walk up to the barn door and rattle the lock, I decided if I was gonna get killed for some mysterious chotchke I might as well know what I was dying for.

"All right, Catherine—just what *is* in that box?"

She pulled the macramé bag a little closer. "Something so ordinary you could pass by it a hundred times a day without even noticing. And yet, I'm sorry to say people have killed and willingly died for it."

Somehow that figured and made me all the more determined to see it for myself. I moved closer to her. "Show me."

A surprising flash of fire ignited behind the thick lenses in the plain wire frames. "No. I'm sorry, but not yet. There's a story behind it, and it can't be told in the little time we have left."

"Little time . . . have left? What do you mean?"

Instead of answering, she pointed toward the door. It was opening.

I hissed to Catherine, "Get back in the tunnel." But she shook her head. "They'll be coming that way, too."

I didn't have time to ask her how she knew, but I was sure she did. I put my forefinger to my lips and motioned both women to be silent, took the Beretta .25, placed it in Clarisse's hand and clicked the safety off the Eagle and the Sig. With a screech of rusted hinges, the barn door swung inward. Because of what I'd promised Catherine, I reluctantly fired a warning shot over their heads. When they answered back with a fusillade of slugs, I took careful aim and shot the first two as they entered. They dropped without making a sound. I looked back and forth between the door and the wide-shuttered windows, trying to guess the next line of attack.

From out of the corner of my eye I saw Catherine gazing at me with an incredible look of sadness. I tried to ignore her, but when she moved next to her sister and whispered something to her, then took the Beretta I'd given Clarisse and stuffed it into her purse, I decided we needed to have a quick discussion about the harsh realities of the type of bad guys who were going to be coming through the door to kill us within the next few minutes. But she was ready for my lecture and in the finest tradition of every Christian martyr who'd been thrown to the lions, proceeded to tell me that death was preferable to taking life. "Killing never solved anything," she stated. "All that bloodshed and death lead to is more bloodshed. Revenge in a never-ending cycle."

"You'll pardon me for not sharing your philosophy," I said as I shot the ear off one of our pursuers as he climbed through a window above the old horse stalls. "But when it comes down to a good old-fashioned case of me or them, I'll take me over them every time." I punctuated my statement with another shot and had the satisfaction of watching my target dive for cover. "See what I mean?" I aimed the Sig at a shadow moving past the window. "You can appeal to the angels of their better nature, but in the meantime I find these more persuasive." I got off two shots in quick succession and heard someone outside the barn cry, "Shit!"

I grinned and winked at her.

"If only I could make you see," she sighed.

But I wasn't listening anymore. I was topping off the clips in the Eagle and the Sig. Then I reached for Catherine's bag and fished around for the Beretta she'd finessed from Clarisse. My fingers brushed against the smooth finish of the wooden box. It felt warm to the touch and sent a tingle through my fingertips.

I snatched my hand back until it came into contact with the cold hard steel of the lethal little Beretta. I turned and slapped it into Clarisse's hand. "Hold onto it this time."

She looked confused and conflicted. "Cody, I think my sister's right. This isn't the way to go about it, we should—"

I pushed her to the floor and fired three shots at a silhouette outlined in the far right-hand window.

"Damn it, Clarisse, don't start going all squishy peace and love on me now. I need you to stay sharp, and Clarisse . . ." She looked at me. "Shoot to kill. Got it?"

She swallowed and nodded. "Okay, Cody."

But I wasn't sure how much would stick if I got into a real firefight while her goodytwo-shoes sister whispered meek and mild in her ear.

Then they rushed us all at once, and I emptied both clips into the opening door and the shadows moving through the wide windows. I heard screams and grunts, but they kept on coming. As I drew a bead on one I'd recognized as one of the ringleaders, Clarisse took careful aim with the Beretta and plugged him right through the chest.

"Not bad for a pacifist." I grinned at her.

Then it was back to trading gunfire. I had this vaguely uneasy feeling our attackers could have pumped a few slugs into me, but for some reason were under orders to take me alive. But whose orders—Tony's or Dietrich's?

Given our present circumstances, I really didn't want to find out, so I said to Clarisse, "Look, grab you sister and see if you can find a loose board at the back of the barn and make for the dunes."

I don't know what she might have said, but at that moment Catherine came up to us, slapping dirt and dust from her cardigan.

"I found it," she said breathlessly.

"What? An Abram's tank or a couple of RPG's?"

"No, another way out."

I sighted down the long, thick barrel of the Eagle and waited until I saw a shadow flit from the door toward the old horse stalls and squeezed off one shot.

I heard hollow-point lead strike soft flesh followed by a scream of "Fuck, I'm hit!"

No shit, Sherlock. I mean you come in here with the express purpose of cancelling our checks and you're surprised when you get shot? I sighed. They're just not making tough guys like they used to.

On the other hand, the two or three dozen rapid-fire slugs from automatic weapons were a timely reminder that fat, hired goons still had teeth.

"Time to go, ladies." I tucked the now empty Eagle into its shoulder holster and fired off a few rounds with the Sig to keep their heads down.

"Okay, Catherine, it's show time. Let's see what you've got to save our butts."

She nodded and without speaking turned and led us to the darkest recess of the barn where several bails of moldy hay partially covered a dozen wooden stairs leading down to a low archway set into the barn's rough stone foundation. The only problem was that most of the steps were rotted and had fallen into an eight-foot stairwell hole. But there was no time to consider alternatives, our pursuers were closing in fast, so I swung myself clear of the rotted stairs and dropped the remaining two feet to the stone floor below. Then I motioned for the women to jump and caught each in turn.

Catherine moved quickly to the thick wooden door set into the cellar wall only to exclaim, "It's locked!" She turned to me. "I'm so sorry, I thought we could get out this way, but I have no idea where the key might be and—"

Sometimes the simplest solutions are the best. I kicked the center of the door, and the panels split down the middle. Two more kicks, and they shattered and fell inward. I shouldered the broken planks aside, and we hurried through the archway and emerged in a shallow depression partially roofed by the trailing vines of a long-forgotten arbor. Brambles and wild grape vines grew in riotous tangles that acted as a natural roof as the ditch ran down from the barn toward the salt marshes and ultimately the sea.

We moved silently at a crouching run, and a hundred yards farther on broke through the tangled underbrush and saw a small dock and a twenty-foot classic sloop-rigged sailboat. "Yours?" I asked Catherine, and she nodded.

We piled on board, and she hoisted the sail. But the tide was coming in, and the breeze was too light to make any headway. "I don't suppose you have an outboard, do you?" She shook her head but pointed to the bottom of the boat. "No, but I do have those." Oars.

I sighed and picked them up. This wasn't the first time I'd been called on to man the oars and, compared to pulling the long sweeps on a Viking raider through raging north seas, it was the preverbal piece of cake. Within ten minutes we cleared the mouth of the marsh, and a northwesterly breeze filled our sail. Just in time, too, because as I looked back I could see figures emerging from the barn and running toward the marsh.

I pointed back the way we'd come. "Are there any other boats there?"

"No, just this one."

I nodded. "Well it won't take them long to whistle up a couple of fast boats, so our best chance is to run this thing into the next inlet we see and un-step the mast and try to find some place to hole up."

Both sisters nodded, but I left unspoken the other thing I was equally determined to do. I was going to find out exactly what was in that damned box.

Chapter 19

The late afternoon sun tinted the western half of Cape Cod Bay in a shifting kaleidoscope of yellows, reds and orange. I stared at the drifting ocher clouds, and in the waning crimson light they seemed filled with images. Scenes of blood and battle. Faces, some fierce, some frightened. Most, I realized, were faded memories of ages past. But one face seemed to hover just beyond my recognition. A cruel face, eyes sharp and hard as broken glass. Mouth twisted with merciless contempt, he seemed to be speaking . . . to me. Harsh, guttural tones as cold as the blood-tipped waves on the bay—

"I'm coming for you."

I knew him from somewhere in my past. Long, long ago, I knew him and I feared him. I could not recall his name or how or where I knew him, except that it was from a time of blood and pain and suffering. A time when the sun hung in a boiling, fiery sky, and when I looked at my hands, they too dripped dark, crimson drops of newly shed blood.

I stared at the setting sun until my eyes burned and watched as the image seemed to coalesce before me. It was coming back to me now. Yes, I knew him. Yes...

"Cody?"

The image dissipated like a puff of smoke.

Clarisse was looking at me with concern. "Are you OK?"

I nodded. "Sure." But I wasn't.

We kept making plans and discarding them. for us between there and Provincetown. What we needed was a safe house—but where? Almost as if she heard my question, Catherine spoke up. "I know where."

"Where what?"

"Where we can go and they won't think to look for us."

"Yeah—and where might that be?"

"My home."

I must have looked as skeptical as I felt because she quickly added, "Don't you see? They've already searched there, and now it's the last place they'd look for us."

Clarisse, who'd been as quiet as a kid in Sunday school ever since we'd been around her sister, grabbed my hand. "She's right, Cody. It's perfect. We can be safe there, just the three of us."

There's a cozy little thought, I mused but finally nodded. "Okay, we leave as soon as it's dark."

Two hours later the sun was fully down and the women were cold. Catherine still had on the same gray cardigan she'd been wearing when we arrived, so I gave my jacket to Clarisse. She tried to get Catherine to take it, but she refused, and I was quite frankly bewildered by this new selfless side of the tough little blonde who'd made a living on the unforgiving streets of NYC. Maybe the old line was right and blood is thicker than water. On the other hand, it's been my considerable experience that too much trust can make that same blood flow all too quickly.

As I gazed at the two sisters, Catherine smiled as if she knew what I was thinking. "Yes, we do make an unusual pair, don't we?"

When I didn't respond, she came over and sat down beside me then pointed to my leather jacket draped around Clarisse's shoulders. "You know, I don't think you're nearly as ruthless and coldblooded as you'd like people to think you are."

I shrugged. "And I'm a sucker for stray puppies, too. But on the other hand, Hitler loved dogs."

"Yes, but you're not him. In fact, I believe you would've fought against people like that."

A cold tickle went down my spine as I remembered the last hour I'd spent in Hitler's Reich. I glanced over at Catherine and saw her watching me, her eyes filled with compassion as if she knew what I'd done and what it had cost. Her hand brushed the back of mine, and I felt it again. That strange Déjà vu tickle at the back of my mind, like a tiny mouse nibbling around the edges of my subconscious.

"Cody, would it help you to talk about it?"

I wanted to shout "No," but another part of me wanted to spill my guts to this strange, quiet little thing. Because for some unfathomable reason it seemed as though she really did care. I glanced over at Clarisse. She caught my eye and nodded her head, pleading silently for me to confide in her sister, which was all the more puzzling seeing as how up until now any time I'd even glimpsed another woman,

Clarisse had given me the evil eye. But apparently jealously was not a part of their relationship. So maybe this was a sign. Maybe it really would help to tell someone. Maybe I should—

Fortunately I was spared that decision, as the bubbling rumble of a large power boat split the night air. A stygian-dark outline with the starboard running lights glowing like Hell's Christmas tree rounded the point leading to our inlet, and in the next moment a blindingly powerful searchlight slashed through the darkness, moving inexorably toward our position.

"Get down!" I hissed and motioned to Clarisse. And when Catherine didn't move, I grabbed her around the waist and pulled her to the ground next to me.

She didn't make a sound, just looked at me with complete trust, lying quietly in my arms. I noticed incongruously that she smelled good, too. A very faint whiff of perfume that seemed to be made up of the marsh grass, sun, sand and sea. A scent that seemed so natural and totally unique—like a half-remembered snatch of another time.

She was as trusting and peaceful as a child, and I had the disconcerting feeling that it might be nice to lie there like that for a very long time and let the world pass by without me.

Suddenly, the searchlight beam swung away from us, and I heard the boat engine rev as they moved on to scour a new location. Then they were gone, and it was time for us to move.

And at that moment I didn't know whether that made me happy or sad.

By the time we coasted quietly up to the small pier behind Catherine's house, the moon was fully up, and a steadily rising wind had blown the low-hanging clouds away.

I tied the bow line to a piling and whispered, "When we reach the house, we're going to be outlined by a nearly full moon."

Clarisse glanced up. "Then why don't we just take the tunnel back in?"

"Because if I was going to set up an ambush for someone who might return, that's exactly where I'd do it. I doubt if they have enough manpower to keep someone here on the off chance we'd come back, but that's just one more reason for the likelihood that they'd rig a booby trap, just in case. So we'll keep low and approach from the south side of the house."

I left the women crouching in the shadows of the bushes and reconnoitered the perimeter, but despite my apprehension the place seemed deserted. My car was where I'd left it, but I didn't doubt it was now bugged with a homing device and possibly even a spy cam that would activate the moment I turned the key. Fortunately, there was nothing in the car I'd need, at least for now. I moved around to the back of the house and beckoned Clarisse and Catherine. By the time they reached me, I'd picked the lock on the back door. Two minutes later, we were all seated on the floor in the small living room.

I crept over to the window and made some mental notes of angles and fields of fire just in case, then turned back to the two women just in time to see—

"Don't!" I took two strides to where Catherine stood with a candle in one hand and a lit match in the other. I grabbed the burning flame out of her hand and extinguished it with my own. "No lights," I hissed. "That's exactly what anyone watching would be looking for."

"I'm sorry," she said calmly. "I assumed you were closing the blinds."

I shook my head. "That'd be another tipoff. They know the blinds were open when they left, so any change would be noticed."

She nodded solemnly. "Of course. I'm sorry."

"Forget it. Why don't you see if you can find us something to eat? Nothing that requires cooking, maybe some bread and cheese or cold cuts. But unplug the refrigerator before you open the door. The light, you know."

Fifteen minutes later we were gathered around a delicious spread of smoked salmon, French bread, Camembert cheese and a velvety-smooth bottle of Merlot.

While Catherine poured the wine, I fished out one of my few remaining cell phones and rang Chuck. This time when he answered he sounded scared. And it took a lot to scare a guy who always smiled as he killed,

"I'm in deep shit Cody."

"And I'm not?"

"Look, I found out some stuff, but I think I asked one too many questions 'cuz today two guys came to my door. Said they were cops and held up badges to the peephole, but I wasn't buying it. I told 'em I wasn't letting any cop with a Dollar Store badge in, and if they wanted to talk to me they could come back with a warrant. I heard 'em arguing outside the door and went to the peephole. One of the guys hauled a pry bar from under his coat, but just then the old lady from across the hall came out to walk her dog. For a minute I thought they were gonna bash in the old bag's head, but finally they turned and walked away. I know they'll be back. Cody, I think these guys were from Tony Bags or even worse—Dietrich."

"Look man, tell me what you found out and then drop outta sight for a while."

I heard him take a deep breath.

"What I got was that he's feeding money to Tony in exchange for something you've got."

"The box," I whispered

"I think so. Most of my snitches were too scared to say much. But one of 'em said that word is Dietrich told Tony's boys to make sure the box came to him intact and unopened. My guy even said he heard Dietrich's private plane left DC this morning. If Dietrich is coming for you, you need to move quick. Do you have some place you can hide out?"

I was about to answer when I heard a sharp intake of breath on the other end. "Shit Cody, I heard something."

I heard banging in the background and then a voice calling, "Open up. Police, and this time we've got a warrant."

"Hang on Cody." His voice came across cyberspace as a nervous hiss.

"Chuckles, get the hell out of there."

"OK, but first I need to . . ."

"Now!"

Then I heard the sound of splintering wood and a harsh nasal voice with a Brooklyn accent—"Hold it right there, dirtbag."—Two shots rang out and then nothing. Dead air. Dead.

I walked slowly back to where the sisters were resting on a small circle of throw cushions on the floor.

Catherine patted a worn, overstuffed velvet pillow. I sank down cross-legged and looked at the food they'd laid out on a low coffee table. I'd lost my appetite, but Clarisse's was in overdrive.

"Mmmm, this is more like it." She spread some of the cheese on a slice of bread and helped herself to another glass of wine. "C'mon, Cody. I got one poured for you too." Catherine nodded. "Yes, please, have something."

The sound of those two shots kept replaying in my head. I wasn't tender hearted or sentimental, but I believed in paying my debts. Chuckles had saved my ass on more than one occasion and been a loyal friend in a business where most guys would sell you out for a good whore or a bad bottle of whiskey. I owed him, and right then there wasn't a thing I could do to help him. Hell, I wasn't even sure I could help the people gathered around the coffee table.

Fortunately, I'd had centuries of perfecting not letting my feelings show. Crucial, because the last thing the sisters needed right then was to think their protector might not have all the answers.

It must have worked, because a few minutes later Catherine studied my face and said, "I knew I was right."

I glanced over at her. "Come again?"

"When I picked you as the one to bring the box here to me, I knew it would be dangerous and difficult, but that's why I sought you out. I knew there was only one person who could overcome every obstacle and see it safely to me—you."

"Ah huh. And you know what? I think this would be a perfect time for me to get some answers to a whole lot of questions, and I think there's likewise only one person who can give me those answers. You."

She nodded. "You're right. You do deserve some answers. So very well, ask your questions, and I'll do my best to answer them if I can."

I didn't like that last part, but I was more concerned with finding out what the hell this was all about, so I let it slide.

"Okay, let's start with this mysterious box. No, on second thought, why don't we begin at the beginning. Why did you choose me and how did you find me?

She sighed. "All right, but you may find some of this a little hard to believe."

"Try me."

She looked at me with a strange sort of half smile. "Do you believe in psychic abilities? That some people can see and experience things others don't?"

I tried to keep my laugh from sounding too bitter. "So, when do you get to the part that I'm going to find hard to believe?"

She smiled. "Well, I don't share this with many people, but I do seem to have a knack for sensing things. For instance, I can always tell when my sister is happy or sad."

"That's true, Cody." Clarisse looked up from her wine glass. "Some days I'll be feeling kinda down and then *poof*, my cell rings, and it's Catherine."

"Remarkable," I said, not really trying to keep the sarcasm out of my voice. "Then I'd say that talent makes you about as unusual as half the population of the world who claim they can sense when a family member needs them. So you'll forgive me if I ask you one more time, what made you seek me out, and how did you hear about me?"

Unperturbed by my snarky comment, Catherine continued calmly. "I saw you in what some might call a vision. You were fighting and winning. I don't know where you were, but I saw your face clearly and knew instantly that once you set your mind to a task, you would never give up. From there on in, it was just good old-fashioned detective work by me, but mostly by my lawyer. He has numerous contacts with people who work outside the law, and from the description I gave him, one of his contacts led him to another who led him to you."

I wasn't happy with that answer, either. It seemed too New Age glib. I was even less happy at the thought that *anyone* could find me with "good old-fashioned detective work." I only took jobs referred to me by someone I knew and trusted. Then *I* would get in touch with the client, not the other way around. Maybe I needed to have a talk with Chuckles who'd done the referral on this. Then I remembered that I might never get that chance. But I had to put that out of my head just then because I needed an answer to the question bugging me the most.

"Okay, so then what's the deal with the box?"

She nodded cooperatively if not enthusiastically. "As I mentioned, that humble box contains an item that has sparked greed, wonder, passion and death across the centuries."

I held up my hand. "Please tell me Indiana Jones does not appear somewhere in this tale."

She smiled enigmatically. "No, or at least not until *you* came along." I rolled my eyes and muttered something very cynical, but she continued. "You are, in fact, correct to think the box is the object of many noble quests and darker desires of men with insatiable lusts for dominance and power."

"And just how would the doohickey in the box accomplish that?"

"They believe that its possession would invest them with incredible power, both temporal and spiritual."

I was becoming impatient. "I don't want to be rude, Catherine, but you seem to be talking in circles. And I'm getting a bit tired of tripping over metaphors and oblique clues. So let me ask you straight out, without any cryptic answers on your part. Exactly *what* is in that damn box"

She looked as though she wasn't going to answer, but finally nodded. "Yes, perhaps it is time. Very well. Contained within that box is nothing less than the—"

"Cody!" I turned toward Clarisse's shout. "There's someone coming."

I went over to the window and peeked out. There were headlights coming up the drive. I pulled out the Desert Eagle and slid a round into the chamber. I guess explanations were going to have to wait.

Chapter 20

The sound of a car door slamming was followed quickly by another. I turned to Clarisse and Catherine and put my index finger to my lips then slipped out the back door. I fixed the silencer to the Eagle and crept around front. There were two people at the door, a man and a woman. That was nice, now they were sending killers as couples. Cute.

I moved toward them. I'd take out the guy first in the hope that the woman would prove more cooperative for questioning. I took my familiar shooter's stance and sighted down the long barrel.

"Seth, I'm telling you this is not the place."

"Will you give it a rest, Tiffany? The rental guy said it was a right, then a left, and it was on a small hill at the end of a gravel driveway." He took a key out of an envelope and fumbled with the door lock.

"You see, the key doesn't even fit, and the driveway, Seth? It's not gravel, it's crushed sea shells."

The man stopped trying to fit the key into the lock and turned back to her. "Okay, Tiffany, you're right, I'm wrong. Again. You are queen of all wisdom in the universe, and I am a total asshole—again."

She turned on her heel and headed for the car. "You said it, I didn't, Seth. Now, come on. I'd like to find the damn place some time tonight."

I could hear their bickering as they turned the car around and headed back down the driveway.

I smiled and un-cocked the Eagle. Time to get back to the questions. And more importantly, some answers.

I made a quick circuit of the house, and when I was satisfied that at least for the present we were alone, I let myself in through the back door and walked into the living room. Clarisse was sitting where I left her, but she was alone.

"Where's Catherine?"

Clarisse got up and put her arms around me. "She was really exhausted and went to bed."

"Did she now? Well, get her up because we're not through with our conversation."

Clarisse hugged me tighter. "Aw, please, Cody, let her sleep. She leads a pretty quiet life and isn't used to this kind of stress. Besides, I'm pretty well done in, too."

She pulled me toward the bedroom. "Come-on, she crashed in the guest bedroom and gave us hers because the bed is bigger." She leaned up and kissed me. "Hey, maybe I can give you something that'll help you sleep."

I stared at the small guest bedroom door and started toward it.

"Cody, please?"

In spite of myself, I yawned. Clarisse and sleep. Yeah that sounded pretty good. "All right then, until morning."

Some time during the night the dreams came. At least that's what I thought they were. At first. Clarisse and I were making love, but I couldn't tell if it was for real or a dream. It was great. In fact, it was better than great, it was fantastic. The best I'd ever had. Suddenly I felt another body pressed against my back. I rolled over in confusion. Catherine?

She was naked except for a gold locket on a red velvet band around her neck. Her hair was undone and flowed in soft waves over her shoulders and breasts. Her lips were parted and sensual while at the same time oddly innocent.

"Catherine, what the hell are you doing? Hey, don't get me wrong, I love a good threesome, but I draw my kinky line at sisters."

Clarisse placed her mouth next to my ear. "No Cody, it's not wrong, it's what we want, both of us. We want you to make love to both of us, just like we were one."

"My sister's right, Cody. This is what we need and more importantly it's what you need."

She kissed me then and Clarisse next. Then I was drowning in a sea of soft arms and legs, sweet lips and perfumed hair.

But later, somewhere within that dream that wasn't a dream, another dream started. The dream I'd spent all the long centuries trying to remember and praying I never would.

The palace of Herod Antipas – Province of Judea - 33AD

I shifted my feet restlessly as the tetrarch of Galilee and Peraea droned on about precedence and the nuances between spiritual and civil law. He was trying unsuccessfully to appear both pious and regal.

As he lectured the Sanhedrin and court about the difference between celestial and temporal rulers, I exchanged a quick glance with his wife, Queen Herodias. She winked, and I grinned because we both knew that despite his attempts to sound impartial, he despised the rebel agitator standing before him because he had once compared the wily Herod to a fox, an animal derided for being unclean.

Thus, I had to restrain myself from shouting to the blathering fool, "By Jupiter, just convict the fellow and be done with it."

How in the name of Mithras and Mars had I even been thrust into this assignment of guard duty and liaison between Herod and my centurion in Jerusalem? Oh, of course, it was by bedding Herod's wife. I glanced over again, and she gave me a sultry gaze through eyes heavily rimmed with kohl and cinnabar. She had looked at me that way after the first time we made love.

"You please me so well, Lucius Varius Severus, that I intend to make sure we have the opportunity to see one another often."

That had been fine with me until I learned what she really meant. She had cajoled her husband into requesting that the imperial governor assign me to oversee communication between Herod and the Roman command in Jerusalem. I had found out today, to my frustration and disgust, that also included escorting prisoners between Herod and Pilate.

I tried without much effort to stifle a yawn. The king didn't look to be winding down soon. The windy bastard was in love with the sound of his own voice and showed no signs of stopping.

Then I saw a silver lining. If Herod kept the rebel agitator overnight, I could at least expect the best of food, wine and, later on, enticing games in the arms of the queen.

That thought cheered me so I was almost disappointed when ten minutes later Herod suddenly concluded his harangue with the words, "Thus, I do not feel the deposition of this agitator falls within my jurisdiction. *Sesquiplicarius*?" As the only junior non-commissioned officer with that title in the room, I knew he was speaking to me. I straightened with a guilty start. "I wish you to return the prisoner to my esteemed friend, the noble Governor Pontius Pilate for whatever punishment he deems fit."

I came awake with a start. I sat up and looked around. The room was empty, as was the bed on either side of me. So it had all been some crazy sex dream brought on by stress and exhaustion? I looked at the rumpled sheets and saw several long brown hairs. I picked one up and examined it. The hair was the same color as Catherine's, and as I looked closer I realized that it was not one but two hairs, and the second one wound around the brown hair was pale blonde.

I pulled on my jeans and tee shirt and went to the find the sisters. They were in the kitchen drinking coffee. They both smiled at me, but something was different. Catherine's hair was still down, and she was wearing jeans instead of the dowdy tweed skirt. The jeans fit snugly and, I had to admit, looked damn good on her. Clarisse on the other hand was dressed more conservatively than I'd ever seen her, in a knee-length plaid skirt and old Fair Isle sweater. Her hair was pulled back and held in place by a headband. A pair of small, pearl studs had replaced the elaborate dangle earrings she usually favored. Conversely, Catherine had swapped her plain gold studs from yesterday for a pair of large silver hoops I seemed to recall seeing on Clarisse.

Well why not? It was evident now the sisters were the same size and probably grew up sharing clothes and jewelry. What I needed to find out was if that included sharing men.

"Good morning, sleepy head." Catherine smiled with an easy grin. "Did you have sweet dreams?" She winked at Clarisse, and they giggled. I was surprised, in fact, just short of stunned. I had been expecting a salacious smirk from Clarisse but embarrassment and contrition from Catherine. Instead, both women seemed perfectly okay with what I was now coming to accept had indeed really occurred last night.

But something else was different. Both sisters had changed. Catherine seemed more at ease and outgoing, while Clarisse's normal flamboyance seemed somewhat muted and reserved. It wasn't so much that the women had switched personalities, it was as though they were meeting somewhere in the middle. Did they share personalities the same way they shared clothes and, apparently, men?

I sat down, and Catherine poured me a cup of coffee. "You take it black, right?"

I nodded. Did Clarisse tell her that, or was it another example of shared knowledge? These sisters were close, maybe too close.

I drained the first cup of coffee and held out the mug for another. This time Clarisse poured. It figured.

"Okay, ladies, here's the plan. They will eventually check back here, so we need another place to hole up for today, preferably someplace with an unobstructed field of vision from all angles. Last night when we sailed back into the marsh, I noticed there were three houses down by the beach. Two had lights on, one did not. And when I reconnoitered later on, it was still dark. I'm guessing it's closed up for the season, so I'm gonna have one of you call a couple of realtors and ask if they know if it's for rent. If it's vacant, we can—"

"It is vacant." Catherine broke in.

"How do you know?"

"Because I know the owner, Dr. Scarborough. I did post-grad work for him. He teaches in Boston, so he won't be back until spring."

I nodded slowly. "Good. We'll finish up here and move there for the rest of the day. Then tonight I'll hot wire some car, and we'll drive down the Cape to Provincetown and take a ferry to Boston."

"And from there?"

"From there, a very small island in a very big world."

The sisters looked at one another. They realized I hadn't mentioned them, and I hadn't because I needed to decide what I was going to do. Leave them in Boston? Could I really do that? Despite myself, I had to admit I'd really developed some feelings for the sassy little blonde, and I knew Catherine wouldn't last twenty-four hours on her own before they tracked her down, killed her and took the box.

The box, humm.

"But before we go anywhere, Catherine, you and I need to finish our conversation about the box."

"Can it wait until tonight?"

"No."

"Why not?"

"Let me be blunt. Because by tonight we might all be dead." I gave them both a hard stare. "Look ladies, I'm gonna do my best to protect you, but to do that I need to know exactly what's going on. Like for instance what's in that damn box and what makes it so valuable that some very nasty people want to kill us for it?"

Catherine bit her lower lip and put her hand on mine. All the little hairs on the back of my hand stood up. "I know you're trying to protect us, Cody, and we love you for it, but I really need to wait until tonight to be able to fully explain it to you."

"Why?" I was getting impatient and annoyed with the ever-growing obfuscation surrounding the damn box.

"Did you dream last night, Cody?"

"What does that have to with anything?"

"Everything. Your dreams are the key to the answer, and you can't truly understand the significance of what's in the box until you fully remember your dreams. That one particular dream you've tried for so long to remember."

I could feel my heart beat faster. How did she know? "All right then, so tell me about the dream *and* the box."

"I can't tell you, I can only show you."

"Then show me, goddamn it!"

Her hand gripped mine tighter. "That's why we have to wait. You need to sleep to dream, and I need to be with you. Near you, next to you, close to you. Very close."

I raised my eyebrow. "As close as we were last night?"

"Perhaps."

I was silent for a few minutes. Other than beating it out of her, I didn't see any way around it. Oh sure, I could simply take the box and open it, but somehow I knew that whatever was in there wouldn't mean much without the explanation. And the only ones who could supply me with that were Catherine and the people who wanted me dead.

"Come on, ladies, let's get a move on."

"Just another few minutes, Cody. There are a few more things I need to bring."

"Listen, we need to leave right now, before the morning fog burns away, and we're caught out in the open like sitting ducks. Or in this case, seagulls."

"I understand. Just one more second."

I followed Catherine's voice to her small study. The walls were lined with bookcases, and she was sitting cross-legged in the middle of the floor with a half-dozen old leather-bound books scattered around her.

"What are you doing?"

"I'm gathering some things I think we'll need."

"Books?"

"Yes, and don't look at me that way. If you're going to understand the significance of the box, I think these will help." I bent down to gather them up, but before I could she shoved them into a large leather book bag "Ready," she said and scrambled to her feet and slung the bag over her shoulder.

I started to speak, then shook my head. "Let's go. Where's your sister?"

"Right here, Cody." Clarisse stood in the doorway with a dusty old backpack and a green Whole Foods environmentally-correct shopping bag stuffed with fruit, crackers and the remains of last night's meal. "There's probably nothing in the fridge at the professor's house, and he may have even taken all the can goods. So like the Girl Scouts say, 'Be prepared.'"

"I thought that was the Boy Scouts, and please don't tell me you were in the Girl Scouts."

"Yup, believe or not I was. In fact we both were, right, Sis?"

Catherine nodded but didn't elaborate, and a few minutes later we'd slipped out the back door and were making our way down the hill through a thinning fog. By the time we reached the beach house the last few wisps of fog were dissipating, so I lost no time in picking the back door lock and ushering the women inside.

The place was about forty or fifty years old, and it was obvious the professor divided his taste between all things nautical and literary classics—also nautical. A huge brick fireplace flanked by floor to ceiling bookcases filled with books about ships, sailing and the sea commanded one wall. The rest of his personal library seemed to consist of scientific treatises on archeology and ancient legends.

Catherine ran her fingertips over the book spines and took two down, setting them on top of her book bag. "We'll need these, too."

I didn't comment, but went about the house checking window and door locks. When I was done, I joined the ladies who were sprawled out on the living room floor watching the ocean through the half-open living room drapes. The wind had picked up and was pushing the grey and silver waves farther and farther up onto the beach.

I sat down quietly next to Catherine and Clarisse and let my mind drift back a thousand years. I could feel the hot sun of Judea on my neck and hear the *clop* of Roman Legionaries hobnail sandals trampling across stone paved floors.

Suddenly, I felt Catherine's hand on my shoulder. "You're back there, aren't you?" My throat felt dry, so I could only nod, but finally I said, "Yes, and I think I'm ready to go farther back. All the way to the beginning." I closed my eyes.

"Cody."

My eyes opened. Catherine was kneeling in front of me.

Suddenly, she stood up, looking pale. "We've got to leave. We're in terrible danger." The color drained from Clarisse's face as well. "She's right, Cody." She jumped up, too, took my hand and pulled me toward the door. "Come on, we don't have much time." I shook off her hand. "No."

Both women stared at me. Clarisse blinked in confusion. "What do you mean, 'No'?"

"I mean that every time I get close to finding out what the hell this is all about, something happens to prevent it. Well, this time no one is going anywhere until I get some answers."

I pushed Clarisse's hand away from mine and started to turn away, but Catherine stepped in front of me. "No Cody, you don't understand. We've only got a few hours at best and it's not just our own lives and safety that are at stake. If the box falls into the wrong hands it could have terrible repercussions for the entire world."

"All the more reason I need to know what's in the box and how I'm connected with it."

Clarisse joined in. "But Cody, there's so much more at stake than just we three." She was close to tears. "Please, you've got to trust us. You've got to—"

Catherine held up her hand. "No Clarisse, he's right. He does need to know." She turned to me. "One warning, though. You do understand that with great knowledge comes great pain."

I laughed bitterly. "Trust me, I know about pain."

Catherine regarded me steadily. "But perhaps not pain like this."

I shrugged. "We're wasting time, Catherine. And if you two are right, it's running out."

She nodded and took my hand. Then she glanced at Clarisse who put several of the large throw pillows on the floor. Catherine knelt and gently pulled me down beside her as Clarisse knelt on my other side.

Catherine pushed a pillow toward me. "Lay back, Cody, and close your eyes." Suddenly I felt an unaccustomed rush of panic. Maybe this was something I really didn't want to know. Maybe it was something I wasn't meant to know.

As if she was reading my mind, Catherine whispered, "Don't doubt yourself, Cody. You've struggled for so long, now it's time to know. It's time to remember. Sleep, Cody.

Sleep and dream. Sleep and remember."

Chapter 21

Jerusalem, In the Roman Province of Judea-33 AD

The agitator had been questioned rather roughly by the elders of the Sanhedrin, and he now stood bleeding in front of Pilate.

I had almost begun to feel sorry for him. True, he had a big mouth and, true, he got the local population stirred up and grumbling against Rome. But then again, these people were always stirred up. I had served in Gaul and Britannia, but this flea-bitten, sun-parched province was by far the worst I'd ever been stationed in.

That's why it was really rather ironic they were making such a fuss over one skinny carpenter turned messiah. That was another laugh. Knock over any ant hill in Judea, and a dozen so-called messiahs would come scurrying out. So, why all the fuss about this one? In a word—politics. I didn't pretend to understand all of the machinations going on behind the scenes among Pilate, Herod and the irritating and ever-present gaggle of Jewish priests. All I knew was that this poor backwater preacher didn't deserve the punishment we reserved for thieves, murderers and enemies of Rome—crucifixion.

Pilate gazed solemnly at the self-styled messiah. "I am going to ask you one last time to admit that you have made rebellious statements against Rome and have instigated the population to refuse to make sacrifices to our divine emperor."

The man shook his head. "I made no such statements."

Pilate rose and walked over to where the chained prisoner stood. He fixed the man with a magisterial gaze, as though truly trying to decide his fate rather than engaging in political theatre for the benefit of those who were unaware of the mutually advantageous arrangement worked out between the Sanhedrin, Herod, and him.

He stroked his chin as if deep in deliberation instead of getting ready to announce the sentence which we all knew was a foregone conclusion. "And you deny trying to pass yourself off as the King of the Jews?"

"My kingdom is not of this world."

Pilate shook his head in disgust. "Since you stubbornly refuse to answer truthfully, I can do nothing more to help you." He motioned to a slave who brought him a bowl of water and a towel. "Let all here see that I have washed my hands of this matter. Centurion!"

Our Centurion, Quintus Livius Faustus, stepped forward and smashed his fist against his breastplate. "Governor, I await your orders."

"Take the prisoner from here, administer the punishment, and take him to the place of execution."

Quintus saluted once more and turned on his heel.

"Lucius Varius Severus."

I straightened with a start. Pilate had called my name. "Sir."

"Gather your squad, *Sesquiplicarius*, and take the prisoner to the courtyard to be scourged."

Scourging is a terrible punishment in itself. The prisoner is manacled and chained to a post or bent over a pillar section—chained by wrists and ankles to large iron staples set into the stone—then lashed with the flagellum. The Roman flagellum was a whip featuring up to a dozen individual rawhide lashes tipped with lead or bone that could—and most often did— rip the living flesh from the prisoner's back.

It was my duty to direct the two legionaries beating the man with alternating strokes, though the punishment itself was taking place under the watchful eye of Centurion Faustus.

He knew I had my own private doubts as to the guilt of this man, so he was watching me intently for any signs of reluctance or weakness.

We had clashed before over the degree of chastisement and retribution to be meted out to those who defied Rome. And while it was common practice to sell the people we conquered into slavery and execute a few of their leaders as an example, I was never quite comfortable with Quintus's penchant for wholesale slaughter and rape. Specifically that of one ten-year-old girl in Britannia whose father, the local chief, had refused to pay taxes. In retaliation, Quintus threw his three daughters, one as young as ten, to the troops.

As *sesquiplicarius,* I had tried to intervene and ordered the men to stop. But when Quintus heard of it, he took all three girls and forced them to endure the whole rape all over again. Two of the girls died, including the ten-year–old. The eldest, fourteen, committed suicide.

Ever since then we had regarded one another with enmity, and Quintus would have stripped me of my rank except I had powerful connections through both the Varius and Severus branches of my family.

So in response, he watched me like a hawk for any breach of duty that could get me sentenced to a military court martial. Thus, as the pair of burly soldiers continued to turn the hapless carpenter's back into raw meat, I made myself stand stoic and unblinking.

When they were finally finished, a slave threw a bucket of cold water on the man to revive him, and an old purple cloak—meant to mock his claims of kingship—was thrown over his bloody shoulders.

With a steady if flat voice, I was ordering the men of the execution detail to form up when I felt a hand on my shoulder. It was Quintus Faustus, and he was holding something.

"What is this?"

He held out his hand to me. "It is a crown for our would-be king."

I glanced down at it, puzzled and repulsed all at the same time.

It was a circlet of interwoven vines like the ancient laurel crowns awarded to victors. But this was no crown of victory.

It was a crown of pain and humiliation because it was made entirely from thorns.

Quintus smiled maliciously and pushed the object into my hand. "I want you to personally place the crown on the rebel king's head. And to make sure it stays there, you are to place it on as firmly as possible."

I stood there staring mutely.

The corner of his mouth turned upward in a sneer. "And that, *Sesquiplicarius*, is an order."

I sat up gasping for breath, my hands spasming as if pushing something away. Catherine wrapped her arm around me and smoothed my hair as a parent would a child after a bad dream. "You saw, didn't you?"

"Yes." The word came out like my throat was made of sandpaper.

Clarisse, on my other side, put her hand on her sisters' shoulder. "No more, Catherine. He's seen enough."

She shook her head. "You know better than that. He must see everything. He'll know no peace until he does, but I'll leave it up to Cody." She turned to me. Her eyes behind the thick glasses were wide and large, filled with a look that was halfway between determination and pity. "Do you want to continue?"

What else could I say but yes? Not because I really wanted to see what I was afraid I would, but because I'd waited two thousand years for this answer, and I couldn't turn back now.

"Let's do it."

But fate had other plans because at the same moment the front door crashed in and two of Tony Bag's greaseballs, a hard-looking case in a black suit and an old man with a face I'd seen somewhere before, strode into the room.

We were seated in the living room. I hadn't even had time to get to my weapons, and Tony's two *goombahs* had frisked me, this time finding my hide-out .25-cal and the throwing knife. Now the old man was watching us with the genial amusement of the cat about to swallow the canary.

"How did you find us?"

The old man came forward and gazed at Clarisse appreciatively. "My goodness, you certainly have gotten to be attractive this time around."

For a moment Clarisse appeared flustered. "Do I know you?"

"If by that you mean, am I another of your clients—or as the ladies in your profession now term it, 'tricks'—the answer is, no. But we have met before." He turned to Catherine, though he still spoke to Clarisse. "But perhaps your sister here can help to refresh your memory."

Catherine stood up, saying coldly, "My sister could remember, but she has wisely chosen to blot things that are foul and evil from her memory."

"But you remember, don't you?"

She nodded. "Sadly, yes." Then she folded her hands in front of her and asked calmly, "May I know how you found us?"

The old man smiled. His teeth were worn and stained, but still looked like those of a shark. "I don't see why not, since soon it won't matter anyway." He pointed to the sofa. "Do you mind if I sit? Old bones you know." No one moved or spoke, but he sat as if he had been invited to do so. "Now as to your question. I'm sure that in your long and varied travels you must have come across the art of scrying?"

Catherine nodded. "Using the reflection of a crystal, a mirror or clear water to divine the answer to a question."

He smiled again. "Yes, very good. And that's exactly what it did. Not quite so accurate as reading the entrails of a dove, the way we used to. But one cannot be too choosy when live doves are no longer sold in the market stalls, and one's only other resource is a pair of buffoons with modern automatic weapons."

"In an attempt to obtain a substitute animal for divination, I directed these cretins to bring down one those flying rats you call seagulls. They couldn't drop one with a dozen shots." He shook his head in disgust. "I've seen native tribesmen do better with an arrow."

Paulie and Tommy exchanged looks, but one basilisk glance from the hard case in the black suit and they dropped their gazes.

I stared at the tall, brutal-looking man. He looked back at me the way a cobra regards a mouse, and I recognized him. No, not him personally, but the hundreds and thousands of coldly efficient killers he represented. He was the ruthless, pitiless henchman who carried out the orders of his mad master with callous professionalism. And I had seen his counterparts in every age, moving with unfeeling competence to do whatever dark deed was required. I had watched his type at work—turning the wheel that broke men on the medieval rack, dragging prisoners behind the horses of Genghis Kahn's Mongol hoards and herding naked, shivering men, women and children into the ovens at Auschwitz.

And now he was here with his master to take care of us.

The old man caught my gaze out of the corner of his eye. He paused for a moment, then smiled benignly, "Forgive my bad manners. I'm afraid I've neglected to make the introductions." He glanced at the two hoods and then at me. "I believe you've already met my two associates, courtesy of our mutual acquaintance Anthony, who is currently spending ten to twenty years in Upstate New York as a guest of the Federal government. And this stalwart gentleman here," he pointed to the man in the black suit, "is from a family that has served me loyally for many generations."

I took a deep breath. I couldn't let them think they were getting to me. "Okay, then, if we're all done with introductions, may I suggest you cut the crap and tell us who you are and just why the hell you're here."

He raised his eyebrows slightly. "My name is Dietrich and as to why I'm here, I should have thought that would be obvious Mister . . . Just what are you calling yourself these days?"

"Cody."

"And is that your first or last name?"

"It's the only fucking name you're going to get, and I'll ask you one last time. What do you want and where the hell do you get off acting like we're old buddies?"

He sighed. "Come now, Cody, please don't be disingenuous, it doesn't suit you. But I must say it saddens me to think you've forgotten me, though I'll admit it has been some time."

I felt a sudden chill. Something about the old man—a fleeting memory hovering just beyond my grasp. His voice, his mannerisms, the way he watched me—gave me a crawling sensation like centipedes running down my spine.

He looked at me and smiled, but his eyes were like two hard little chips of obsidian. "As pleasant as this has been, I'm afraid we must get down to business." He turned to Catherine. "I believe you have something I require, Miss Franklin"

"I have nothing that belongs to you, Mr. Dietrich."

He stood up. "On the contrary, Miss Franklin. The content of the box our friend here has recently delivered to you originates with me." The false smile fell away, and the rest of his face became as cold and pitiless as his eyes. "And now I want it back,"

Catherine swallowed hard, but said in a tightly controlled voice, "Assuming you do know what the box contains, you must also know it would do a man such as you little good."

"I'm afraid you are quite misinformed about that, Miss Franklin. There is much the object resting in the box could do for me now and in the years to come." His eyes unfocused for a moment as he stared at a vision that only he could see. Or would want to.

Finally he blinked, and his attention transferred to Catherine more intently than ever. "But you are correct in one respect. The contents of the box could not give me all I desire. Were it the only such object." He paused a moment as if for dramatic effect, then assured that all eyes were upon him, he continued, "As a researcher and curator, I'm sure, Miss Franklin, you are familiar with the legend of the Spear of Destiny?"

Catherine took a stumbling step backward before recovering. She refolded her hands, but I could see they were trembling. "Of course, it has long been the target of unstable minds and sensationalist novelists."

"Quite true, but then as a learned researcher and archeologist, you must also admit that whether or not the Spear is imbued with the powers ascribed to it, it really does exist."

She nodded. "Yes, you're correct, it has been in the hands of ruthless, power-mad men for most of the last two thousand years. So I'm not at all surprised you wish to join that list, Mr. Dietrich. But here's where I must disappoint you. The object in the box is *not* the Spear of Destiny."

Rather than becoming angry, Dietrich smiled. "No, Miss Franklin, this only confirms my assumption that you are an honest and truthful woman. You see, I believe you completely when you say the Spear is not in your possession. And do you know why I am certain of this?" He paused. "Because I have it."

Both Catherine and Clarisse were visibly shaken. And from the sketchy details about the Spear I'd picked up through the ages, I wasn't feeling too good about it, either. I glanced at the sisters. Were they really aware of what potential power lay dormant within the spear?

Catherine recovered first. "Very well then, but if what you say is true, why would you need the contents of the box?"

"A fair question." He smiled. He was enjoying this game of intellectual cat and mouse. "Let's go back to the beginning, shall we? And just to give everyone a chance to participate in our lively little discussion group, perhaps the lovely Clarisse would like to tell us all what exactly the Spear of Destiny is."

I could tell he was testing Clarisse's intellect to see if she was as smart as her sister or simply a good-looking bimbo. But she surprised him.

"The so-called Spear of Destiny refers to the spear a soldier named Longinus—the Roman Centurion in charge of the Crucifixion—used to pierce Christ's side on the cross. His blood flowed onto the spear's blade, and so the legend was born that whoever possessed the spear could rule the world."

"Excellent, my dear." He beamed. "Just one minor correction, the soldier Longinus was not the Centurion presiding over the execution. But please continue."

Clarisse shot me a glance that seemed to say, "Pay attention, there's a clue here."

I nodded imperceptibly, but was still not sure that I wanted to go where a clue might take me.

She continued. "Legend has it the first person of importance to use the spear was the famous Carolingian king, Charlemagne, who used it to gain power and start what the Germanic tribes called the First Reich of empire."

Dietrich interrupted in a low voice, "So says the legend, but the Frankish king was not the first to realize the spear's power." He stared off in the distance again as if remembering and then snapped out of it. "Forgive me for interrupting with an old man's wool gathering. Please, do go on. You're doing splendidly."

"And, yes, you're right." Clarisse nodded. "Charlemagne was not the first to recognize the spear's power. Earlier references can be traced back to Constantine the Great, the first Roman Emperor to convert and adopt Christianity as the state religion in the 4th century. The legend then goes on to assert that forty-five kings and rulers such as Alaric— who defeated and sacked Rome—Charles Martel, Charlemagne and Frederick Barbarossa all possessed the spear, which made them invincible in battle. Over the years the legend grew that whoever had the holy lance would be able to conquer the world. Napoleon attempted to obtain it after the battle of Austerlitz, but it had been smuggled out of the city prior to the start of the fight, and he was never able to find it."

Dietrich grinned broadly and turned to his bodyguard. "What do think, Robert? Isn't this charming young lady well versed in history?"

"Yes, she is, Mr. Dietrich." Robert's mouth smiled, but his shoe-button eyes remained dark and flat.

Dietrich turned back to Clarisse. "In fact, my dear, I would say that you are a veritable fountain of information."

He chuckled. "Indeed, how clever of me. Miss Fontaine is a *fountain* of facts and historical anecdotes."

He laughed, but there was no humor behind it. I'd heard that laugh before. It was a mocking laugh. One that always preceded cruelty.

He wiped his eyes with an intricately monogrammed silk handkerchief. I caught a glimpse of the initials. *QLF.* They were done in a formal style vaguely reminiscent of letters I'd seen on a public building a long time ago. But whose name did they represent? The gloating man in front of us had given his name as Dietrich.

He tucked the handkerchief back in his pocket and nodded to Clarisse. "But I am interrupting your dissertation. Pray continue."

Clarisse glanced questioningly at her sister, but Catherine nodded, so she resumed. "But there is also a dark side to the spear. While it would grant its owner victory and power, the legend also held that if the owner ever lost possession of the holy lance, death would soon follow. For instance, Charlemagne carried the spear through dozens of battles and won each time, but when he accidentally dropped it, his death came swiftly. Likewise Barbarossa, who perished only minutes after it slipped out of his hands while fording a river.

"Somewhere during the Middle Ages, the spear's shaft disintegrated from old age or was either lost. It was replaced several times. But since the blade had felt Christ's blood, it's what was important, not the shaft. Also during that time period, a golden overlay was attached to the blade."

Dietrich gazed at Clarisse with what appeared to be sincere admiration. "Please forgive me for ever having doubted you, my dear. You are a remarkable young woman who has proven that a pretty face and superior intellect are not mutually exclusive."

That was somewhat along the line of what I'd been thinking. And now I was more than a little curious as to how the tough, streetwise hooker came to have more historical knowledge than a Harvard professor. If we ever got out of this, we were definitely going to have some serious conversations about her resumé.

Deitrich glanced over at me. "Wherever did you find such a treasure?"

"Just lucky, I guess."

A cold smile played across his lips. "Yes, you always were." A moment later he turned back to Clarisse. "Can you tell us more?"

She answered with a slight incline of her head and resumed her narrative. "The spear remained in Austria until Hitler annexed the country in the *Anschluss* of 1938. However, scholars believe he incorporated the country of his birth into the Third Reich primarily to acquire the spear, which he'd first seen in 1912 while a starving young artist in Vienna. As history records, he went from victory to victory until, fearing the spear might be damaged in the increasing Allied bombing raids, he gave it to Heinrich Himmler to secure in the heavily fortified castle of Wewelsberg. From then on, Hitler's previously invincible army went from constant victory to constant defeat. And when General

George S. Patton captured the castle at the war's end, it was said that at the moment he took possession of the spear, Hitler blew his brains out."

Dietrich was listening to Clarisse but watching me. Did he know what I was thinking? That, sadly, I hadn't lived to see that moment, but had I known what the little Austrian corporal was going to do, I would have gladly taken that damned spear and rammed it up his ass.

Dietrich's eyes held mine for a moment longer then shifted back to Clarisse.

"Patton was fascinated by the spear and had its authenticity verified, but before he could use it for his pet project—he defeat of Soviet communism—he was ordered to secretly send it back to America. Shortly after he did, he was killed in a freak auto accident. Coincidence? There are many who don't think so."

"So then what happened to the spear after that?" Dietrich leaned forward.

Clarisse's lips twisted into a wry smile reminiscent of the streetwise, cynical blonde I'd known. "Well since you claim to have it, why don't you tell me?"

"Bravo!" Dietrich applauded. "Well said. I do like a girl with spunk. As you have so brilliantly recounted, Patton though a personal believer in the spear's power, followed orders and sent it to Washington. I live in Washington. And I know whom to bribe, whom to threaten and whom to blackmail. Let's just say that in short order the spear was mine. Or as I like to think of it, returned to where it belonged."

"But what of the spear currently on display in the museum in Vienna?" Catherine spoke up.

"It's a fake. I know because I'm the one who had it made so the State Department would have something to return to them after the war. Oh it's meticulously crafted and good enough to fool the thousands of tourists who view it every year, but a fake nonetheless."

Catherine was trying not to look frightened, but I could tell she was. "Then assuming that you really do have the original spear, what do you plan to do with it?"

He stood up, and his movements seemed surer and swifter than before. "I intend to reunite it with what is in that box." He stretched out his hand, his false *bonhomie* gone. "Now."

Chapter 22

I had been ready to try to jump Paulie or Tommy and take their weapon, but as if she knew what I was thinking, Catherine caught my eye and gave a small shake of her head. She was probably right. I most likely could have taken one or both of Tony's boys, but the hard case, Robert, was a different matter. I had a feeling he was as tough as he looked, maybe tougher. So in the end Catherine made the only decision possible, she gave Dietrich the box.

The old man held it on his lap and caressed the dark wood. "I've waited a very long time for this." He shifted his gaze to Catherine. "I almost had it in San Francisco. Do you remember?"

Catherine said nothing, but Clarisse looked uneasy.

"Let me see, I believe it was in 1930. And as I recall, you and your fifteen-year-old sister were living in a large house overlooking the bay. You were especially lovely that time. Let me see, how old were you then?"

Catherine stared back at him without expression. "I turned twenty-five years old the day you killed me."

What . . .? "Killed me"? What the hell was she saying? Could there really be someone else who was doomed to wander through time, living, suffering and dying only to be reborn over and over? I stared hard at Catherine. Her eyes briefly caught mine, but the gaze she returned was enigmatic. On the other hand, Dietrich found it amusing.

"Oh dear, please don't put it that way, you're going to make me sad." He smiled insincerely. "Of course, if you had just given me the box, there would have been no need for unpleasantness. I do have one question, though. Who did you give the box to, that lawyer?"

"No, I gave it to my sister with instructions to keep it hidden until she received a letter relating an incident from her childhood that only she and I would know. Then she was to have our family lawyer send it by special courier to the person who sent the letter."

"You."

"Yes, me."

It was obvious by now that Dietrich knew more about Catherine and the box than I did, which wasn't difficult, of course, since what I knew was next to nothing about either. And rather than learning more, it seemed that with every word the two of them spoke, my unanswered questions multiplied.

Dietrich proved it with his next statement. "Well, well very clever. I always felt there was more to you than meets the eye. And speaking of meeting, do you remember the first time we met?"

"I wish I could forget it."

"It was the day I first held the object in this box. Of course, I had no way of knowing then how important it would become." He turned to me. "And I'm sure you'll never forget that day. Will you, Lucius?"

I blinked in confusion. The name he'd called me. *Lucius.* How could he know that? No one had called me by that name for twenty centuries. Who was this old man, and how did he, how could he, know me?

He opened the box, pulled back the coarse, stained cloth and thrust it toward me, revealing the contents. I felt my face burning, and the room seemed to waver and churn around me. Then blackness as if I was falling down a deep, dark well.

Jerusalem, In the Roman Province of Judea–the road to Golgotha

I stood in the archway of the courtyard leading to the street we would herd the prisoners through on their way to the place of execution—a small hill outside the city walls known locally as Golgotha. An Aramaic word that meant "place of the skull."

But before the ritual procession of marching the condemned through the city for the population to mock and abuse, I had been ordered to start the entertainment by tormenting the poor wretch standing in front of me. Our Centurion Quintus Faustus, my superior, was waiting with sadistic anticipation for me to crown the rebel agitator with a coronet woven of tough vines, each with dozens of needle-sharp thorns.

"Well, Severus, we are waiting for you to obey your orders."

Trying to keep my face expressionless, I took the crown gingerly and placed it as gently as possible on the beaten man's sweat-matted hair. A few of the thorns pricked the top of his head, but with the more serious wounds still dripping blood from his back, he barely noticed it.

This did not please our Centurion. "What are you trying to do, *Sesquiplicarius*, tickle him? He is an enemy of whatever order exists in this flea-bitten country, but more importantly he is an enemy of Rome."

He stormed over to where I stood and grabbed both my hands. "You will press that crown firmly on his head, or you may find yourself wearing it. Do you understand me?"

He saw my hands twitch with longing to fasten them around his neck and that was just what he wanted. If I raised a fist against him, he would have me in chains, sentenced and executed long before my family would even receive word of my death. He leered at me, daring me to move against him. There was nothing I could do. I pressed the crown down on the prisoner's head. The blood began to flow.

But Quintus was still not satisfied. "Not good enough, *Sesquiplicarius*, not nearly good enough." He struck the crown with his vine staff of office, and the man swayed. "Do you see how easily it is dislodged? Why, a strong breeze could send his royal cap sailing away, and then how would he show the world his regal status?" He pressed down with the vine staff. The man winced. "There, you see how it is done?" He glared at me, eyes glittering with malice, but he spoke in a low, controlled voice. "Do as you are commanded, Lucius Varius Severus, or you will find yourself on a cross next to his."

I had no doubt Quintus was not making an idle threat. He would happily do just that. So I took both sides of the crown and pressed it into the prisoner's scalp. He moaned a little and closed his eyes with the pain of it as his blood flowed freely through his tangled hair and pooled around his sunken eye sockets before dripping over his cheeks like crimson tears.

Then he opened his eyes and stared into mine, and I felt an almost irresistible urge to apologize for the pain I had caused him. I started to form the words, but Quintus came and stood on the other side of the prisoner as if just daring me to utter one word that could brand me a traitor to Imperial order. So with a tight and empty feeling in my chest, I turned away from the deep dark eyes that had already forgiven what I could not forgive myself.

To cover my feelings of unease, I shouted to the troop to form up and started the procession moving out of the courtyard and into the streets of Jerusalem.

The prisoners staggered under the weight of the crossbeams lashed across their shoulders.

It was as the street rose up near the city gate that the man stumbled and fell to one knee. Immediately, a young woman who had been keeping pace with us as we made our way through the narrow streets knelt down beside him and began wiping the blood away from his eyes and face with a strip of fabric torn from her cheap, homespun dress.

Quintus saw her helping him and shouted at me, "Remove that woman, *Sesquiplicarius,* or I will do it with the point of my sword."

I strode over to the woman who was in truth little more than a girl of fifteen or sixteen and curtly ordered her away from the man. When she continued dabbing at his face, I grabbed her roughly by the arm and shoved her away. She fell sprawling in the dust and refuse of the street. And that was when she looked at me.

She was not a great beauty, just a plain and timid little creature. But her eyes were large, dark and liquid with a compassion that seemed to promise redemption for the whole world—even for a Roman officer who was about to crucify someone for whom she so obviously cared. She looked at me with a sadness so deep I wanted to hide my face in my cloak and weep. But I did not. I could not. I was a soldier of Rome and sworn to uphold the Emperor and our invincible Roman Empire.

And so I tore my gaze away from hers, and we marched on. I could feel her staring at my back and tried to put her out of my mind.

I should have known it would not be that easy.

It was dark now, but it was still day. How could that be?

Then again nothing about this day was normal.

I had viewed and taken part in many executions, from a simple sword thrust to the ritualized strangling of an important enemy of the state, but crucifixions were always the worst. Certainly for the victims, but unless you were especially cruel or a nascent sadist such as Faustus, they were not particularly pleasant for the execution party, either.

It had been a long day, first hot and still but now dark and stormy with a chill wind and great black clouds blotting out the sun.

The rebel king had survived longer than any of us had expected. Normally, a prisoner who had been as brutally scourged as he had been would have expired within hours of being put on the cross. But he was still alive.

He had been speaking, at first to some of the condemned near him, but over the last several hours his words had slowed to a mumble I could not understand, though a part of me wished I could.

But now the end was near. I had seen many crucifixions, and though the man had sadly proved remarkably resilient, each breath he now drew was clearly a struggle. I found myself hoping the end would come quickly now, to save the poor wretch further agony. I couldn't say why this execution bothered me, but it did. Perhaps that was why I had let the girl stay.

It was the girl from the street, the one who had wiped the blood from his face. She had knelt at the foot of the cross since we first raised it into place and had not left.

Quintus Faustus had told me to drive her off and then left to return to the Governor's residence, but I hadn't obeyed.

Instead, after some time I had gone over to where she knelt. I told myself I needed to question her to see if she was connected to any other subversive groups who might be planning trouble, but in truth I was curious. There was something about her.

"What is your name, girl?"

"Rachel, sir."

"And exactly what is your connection with this man?"

"I love him, sir."

"Ah, then that explains it. You are his wife?"

"No, sir."

"Humm, his woman then? You are quite young to be tramping the countryside with a man not your husband."

"No, sir, it's not like that at all. I am not his woman, though I wish I was."

"But you said you are in love with him?"

"And I am, but not only in the way you think of it, but I also love his spirit, his soul. The words he preaches."

"Careful, girl, if the Centurion heard you speaking this way, he'd nail you up alongside your leader."

She shook her head sadly. "You Romans don't understand. He never preached rebellion. He preached love. The same kind of love I have for him and what he stands for."

I took off my helmet and ran a hand through my hair. "You're right, girl. I don't understand what you or he is talking about with your spiritual love and words that seem to mean things other than what they sound like. I find this whole country incomprehensible with its one god and strange religious laws." I replaced my helmet and adjusted the chin strap. "How do you know this man? If you are not his lover, then what are you to him?"

"Even though I am nothing, I am something to him and even though he never loved me as a man does a woman, he does love me."

"Stop talking in riddles, girl," I snapped irritably. "Where did you meet him, and how did you come to follow him?"

"I was raised in the same village he comes from and knew him as a young man when I was a child. I think I loved him from the first. When he began his preaching I longed to become one of his disciples and travel with him as Mary did. But of course I could not. I was just a girl, and my parents would never have permitted it. But when we came to the great temple in Jerusalem for Passover, and I heard of his trial, I rushed to help him." Tears welled up in the corners of her eyes. "But once again, I could do nothing. I tried to comfort him when he stumbled in the street, but you . . . "

She dropped her gaze, but I could feel my face burning with shame, and it made me angry and contrite at the same time. She knelt there before me, next to the dying man on the cross, and I didn't know what to do. But for some inexplicable reason I felt I wanted to protect her. From what I didn't know, and then a moment later I did. Centurion Quintus Livius Faustus had returned.

He had brought along a *Sesquiplicarius* from another cohort, and I breathed a sigh of relief thinking he was going to relieve me. I was already imagining cups of wine and the mindless chatter of the tavern whores who knew or cared nothing for strange gods or desert messiahs, but that was not Quintus's plan.

"*Sesquiplicarius* Severus, is that rebel not dead yet? What have you been doing out here all this time?" He strode up to the cross and peered at the man. "Why, you haven't even broken his legs."

It was common practice to hurry an execution along and at the same time inflict the most pain by breaking the condemned's legs so that, unable to shift his weight, he would asphyxiate in agony. But Centurion Faustus was correct. I had not done that.

He turned from the man and walked back to me, looking me up and down. "You know it is my opinion, *Sesquiplicarius* Severus, that you are becoming derelict in your duties. I am wondering if perhaps you've been playing a double game with these rebel agitators."

"That is not true, sir, and you know it."

"Do I now?" He smiled and took the other *sesquiplicarius'* spear and thrust it into my hands. "Then kill the false king. Shove this spear into his side, and let's be done with this."

I looked at the weapon, a broad-tipped Hasta—six and one half feet of tough ash shaft, tipped by a triangular iron blade. I had carried it for my first five years in the Legion and was more than proficient in its use. I looked up at the man on the cross and then at the still-kneeling girl and handed the weapon back to Faustus.

He laughed with contempt, "Just as I thought." He handed the spear to the junior officer of the Fifth Cohort. "*Sesquiplicarius* Longinus, finish what Lucius Varius Severus could not."

Without a word, Longinus marched up to the man on the cross and drew back his arm.

Suddenly the girl jumped up and ran toward him screaming, "No, please!"

But it was too late. Longinus thrust. Blood and water gushed from the man's side. Longinus frowned at the lack of reaction and prodded him again, but he was already dead.

The girl began sobbing and reached out to clutch the feet of her dead messiah, but Faustus snarled, "Drive her away, Severus, or kill her."

I tried to pull her from the man, but she kept running back.

Faustus snorted with scorn. "You can't even control a woman. Longinus, take the bitch and have her lashed then throw her to the troops."

I turned on him. "No!"

"What was that, *Sesquiplicarius*? Did you just refuse to obey an order from your commanding officer?"

I swallowed hard, but stood my ground between the Centurion and the sobbing girl. "Attend to your duty, Lucius Varius Severus. I'm giving you an order. If you do not obey, both you and she will end this day nailed to the highest cross on this hill. Is that clear?"

"Lucius, Lucius? Do you hear me Lucius? Or perhaps I should call you by your present name, since you never did do well at responding to that name."

I opened my eyes. The old man stood in front of me holding the open box. I stared at him, and he smiled a two-thousand-year-old malicious smile at me.

The cruel, malevolent smile of Centurion Quintus Livius Faustus.

Chapter 23

"**Y**es, it is exactly what you think it is. Go ahead, pick it up." The old man moved another step closer, still holding out the open box.

He was right. It was what I thought it was, but I didn't want to touch it. The last time I had was in another life, my first one, two thousand years before. I had been forced to handle it then, and I had no desire to repeat the experience.

"Look at it, Lucius Varius Severus. You were the last one to lay hands on it before you placed it on *His* head."

He was right about that, too. I had, and it had haunted my subconscious mind throughout the centuries with half-remembered snippets like fever dreams, always hovering just out of reach. And who knew what other horrible memories lurked there—in that deep dark place of my soul where I feared to go but couldn't escape.

I stared down at the box; that circlet of thin branches of the Jujube Tree, a bush that grew wild around the walls of Jerusalem. I hadn't woven it and I hadn't wanted to put it on his head. But I had. And now it had returned to me.

It rested in the center of the plain wooden box on a scrap of coarse, brown homespun cloth torn from the dress of a devoted young woman. It was stained with the blood of a carpenter and stiff with age, but I recognized the fabric and the object that rested on it.

The object that the Bible named as The Crown of Thorns had unraveled on one side where several thorns had broken off but, other than that, appeared almost as it had that hot, still day two millennium ago.

The old man saw me gazing at it. "Yes, it is missing several thorns. You see, over its many years, occasionally one of its owners would give a thorn to a powerful churchman or king in return for earthly or spiritual rewards.

"Go ahead, pick it up." He pushed the box closer to me, but I didn't move. "You seem reluctant, Lucius. Why? Do you still feel guilt about what you did? Then perhaps you'd be happier placing it on your own head. Or would you prefer I did it for you?"

The box was only inches from my face now, and I could see the thick tarry streaks on the underside of the circlet. His blood. I took a step backwards.

"Get it away from me. I wasn't the one who ordered it to be made or ordered another to place it on his head. That was you, *Centurion*," I spat the word.

"True enough, *Sesquiplicarius*. Then you were only following orders? I would have thought you'd worn out that excuse during your service to the Third Reich."

He smiled. He was enjoying this.

"You're surprised I know about that? Don't be. I've followed your career with great interest down through the centuries, Lucius. You see, I've always considered you a protégé, perhaps even like a son."

"I'm no son to you, unless it's son of a bitch to a world class bastard." And then it struck me. "Wait, if you're like me, how could you know who I was in each lifetime?"

"Who said I was like you? Whatever the rebel Jew did that has caused you to continue to be reborn over and over again until the end of time, he did something quite different to me."

He placed the box on the coffee table. For the first time since he'd entered, the smug, superior smile was gone. Instead he looked old and desperate and bitter.

"Just before he died, he spoke to me. He spoke so softly, I had to get quite close. In fact, during the many years since then, I have often wondered if he really spoke at all or if I just imagined it." He stared through me to a bleak hillside twenty centuries before. "But I didn't imagine the result. You see, Lucius Varius Severus, I have not been reborn after each normal span of years like you. I have lived each one with full consciousness every day, without the comfort of the final repose of death, for the past two thousand years."

"But you . . . you look old, but not two-fucking-thousand years old."

"Ah, that is the curse. For although he gave me immortality, he did not give me eternal youth. I do age—very slowly. As near as I can calculate, I age about one year for every quarter of a century. At first I thought it was wonderful and marveled at what a fool he had been to reward his executioner with centuries of life. But as the years rolled on and I continued to age, I changed my mind. It was not a boon but a curse. Several hundred years ago when I entered old age, I began to worry. Each night I went to bed wondering if I would continue to age until I became old and decrepit and senile. One night, after several bottles of whiskey, I decided I'd had enough and put a pistol to my head."

He pulled back the thin wisps of white hair and showed me a puckered scar.

"Fortunately, it missed most of my brain, but I spent the next century in a coma. Had it not been for the care and loyalty of Robert's great-great-great-great grandfather, I might have awakened to find myself in some charity ward with my vast fortune scattered to the four winds. But I learned then that I could not die. Not by nature and not by my own hand." His eyes grew wide with a terror only he could see. "Instead, I will continue my slow aging, growing more wizened and feeble with every century—turning into a creature of horror and pity—until the end of time."

His legs began to tremble, and he sat down. His bodyguard, Robert, opened a silver flask and poured him a capful of its contents. He gulped it down, and gradually the trembling stopped.

"That is why I had to secure the crown. According to the legend, once the spear is combined with the crown the one who possesses it will obtain almost unimaginable power."

"And you think that will break your curse?"

"Yes. It will." He rose and gripped my hand. "It must and it will!"

I shook him off. "You're deluding yourself. Power won't give you back your youth. You were cursed because you were evil. You still are."

His mouth twisted with anger. "Then you should be afraid of me, Lucius, very afraid. And as well as you know me, you must also know that if I do not get what I want, I won't hesitate to kill you all."

He reached into his coat pocket and pulled what was no doubt an original 9- millimeter Luger Parabellum, an accurate and deadly weapon. I knew because one had been issued to me as an officer in the *SS*. He pointed it first at me and then at Clarisse and Catherine.

"Wait a minute, what the hell do you want?" I asked coldly. "You've already got the damn box. Why threaten us?"

He waved the gun at Catherine. "She knows. She was there. She remembers it all. She knew him, and she is the only one who can tell me how to use the power of the spear and crown to break the curse."

For the first time Catherine spoke up. "And if I do not, Mr. Dietrich?"

"Then I will kill Cody, your sister and you."

Dietrich was taking no chances. The man I had known as Quintus Livius Faustus had been careful. As commander of my cohort he'd been relentless and aggressive in battle, but never foolish. And the only lesson I ever learned from him was never underestimate my enemy.

That was why I found myself tied to a straight-back kitchen chair with electrical tape. After pulling the Luger, Dietrich had instructed Paulie and Tommy to tie me securely which, given the problems I'd caused them in the past, they were only too happy to do.

Then he went to work on Clarisse and Catherine.

Tommy put one beefy arm around Catherine's neck, immobilizing her, and Paulie held Clarisse while the dead-eyed, expressionless Robert hit her, first with his open hand and then with the back of it. He did it mechanically and seemed to take no pleasure and even less interest in the pain he was causing, but I could see Dietrich's eyes gleaming just as they had that day so long ago when all of this began.

I struggled against the sticky elasticity of the tape and succeeded in stretching it an inch or two, but the only result was that Tommy came over and wrapped another dozen yards of it around my wrists.

Dietrich held up his hand and Robert stopped in mid-stroke, more like a robot than a human being. He moved slowly over to where Clarisse slumped in Tommy's grip and carefully lifted up her bruised chin.

"I really do hate to do this to such a lovely young woman. Though I must confess, you aren't quite as lovely as you were five minutes ago. What a pity." He sighed dramatically then turned to Catherine. "You have the power to stop this right now."

She stood rigid in the center of the room, her face pale and creased with pain. In fact, she had winced each time her sister was struck, as if she felt every blow her sister had received, Given the incredible closeness of the two sisters, I was becoming increasingly certain that she had. But Dietrich was not convinced.

"Can you really be so callous as to allow your sister to suffer so, when you could put an end to it with just a few words?"

Clarisse lifted her head and said through swollen lips, "Don't tell the bastard a thing, Cathy."

Dietrich nodded to Robert, and who raised his hand again.

"If I told you," Catherine stated coldly, "you wouldn't understand anyway."

"Try me."

She looked at me, made the slightest of gestures with her chin, then began to speak. But I'd seen what she'd noticed on the end table behind me—a pair of nail clippers. So while all the attention was focused on her, I tilted my chair back slightly and plucked up the clippers with the fingertips of my right hand. I tried to concentrate on not letting them slip from my sweat-slick fingers as I felt for the edge of the tape and made the first careful cut. The click sounded so loud in my ears that I was sure the rest of the room must have heard, but all ears were tuned to what Catherine was saying.

". . . So the final part of the ritual involves holding the crown in your left hand and the spear in your right. To achieve full power, the ceremony should be performed in a cathedral, but if that isn't possible any consecrated church will suffice. The main element is to lay both objects on the altar, repeating three times the words spoken by Constantine the Great when he saw the fiery cross in the sky and converted on the spot to Christianity, *In hoc signo vinces*. In this sign you will conquer."

Dietrich's eyes opened wide, and he rubbed his hands together. "Of course. I should have guessed as much. What other words could serve so well to unlock the power of the spear and crown? Excellent, my dear, first rate. I knew that with a bit of persuasion I could depend upon you to unlock the secret."

Catherine stood rigidly. "And now keep your part of the bargain. Release my sister and Cody."

Dietrich looked up in mock surprise. "Bargain? I really don't recall any bargain."

"You promised you would let them go if I . . ."

He held up his hand. "I'm afraid you're guilty of that all too human failing of hearing what you wanted to hear."

"But I told you everything. Surely there can't be any reason to hold us any longer?" He smiled in the way that had always meant something bad for someone. In this case, us.

"You're quite right, my dear. I don't have any further use for any of you. Robert, shoot them all."

I had only snipped about halfway through the tape, but in a few seconds it wouldn't make any difference. I put all my effort into my arms and jerked them upward and out. The tape and a small portion of my skin ripped from my wrists, and even though my feet were still bound, I gave one hopping leap and crashed into Robert. I grabbed him by the shirt and tried to drag him down with me, but without the use of my legs it was hopeless. He twisted out of my grip and slammed the barrel of his pistol against my head. I went down.

Dietrich came over, clucking his tongue. "Lucius, my boy, always reckless and impulsive. Whatever shall I do with you?" He stroked his chin. "Ah, yes, I remember.

Robert, shoot him."

Robert raised his pistol and dispassionately sighted down the barrel. I saw the barest flicker of a grin as he squeezed the trigger and fired.

At that same instant I heard a feminine voice scream, "No!" The shot rang out, and Clarisse fell into my arms. She had jumped in front of me.

The bullet passed through her body and lodged in the fleshy part of my forearm, though not deeply. But as I held her, I saw the red blossom spread from a small hole in the front of her sweater and grow larger and larger.

And in that moment I realized I loved her.

As if she sensed it, she smiled, raised her hands and cupped one hand over her left eye and then her right, showing me the two small dots that rested there. Contact lenses.

I looked into eyes which were now a deep emerald green. It was Her. All along, she'd been the one I'd searched out in every life. I couldn't see it because she must have deliberately used the contacts to hide it. Why?

But that didn't matter now because I had her, even as I knew that the curse of my existence was repeating itself. I was going to lose her. Again.

"Please, Clarisse, hold on. You can't leave me—not again. Please, baby, I can't live without you."

She smiled and whispered, "Took you long enough to figure it out, tough guy."

I tried to smile, but my throat kept closing. I raised her head level with mine and kissed her as the blood trickled from her lips and onto mine. I pressed my lips tighter as if I could somehow stop the bleeding with my breath.

Her beautiful green eyes fastened on mine. She whispered, "I love you."

"I love you, too."

But I was talking to a corpse. She was dead.

I don't know how long I knelt there holding her lifeless body, but when I looked up I saw Robert standing over me, one hand on the collar of Clarisse's sweater and the other pointing the gun at me. He pulled at her sweater to get a better shot at me, and suddenly my world turned red as the same mindless Berserker fury of my Viking days overcame me. All I wanted to do was rend and tear and kill.

So as he pushed the gun toward my face, I screamed and bit down on his hand. Hard. For once his inscrutable reserve cracked and he screamed, too—in pain. He slammed my head with the pistol, but I wouldn't let go, and when I finally did I spat out a chunk of his flesh. At the same time I wrapped my hands around his neck and squeezed with the strength of the damned and doomed.

Tony's two gunsels kept trying for a shot, but as we rolled and struggled they couldn't get a clear one. In a last desperate move, Robert pulled a stiletto out of a leg sheath and stabbed it into my arm. I yanked it out and cut his throat with it. He died gurgling on the carpet.

For a moment everyone was too stunned to react, and in that moment I used the knife to slice through the tape on my ankles. Then, before Tommy could bring his gun around, I threw the knife, burying it in his gut. He fell to the floor howling with pain as I scooped up Robert's fallen pistol and pointed it at the three remaining enemies.

"Give me one good reason why I shouldn't kill you all slowly."

I felt Catherine's hand on my arm. "Cody, please don't. Clarisse wouldn't have wanted this."

I could barely speak. "You don't understand. She was the one. All this time, and I didn't know. I had funny feelings and strange hunches, but I didn't truly know until a few minutes ago. And now she's gone and my life here is over, so I might as well take these vermin with me."

I turned to Dietrich. "I think I'm going to put your claim of immortality to the test, Centurion. Maybe you can't die, but let's see how you enjoy the rest of eternity with your head blown off."

He paled, but quickly recovered. "Do you really think you are better than me, Lucius? You who have murdered hundreds over the centuries." He smirked. "You who claim undying love for The Girl. It is all hypocrisy and self-delusion. You lie not only to the world but to yourself. You are no better than I. You are a born killer, and were from the first day you received your badge of command."

He reached into his pocket and pulled out a small silver disk. "This is your emblem, which I have kept all these years." His voice rose triumphantly. "You killed under this badge. You killed the enemies of Rome. In fact, *Sesquiplicarius*," —he pointed to Catherine with one hand and with the other thrust the disk into my hand— "You killed *her!*"

The room spun and the universe turned inside out, until all that was left was darkness.

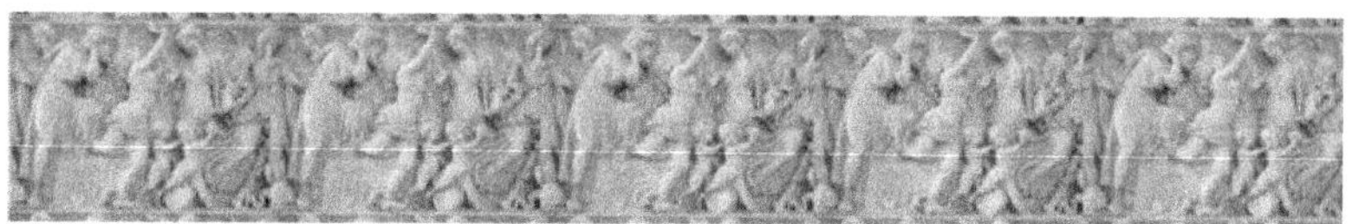

Chapter 24

Jerusalem, In the Roman Province of Judea–Golgotha

My head was pounding like a like a hammer on an anvil, and my throat felt as dry as the dust-laden wind that blew across the hill of Golgotha. It whipped the cloaks of the guards and made the tattered remnants of the condemned's rags snap and flutter like the baleful pennants of death.

The Centurion had given me an order, but I wasn't going to obey it. I'd had enough of pain and brutality for one day. In fact, I thought as I backed away from the pitiful grove of crosses, I had had enough of the Legions of Imperial Rome itself. I was going back to the barracks to write to my uncle, Marcus Severus, to use his influence to get me reassigned to an easy post with the city watch. I wanted to shake off the dust and stench of death in Judea and never leave Rome again.

Perhaps that was why I didn't hear the Centurion the first time he called, "Where are you going, *Sesquiplicarius* Severus?"

Or maybe I just didn't want to hear him. I kept walking.

"Lucius Varius Severus, you will turn and face me, you cowardly dog, or I will run you through from behind."

I stopped and turned. He knew that was a lie as well as I did. First of all, I had been decorated for bravery in the field, and second, there were very few cowards in the Roman Legions. Cowards were executed. In fact, had I not been cited so often for courage, Faustus would have gladly condemned me himself. But he had no basis. I knew it, and he knew it. So instead of running me through, he glared at me, face red and eyes blazing. I thought about unsheathing my *gladius* short sword and slicing through his neck. It was a pleasing thought, but I kept my expression blank.

He strode up to me until his nose was only inches from mine. His breath stank of garlic and sour wine.

"I gave you an order, *Sesquiplicarius*, and if you do not carry it out immediately, I will convene a field court-martial here and now and have you nailed to a cross next to the dead Jew."

He grabbed my arm and pressed my right hand to the hilt of my sword. Then he dragged the girl, Rachel, away from her vigil next to the cross and threw her at my feet.

"Draw your sword and strike." When I didn't move, he screamed, "Guards, bind this man and prepare a cross."

Still I stood frozen to the spot. I didn't doubt that this was the excuse he'd been looking for, but I couldn't kill her.

She looked up at me, tears of pity and compassion glistening in her eyes. "Do what you must. He would forgive you, as will I."

She opened her dress of coarse brown homespun and held the folds away from her bare throat. "I would only ask you a boon that you strike quickly and cleanly."

I shook my head. A detail of guards formed up behind Faustus.

"You must. If you do not, you will be crucified. And I will suffer an even more horrible death."

She was right. Still I hesitated. More guards approached. They were carrying wood for a cross.

"Before He died, He spoke to me. Of you."

Bewildered, I turned back to her.

"He had looked into your heart and found goodness that you were trying to deny. He said to me, 'Help him, Rachel. He is worth saving.' And that is what I will do, no matter how long it may take."

"How can you help me when you're dead?" I asked hoarsely.

"There is no real death. The spirit is eternal." She smiled at me one last time then gasped, "Now strike!" and pulled my sword to her breast.

The movement of the sword and sharp sound of command brought back years of instinctive training to never hesitate and my blade plunged into her chest up to the hilt. Her dark eyes sought mine for one last instant, and then she was gone.

I stood I don't know how long, holding the dripping blade before I noticed a hand on my back. Now that I had killed her, he was all smiles and praise, but I had no illusions. It wasn't about my courage or even disobedience to a direct order. It was about the loss of my soul. He had told me to murder an innocent girl, and as far as he was concerned, I had done it. And now in his twisted view I stood no better than he. I too was a killer. A callous thing without pitty. Now he had dragged me down to his level, and my shade would accompany his as we wandered amongst the damned in Hades for eternity.

"Well done, Lucius Varius Severus. A perfect thrust. Why, you ran her through from chest to backbone. I believe I shall have you teach that killing thrust to all our new recruits."

He rubbed his hands together and clapped me on the back again. "And now it's time for the tavern and wine and whores. In fact, the first round of both is on me, Lucius." And, still laughing, he sauntered down the hill back toward the city gate.

I wanted to rush after him and hack him to pieces, but I couldn't move. I stood rooted to the spot.

After I don't know how many hours passed, finally I bent down and picked up Rachel's thin body and carried her to a grove well away from the place of execution and buried her under an olive tree.

Then I sat next to the grave, stared at the midnight scattering of cold, indifferent stars and wept.

The world of the present came back into focus, and I brought my hand up to my face. It was wet.

"I killed her. I couldn't protect her then, any more than I could protect her now. This life has been a joke and a failure, just as every one of them for the last two thousand years." I raised the gun. "And now it's over. I'm going to kill the rest of these monsters and then the most pathetic monster of them all—Me."

Catherine stepped in front of me. "Cody, your life here is not over. Look at me."

I started to turn away, but she said very softly once more, "Look at me, Cody, please," and took off her glasses. Her eyes sparkled. They were a bottomless, bright green— just like Clarisse's.

"It—it's impossible. Unless you were . . ."

"Yes, twins."

I stared in amazement. The thick glasses had hidden the truth in her eyes, just as the contacts had with Clarisse. Catherine looked younger now, and her hair fell the same way as her sister's had and seemed to reflect gold highlights where the mousy brown had been.

"Clarisse isn't dead. She is me and I am her. You see, when I was reincarnated in this life a miracle happened in the womb. I became twins. And not just identical twins, but two halves of one coin. We shared the same mind and memories. One person in two bodies."

I stared at her in disbelief and only the fact that her revelation left everyone else in the room equally stunned prevented them from jumping me while I stood there, incredulity warring with hope. .

"I'm sure you've heard about twins changing clothes and hairstyles and their parents not being able to tell them apart. Well, we went them one better. We would exchange bodies. I would be Clarisse and she me. In fact, when we both entered adolescence we decided we would develop two distinct personalities, and so Claire Franklin became the sexy, cheerleader party girl, Clarisse, while Cathy morphed into the quiet, studious little bookworm. And any time Catherine got bored with being little Miss Goody-two-shoes and Clarisse needed a break from parties and dates, we'd switch."

"So, what—I mean, who are you now?"

"I'm both of us, Catherine and Clarisse. So you see, she isn't dead. Each memory and every bit of her soul are right here in this body with me. We remember the first night we met you at the apartment of that horrible Little T, Tony Junior. And as Clarisse, we'd like you to know we were never a prostitute. That was a ruse."

I shook my head. "I don't get it—why? Why pretend something like that?" She took my hand and held it between hers. "It was a test, Cody."

"A test? For who? What sort of a test?"

"A test for you. A test to see if, after all your many lives which ended indisappointment and frustration, you could fall in love and care for someone you were not predisposed to love. And, if need be, die for her."

"Clarisse, the tough-talking New York hooker."

"Yes. We made her all the things that The Girl was not and still, despite the fact she was a vain, faithless liar and thief, despite your thinking she had cheated on and betrayed you—in spite of all that, you came to truly love her. Thereby proving to God and us, but mostly to yourself, that you can feel love and compassion without the ghost of the past controlling your present. And more importantly, your future."

She leaned forward and kissed me, and when I pulled back I noticed that shimmering just beneath Catherine's features were Clarisse's, impish little smile and all. Two people in one body. And one person who was more complete than any I had known throughout the ages.

I started to wrap my arms around her and noticed movement out of the corner of my eye. I had almost forgotten.

"Hold it right there." Paulie stopped inching toward the door while Tommy still sat on the floor clutching his stomach. I looked at the two of them and then back to Dietrich. He was the only one I wanted.

"Go on, get out of here both of you." Paulie backed up a step, but I added, "Take him with you, and tell Tony Bags it's over between him and me. We're even, and he'd be smart to quit while he's ahead."

I watched the pair limp out the front door, then turned my attention back to Dietrich. "But you and I, Centurion, have unfinished business." Dietrich's gaze darted franticly around seeking a weapon or an advantage, but there was neither.

"There is that little matter of a hill in Judea. An innocent man and a blameless girl.

You contributed to both their deaths and now it's time to see just how much of you I have to chop off before, like Humpty Dumpty, all the king's horses and all the king's men won't ever be able to put you back together again."

I walked across the room, retrieved my bloody throwing knife and started toward him. I could smell thousands of years of fear. He reeked of it.

"Don't watch this Catherine," I called back over my shoulder. "Go into to the bedroom, and I'll come to you once it's done."

But instead I felt her move up behind me. She wrapped her arms around my waist and buried her face in the back of my shirt. "Don't, Cody. Please, let it go. You don't have to do this anymore."

"You're wrong, Catherine, I do. For Clarisse, for you, for the girl on that hillside two thousand years ago."

"She doesn't want you to do it." Catherine turned me toward her and looked at me, then at the cowering old man who had been the cruel Centurion and God knows what else over two millennium. "But not for that wretched old man, Cody. For you. You've proven you can love and be loved. That you even have the power to forgive.

I glanced from her sweet face to the old man's frightened one. The Roman soldier, the Gladiator, the Viking and a hundred other warrior lives I'd lived screamed for his blood. And the only thing that stood in their way was the quiet girl beside me. And somehow, it was enough.

I let the knife fall to the floor and pointed to the open door.

"Go. Get out. Leave this house, this state and this country. Don't ever let me see you again."

He started to move and I saw the look of triumph on his face. He shot me one brief glance that mocked me for being weak and a fool.

"Yes, I know what you're thinking, and maybe I am. But think about this. You have the body of a man in his late nineties. What will that body be like a hundred years from now—a thousand years from now?"

Dietrich stopped, and a look of horror slowly passed across his features as the reality of it finally sunk in. He recovered momentarily and blurted out in a desperate rush, "I'll be back. I'll hunt you both down until I obtain the crown and when I bring it and the spear together . . . "

"You'll find it will do you no good," Catherine said quietly. "What I told you when you held us hostage was all lies. Old myths and legends, with no basis in fact. Credible only to the greedy and power mad. Like you. Even you, deep in the depths of your shriveled soul, must realize that objects of veneration and hope could never aid those who would use them to smash and destroy. The crown will be returned to its place of beginning in Jerusalem, and you'll return to living your shriveled, lonely existence as the years continue to trickle past without end."

He gave a sound which might have been a sob or a cry of anguish and stumbled through the front door.

Trembling, Catherine came into my arms and pressed her face against my chest. I held her for a few moments. "What you told him, that's not really true, is it?"

"No." She took a step back. "The power of both those objects—for good or evil—is all too real. Call it coincidence or perhaps the power of belief to affect an outcome, but it is well-documented that every king and general who possessed the spear was invincible in battle. As for the crown? Well, again it could be the power of faith persuading the mind to heal the body, but there are many recorded examples of merely a single thorn from it producing miraculous cures."

"So Dietrich really could've used the icons to reverse his aging and bring him power?"

"I'd prefer to think not, but I felt it was a chance the world couldn't afford to take."

I pulled her close again and stared through the open door to the sea beyond. Finally I asked, "Do you really think it's over?"

"The endless cycle of death and rebirth?"

"That, and my payment for the hundreds of lives I've taken."

She looked up at me. "Do you regret that?"

I thought for a moment. "Some, yes. But by ending most of the lives I have over the centuries I made the world a better place."

"But not all."

"No, not all. Some were soldiers on the other side of whichever army or warlord I fought for, and some who . . . " I thought of the massive monk swinging his gold cross. "Some were just in the wrong place at the wrong time."

"But this time when you could have killed and had every reason to, you didn't."

I drew a deep breath and could smell the sweet scent of her hair. "That's because you were there. Every decent thing I've ever done has been because of you."

She shook her head. "No, Cody—you cared for, protected and came to truly love a woman who seemed to be even worse than you, and in doing so proved that the man who died that day in Jerusalem was right about you."

She kissed me, and I felt all the years of battle and death begin to fade.

We stood like that until the sun sank over the whitecaps of Cape Cod Bay, and the moon rose like a silver ghost. Then we gently covered Clarisse's body, and with Catherine beside me, I carried her up the hill to Catherine's house.

"We'll bury her next to the wild rose bush." She pointed to the side yard. "She always liked them, and we used to joke that they were like the Clarisse side of our personality—wild and beautiful."

We did. Afterward, we stood silently next to the grave and watched the distant waves rolling in the moonlight.

I thought of all the lonely years spent searching for her, and the all too brief times of being together and, of course, the bittersweet parting as death claimed its price for our happiness.

She knew what I was thinking. She always did. "It's not going to be like that, Cody. This time is different. I know it."

"Then you really think I've squared accounts? I mean in spite of all I've done? What I wasn't strong enough to stop on that hill all those years ago?"

"He forgave you. It was you who couldn't forgive yourself." I gave a bitter laugh. "What makes you think I can now?"

She took a step back and pointed to my empty shoulder holster. "Because you know there's something else now—us."

"So, you think we can live a normal life together, have kids, grow old and then . . . ?"

She smiled. "Well, we've had two thousand years to practice getting it right, so I think we've got a pretty good shot."

I pulled her close and kissed her. "You know what? I kinda think you may just be right."

She smiled, a tiny impish grin. "Well, we may only have one lifetime, but I think one way or another, we've got forever to find out."

About the Author

Ric has a 40 year professional career history in advertising, publishing and marketing in Boston, New York and San Francisco. He has degrees in history and psychology and has been trained in debating, public speaking and stage acting. A large part of his 40 year career was spent in numerous professional and business settings as a presenter and featured speaker at seminars and professional meetings.

Ric has been a visiting professor at Worcester Polytech Institute. He also teaches a popular course on marketing for authors at prominent venues such as the venerable "Cape Cod Writers Conference". Ric is a published author of a Mystery Series and multiple other novels.

Tell-Tale Publishing would like to thank you for your purchase. Please remember to support your author by leaving a review on Amazon, Goodreads, or other review sites. It helps keep their books on the shelves! If you enjoyed this novel, please visit Tell-Tale, so you can see what other authors have to offer.

www.tell-talepublishing.com

www.ingramcontent.com/pod-product-compliance
Lightning Source LLC
Chambersburg PA
CBHW060820120726
47909CB00006B/2015